Peter

&

Paul

A few excerpts from **5 STAR** reviews on Amazon

Peter & Paul
THE KINGDOM
Sequel to
Yeshûa
Personal Memoir of the Missing Years of Jesus

This book is a truly remarkable work by a remarkable author. I highly recommend it.

Fred Schäfer,
Author of The Invention of the Big Bang.

The author is extremely well educated in matters of science, physics and metaphysics and … did a tremendous job of making those times live once again.
…a new perspective of looking at those first centuries of the Way for the author did a tremendous job of making those times live once again.

Joan A. Adamak
Author and Book Reviewer, "VINE VOICE

Stan I.S. Law's… intellect and knowledge on the topics he writes about, never cease to amaze me! …even those who don't practice a specific chosen faith can enjoy the story… that will keep you entirely engaged…

Mary Leckie
Author

Historically and scripturally accurate, Stan I. S. Law's book has investigated and illustrated the perils that Peter and Paul faced as they traveled throughout the early civilized world helping to grow the Christian Church. Equal parts canonical Scripture, Gnostic texts, and brilliant imagination combine together within this book… Two big thumbs up to Law for another amazing book!

Jeff Byrnes
Editor and Publishing

…Not all Christian history is derived from the Bible itself, and Stan Law does a fantastic job of drawing from other sources, which he names, as he put together this most interesting story.

TrishFLReader
TOP 500 REVIEWER

To be able to explain a man's life in a way that makes sense and creates a whole picture is a remarkable feat. Stan I.S. Law has a genuine talent for such feats..

Amy Taylor
Author, reviewer

Whether you are deeply religious or you are just looking for a novel that explores religious faith and historical characters in interesting ways, "Peter and Paul" is an excellent read that sucks you into the world of the Apostles…

L. Clifford
TOP 1000 REVIEWER

The writer brought these two Biblical characters to life. It was wonderful learning about their thinking and growth in the early church.

Chris Careme
Amazon.com

By the same author

ALEC (Alexander Trilogy, Book I)
ALEXANDER (Alexander Trilogy, Book II)
SACHA—The Way Back (Alexander Trilogy, Book III)
YESHUA—Personal Memoir of the Missing Years of Jesus
PETER AND PAUL (An intuitive sequel to Yeshûa)
ONE JUST MAN (Winston Trilogy Book I)
ELOHIM (Winston Trilogy Book II)
WINSTON'S KINGDOM (Winston Trilogy Book III)
THE AVATAR SYNDROME (Prequel to Headless World)
HEADLESS WORLD—The Vatican Incident
(Sequel to *The Avatar Syndrome*)
MARVIN CLARK–In Search of Freedom
THE GATE—Things My Mother Told Me
NOW—Being and Becoming
GIFT OF GAMMAN
THE PRINCESS
ENIGMA of the Second Coming
WALL—Love, Sex, and Immortality (Aquarius Trilogy Book I)
PLUTO EFFECT [Aquarius Trilogy Book II]
OLYMPUS—Of Gods and Men [Aquarius Trilogy Book III]

Short stories

THE JEWEL & OTHER STORIES
CATS AND DOGS
Sci-Fi Series 1
Sci-Fi Series 2

Non-fiction Books by Stanislaw Kapuscinski

VISUALIZATION—Creating Your Own Universe
KEY TO IMMORTALITY
[Commentary on the Gospel of Thomas]
BEYOND RELIGION: Volumes I, II and III
[Collections of essays on perception of Reality]
DICTIONARY OF BIBLICAL SYMBOLISM
DELUSIONS—Pragmatic Realism

Poetry in Polish
[with illustrations by Bozena Happach]
KILKA SŁÓW I TROCHĘ GLINY
WIĘCEJ SŁÓW I WIĘCEJ GLINY

INHOUSEPRESS, MONTREAL, CANADA
http://inhousepress.ca

An intuitive sequel to
YESHUA
Personal Memoir of the Missing Years of Jesus

PETER & PAUL
THE KINGDOM

Stan I.S. Law

INHOUSEPRESS, MONTREAL, CANADA

CONTENTS

Part One – 30-34 A.D.
Tiberius 14-37 AD

PART TWO – 35-50 AD
Tiberius   14-37 AD
Caligula   37-41 AD
Claudius   41-54 AD

CONTENTS continued:

Part One
30-34 AD

1

THE DARK DAYS

"**I** miss fishing," he said out loud to no one in particular, his mind drifting back, far, far back to a different life, a different reality. His eyes searched aimlessly, reaching beyond today, beyond the immediate, a wistful smile barely widening his mouth.

"I miss fishing," he repeated, seemingly to himself.

They were all gathered, still together, in Bethany, where the Master had left them. Only one week ago. He didn't say goodbye. No, not goodbye, just so long. In fact He'd said that He'd never leave them. Never.

It didn't feel like it.

"I miss fishing," Shimon said, once again, the tone of his voice filled with longing. It was beginning to sound like a far-eastern mantra his Master once told him about.

Then he sighed deeply. He always sighed when he thought of the Mount of Olives. That was where he escaped into memories of way-back-when. Memories of when he'd first met the Master. Then he relaxed and allowed his mind to go even further back. Back to when he cast nets in the Lake Gennesareth. The lake of his childhood.

"I'll make you fisher of men," He'd said.

Only He didn't. And now, He'd left. And I am still here. Alone. Quite alone. Why do they look up to me? I am nobody. I'm ignorant. I know nothing. I am a fisherman. A fisherman of fish, in my lake.

His eyes reached far from shore, fishing for memories.

He used to enjoy overnight fishing the most. Heaving off with the last rays of the sun dying over Mount Tabor, just missing the peak on the south side. Even from the shore the view was breathtaking. From the shore of Bethsaida—the Place of Nets; little more than a village. Soon after they cast off, they'd watch the night fires beginning to twinkle, afar, long, long ago, before Tiberias grew into a city.

He missed the western breeze carrying them to the middle of the Lake on a broad reach. Just a small sail, knit by his mother and sisters, was enough. They were in no hurry. They had all night. They didn't have far to go.

In their prouder moments, his friends liked to call it the Sea of Galilee. It sounded more important. Some sea—from every place on its near-lustrous surface you could see the shore, and not very distant, at that. But it was their lake. Theirs for generations. Sweet water where his father, and his father before him, fished for fresh-water fish.

He was a fisherman then. Carefree.

And then He came. Quiet, unimposing. Just his eyes. There was heaven in those eyes. Infinity? Andrew had seen him first. You couldn't escape those eyes…

"Shimon?"

Shimon, He called him, long before He'd changed his name to *Kepha*. All too soon the Romans began to refer to him as *Petrus* taking their translation from *pietra*. The Greeks would give him their own version, naming him *Petros*, from their own word for rock or *petra*. Later, much later, some Gentiles coming from afar would call him *Peter*. So the Master had said. He seemed to reach out into the future. Wherever he'd go, He'd said, people would give him names of their own. Yes, He'd sensed the future and Shimon was afraid.

Yet, it all happened in just three short years. Just three…

When did He first call me Kepha?

"What? Shimon, you must eat!"

Andrew proffered a wooden bowl of steaming soup.

Later? It all happened in just a few years. Just a few…

He didn't feel like a rock. He felt weak, fragile, inadequate, scared… like that night on the boat when…

"Shimon?" the sound of his name reached him from afar—perhaps the other shore? He ignored whoever tried to invade his memories. It was good to remember, even knowing what followed. After all, He did come back. He was real...

"Shimon?" this time the voice was louder.

It must have been Andrew with something of no importance. It could wait... Back then he was happy. So happy. No decisions, few responsibilities... His mind drifted back, again, far, far back...

"Shimon, you haven't eaten in three days..."

Andrew was worried about his older brother. He'd aged, fast, during just these last few days. Already his short trimmed beard was showing signs of gray hair. Andrew suspected that since the Master's departure Shimon felt great weight pressing him down to earth. Literally, down to earth. Perhaps he was trying to reconcile heaven and earth into a single entity, like two sides

of a single coin. Perhaps it was all the decisions he had to make. Everyone wanted his opinion, his advice.

I'm a simple fisherman, Andrew heard him say. Many a time. *A simple fisherman...*

But no one believed him. He really had to be *Kepha*, a rock; strong; unbending; not to cave in under all the expectations.

Shimon looked up for an instant.

"Three days? Out there, in the desert, He hasn't eaten for forty days..." Shimon murmured, surprised.

The next moment his eyes lost focus and drifted back, to the world of his own. Then, a gentle smile broadened his mouth. Andrew wondered if his brother would ever share his daydreams with him.

The wind was rising...

Just sitting there, amidships, on the rough-hewn board spanning from side to side, his two friends stretching abaft. A gentle sway of the dying wind... then silence, darkness, the sky punctured only by the stars of Yahweh. We cast our nets and waited, he recalled, catching a few hours of sleep.

"Not I. I'd sit silent, listening to the stars," he murmured, hardly aware of Andrew's presence. And then he repeated softly, "I miss fishing."

I miss fishing... It really did sound like a mantra.

The waters rose with unrestrained anger and instantly he began drowning. Have faith, He said. Have faith. Trust me. The power lies within you.

Yeshûa was standing, seemingly on the water. He watched the Master walk towards him hardly touching the waves. Almost floating.

"Come to me", Yeshûa tempted, his voice relaxed, encouraging him with a smile. "Don't be afraid..."

"Shimon!" This time Andrew's voice was more insistent. It no longer sounded like the Master. Andrew didn't like Shimon drifting off, so often lately, when there were decisions to be made. As the younger brother he felt the need to look after Shimon. Funny how roles change. Until the Master left them, Shimon was the one who looked after all of them.

"He hasn't left us," Shimon murmured. "He's still within us."

"What's that?"

Andrew looked concerned. He was really worried about his brother since He'd left. Since He'd left them alone. It seems, Shimon missed Him the most. Shimon and John, but mostly Shimon. Still, they had to cope. And Shimon had a lot on his mind. The Master had left his brother in charge.

Shimon was really not himself, lately. Not since the Master's departure, or even before. He seems to have lost all confidence ever since that night he'd spent in the courtyard. Even now he seemed to grow weak and agitated each time some cockerel sang; even when he was asleep.

Each time a rooster crowed Shimon's face would turn pale.

Actually it's been a while. Apart from Andrew, the others didn't really know what had happened. Shimon had no inclination to tell them. Three times... three times the cockerel sang. Three times...

"Never mind."

Shimon was tired of explaining it to his friends. He blinked a few times to shake off the images of Gennesareth. For a while they wouldn't let go. Then he thought of the others, and the boat dissolved in the water. The others wouldn't understand. They'd spent just as many years with the Master as he had, yet they didn't seem to understand his teaching at all. "Why can't they understand my words?" He'd asked them, many a time. Ah, yes, many a time. *Why can't you understand my words?*

To understand that none of this is real?

My kingdom is not of this world...

Andrew drew back from his brother recognizing the signs when Shimon was in a morose mood.

"I suppose Stephen arrived?" Shimon asked without looking up.

"Not yet, Shimon. We expect him shortly."

Andrew just didn't have the heart to tell Shimon that Stephen had been murdered. Stoned to death. In the days that followed the Believers had scattered throughout Samaria, yet preaching the Word as they went.

"You can never be sure, these days. The roads, such as they are, seem the favorite haunt of the bandits in search of easy money," Shimon murmured. He ought to know. He'd been beaten up, twice, by total strangers.

Love thy enemies...

Again, Shimon's lips widened in a wistful smile. That last thought, His last command, seemed almost like a joke; a joke that was painful and not at all funny. Yet, Yeshûa had insisted.

"I'm sorry, I thought he'd already arrived," Shimon replied, another sigh escaping his parched lips. He still had time. Andrew would look after things. Shimon didn't want to treat his brother badly, nor to ignore him. He loved his younger brother. And, after all, it had been Andrew who recognized the Master first. Back then, on the shores of Gennesareth. Before anyone even began to suspect who Yeshûa was.

Ah, yes. Back then, by the Lake. But now it was time for Shimon's daily walk. The time he hated but promised himself to do no matter what.

He made a point of going out, every day, alone, even if just for an hour or so. He hated this commitment he'd made to himself, but knew that if he didn't take at least one walk, outside, he'd crawl into a freshly dug grave and hope that no one would ever find him. He was afraid. He couldn't even define what he was afraid of. Not precisely. Perhaps just of not being able to conquer his fear? He almost smiled at the thought. Could it be that simple?

Be not afraid...

He'd said that. And Jeremiah and Isaiah before Him.

Yeshûa was never afraid. He walked into crowds, hordes of total strangers; crowds often showing signs of anything but friendly disposition. Yet, He was never afraid. How did He do it, Shimon asked himself many a time. How on earth did He do it?

"It's not real, Shimon," He would say. "None of it is real," He'd often repeated, a mysterious smile lighting up His face, his sky-blue eyes piercing Shimon to his soul.

It's not real...

He was always like that. Nothing seemed to matter much. Not really. Except loving one another. How on earth can one love a total stranger?

You love your children for—as well as in spite of things?

None of this is real...

It was real to Shimon. It was real and, most of the time, scary. That was why Shimon went out every day. Since He'd left, Shimon had to conquer his reticence of meeting other people. Especially meeting strangers. His band of men went out to preach, daily, but not he. They understood. He was in charge. He had to hold down the fort. Fort? What fort? A mud hut just big enough to hold a dozen people; sitting on the floor, side by side. Yet he did go out. Once a day. He'd never met anyone who'd given him a glad eye. Not since he'd left Bethsaida. His home. His lake. His family. Now?

Even surrounded by ten of his best friends he felt alone.

He looked left and right, and breathed easier. The street was empty. Yesterday he turned left; today he'd go right, wherever it led him. He promised himself that he'd stop stealing glances over his shoulder. At least for twenty paces at a time. It wasn't easy.

He imagined that He was walking with him—that made him feel better. Much better. If he really concentrated he almost heard His steps—right there, besides him.

"I'm always with you," He'd said, once. Seems like so long ago. He simply couldn't believe that just a few days had past since He'd left them. It seemed he couldn't believe a great many things. Like loving your enemy...

I am always with you...

This time Peter was sure he'd heard His voice. He nearly spun on his heals to see His face. Then he remembered the twenty steps. Six remained. He smiled at his own thoughts. If only, he thought. If only my faith were stronger.

It was a quiet late afternoon, hardly a breeze in the air. He was crossing the square, keeping close to the wall to take advantage of the shade. Half-dozen children were playing hide and seek, in the side street, using the merchants' carts as hiding places. Nothing much happened. It was too hot for adults to take even a leisurely stroll along the dusty streets. And then they came.

Instinctively, Peter backed up into the penumbra of a doorway. Two men were dragging a woman, perhaps no more than twenty years old, by both arms. Five other men followed, grim smiles on their faces. Her bare feet were rubbing against the hard-beaten sand. They must have been sore, skinless, by now. It wouldn't be long any more.

Two of the men tied her arms, then legs, then pushed her against the stone wall, which was already splattered with blood from previous occasions. The other men watched, their smiles getting wider. Then one of the men picked up a stone and threw it at her. He didn't have a good aim—it missed her by a handbreadth. She didn't utter a sound. Resignation? The other men were better. Perhaps they had more practice? By the tenth stone she lay crumpled, unconscious—by twentieth, probably dead. Nobody cared. The men wiped their hands on their coats and walked away. No one even stayed behind to bury her body. She was left there as an example.

The children played on.

He would have forgiven her, whatever the transgression. The body doesn't sin, He'd said, only the mind. Or, He would have stopped the men from doing anything. He had that power.

And I just stand here, cowering, Peter thought. A deep, tearing, silent sob heaved his chest. Oh Master, please give me strength. Give me courage. You called me a Rock, yet my heart is like clay.

Yeshûa was never afraid. Never. It was as though He were immortal. It was as if he could never die. And yet...

It all seems such a very short time ago.

***

2

SANHEDRIN

You could tell how important they were by the grayness of their beards—never cut, cultivated as though adding legitimacy to the tasks they performed. Their job was but one: to maintain status quo. To maintain traditions they'd built up over the years, ever since Moses led them to the Promised Land, even if he didn't reach the destination himself.

This was an ancient and proud assembly.

They sat in a semicircle, mostly straight, though now some with a pronounced stoop—their hair turned gray. There was no perceptible expression on their faces. It was as if they were frozen in time, perhaps ready to be reawakened when the time was ripe.

They where the Sanhedrin. The wisest of the wise.

The Sanhedrin met in the *Lishkat Ha-Gazith*, known to the Greeks and other gentiles as the Hall of Hewn Stones. The vast chamber was built into the north wall of the Temple Mount. Half of the Hall was inside the sanctuary, the other half projected outside. Access to the chamber was both, from the outside—i.e. from the courtyard of the gentiles—and from the Temple. As its location suggested, the Sanhedrin dealt with civil and sacred matters alike.

Usually twenty-three elders met to deal with everyday affairs. On such occasions, behind the columns there was ample space for the members to stretch their stiff bones, before resuming their deliberations. On special occasions, to deal with matters of particular importance, the Great Sanhedrin would swell to seventy-one members.

When the session called for full complement of sages, they often spilled down the broad steps onto the courtyard to discuss matters, before resuming their seats to cast their votes.

At the head of the Council, exactly in the geometric centre of the semicircle, sat the President, or *Nasi*, with the Chancellor, *Av beis din*, sitting at his right hand. When in session, the other sixty-nine general members took their place on either side, embracing the inner space with two long, curved arms. The number seventy-one precluded the possibility of a tie in their judgment. Usually one of guilty. The innocent had no reason for being there.

The members of the Sanhedrin were not elected. Anyone proving superior scholarship of Jewish Law could displace any current member of the assembly. Both, Pharisees and Sadducees could apply. And the priests, of course. What mattered was knowledge, not affiliation to a particular sect. The Greeks found this a strangely, if not surprisingly, democratic notion.

No one, not one sane man or woman, would want to stand facing the semicircle of judges. Only one Man dared, and He was dead now. No matter, the Sanhedrin continued to sit together. Their eyes were cool, indifferent, without feeling. The Law was supreme—or their interpretation of it. The Law descending directly from Yahweh. Neither love nor mercy entered into their deliberations. Just justice. The old, traditional, heartless, absolute justice.

Judge not that ye might not be judged...
Shimon was regarding the assembly from the courtyard of the gentiles, a misnomer, as usually only Jews could get

access to it. He recalled the Master exchanging words with the sages not so long ago. They had been stunned by his knowledge of the Law. Had the Essenes instilled such proficiency? He never said. He just knew. Perhaps the knowledge always resided within Him?

Yet, He, too, had been found guilty.

On the way here Shimon played with the idea of challenging the Sanhedrin declaration that the Believers were not true Jews. That they didn't conform to the Hebrew Law. He approached the Council through the southern gate, keeping close to the sides of the pillared court, taking advantage of the shade offered by the red-roofed Royal Stoa.

He walked slowly, alone, unwilling to expose his brethren to the wrath of the Council. He'd spent the night in prayer, asking for the courage to intercede on behalf of the Believers. No matter what.

Only he didn't make it. His knees gave way as he slid down, his back against the column, his legs trembling, refusing to support his gaunt body.

Master, willst thou not help me?

Silence.

Silence reverberated across the courtyard. It surrounded him and pushed him against the stone floor. He could actually hear the stillness. Intense absence of sound. An emptiness. Like in his heart.

Master, willst thou not help me?

Not yet...

Not yet?

Soon.

The sounds he heard were not from outside. They were born inside his head. Or was it just vain hope? He knew that help was coming. It had to be soon. *Shavuoth*. It had to be that. All his brethren were waiting for *Shavuoth* to come. They were counting the days. They were holding their breath.

Shavuoth. The day of hope. Of redemption.

Of help.

Sitting, his back against the column, Shimon shrugged. What could one man do against seventy-one? Even the Master couldn't convince them of His righteousness. They, the judges, were set in their ways. A thousand years of tradition was on their side.

Recently Shimon, and the other ten, were loosing more brethren. After Stephen was murdered, stoned to death, two other Believers died in a similar way. No one claimed responsibility. No one assumed the blame. They were murdered by cowards. Seemingly in an act of robbery but Shimon and his friends knew better. You cannot be robbed when you have no possessions on you. No money, no silver, no gold. Not a single shekel. All their wealth was only in their heart. Yet they died.

The Believers, though still small in numbers, were all leaving Jerusalem. Too close to the power of the Sanhedrin. Too close to the priests. Who knew what went on in their midst?

The Sanhedrin was in full session. They got through the usual complains about abuses against the Jews by the Romans, about which they could do nothing, and got down to more pressing matters.

There were many sects springing in Judea, and even right here, in Jerusalem. They had to be dealt with. They knew what to expect from the established Pharisees, most of them were Pharisees themselves, but there were the, often difficult to deal with, Sadducees. They kept their noses in books—in the letter of the law, literally. Also the Essenes kept insisting to be heard with their prophetic bias, while the Zealots were raising their rebellious heads. Zealotry was mostly political, but its members were practically terrorists, inciting people to rise against the Roman occupation. Didn't they realize how powerful Rome was? Didn't Jerusalem suffer enough strife and mayhem in recent years?

And then there were the followers of Yeshûa. They were by far the worst. They were the most enigmatic, refusing to be categorized in any recognizable fashion. Yet, the council felt instinctively that they were the most dangerous. They were the most likely to upset the established ways. The ways dating back to Moses himself.

Their ways. Their power.

Nasi, the President, raised his hand. He had to do it three more times before the assembly came to order. He motioned the Chancellor to rise and present the remaining Order of the Day to the Assembly.

Most listened.

But the moment the Chancellor sat down, at the two extremities of the semi-circles whispers resumed with rising ferocity.

"You can't leave it to the old man."

"You're right, he's much too gentle."

"Not here, let's go outside..."

"And if we let them continue with their preaching, people will begin to listen. They can be pretty convincing," the younger Pharisee said, stroking his beard. He was an expert in Law, though his beard didn't show as yet any signs of gray. He looked more like a successful merchant, which he also was, than a member of the Sanhedrin.

"My men got rid of three of them. But it wasn't easy. They cannot connect their actions to us..."

"Of course not." His interlocutor leaned closer to his colleague and lowered his voice. "I got the fellow who got Yehuda to sing for thirty shekels."

"Yehuda?"

"Judas Iscariot, you've heard of him?"

"Ah, yes... he's pretty famous now..." the councilor confirmed sarcastically. He really meant 'infamous', although he'd served their purpose.

"Anyway, the man I have in mind is a truly low-life character. He can do a lot of harm to them, but he's now asking for fifty."

"Fifty?! For what?"

"For getting, ah… to get rid of three more. Maybe four, if I press him hard enough."

"Couldn't you threaten to expose him, to, ah… to us?"

"What, and let him recognize me?"

"Hmmm. It's never easy, is it…" His hand reached up to stroke his lengthy beard. They all liked doing that. It seemed that beards were they status symbol. "I'll see if I can get you twenty-five."

"Fifty. I did the Yehuda thing all on my own."

The younger councilor gave him a dirty look. After a short while, he replied. "Fifty it is." And began turning away to put some distance between himself and the other conspirator. It didn't pay to be seen talking to men who did the necessary but dirty work.

"In advance," he heard behind his back.

He nodded without slowing his pace.

During the session of the Sanhedrin men moved around a lot, exchanging opinions, arguing, before taking the vote. Three other exchanges similar to the one above took place concurrently on the other side of the steps. Similar deals were being made. There was an atmosphere of success in the air. A dozen murders wouldn't put a stop to the Yeshûa followers' ramblings, but it would scare them out of Jerusalem. No one wanted troublemakers on their own doorstep. Romans were problems enough.

Shimon raised himself slowly to his feet. Then he sank back again. Another day, another failure. His chest heaved in a protracted, silent sob. More like a whimper, really. He was who he was, no matter what Yeshûa had called him.

Why won't you help me?

He got to his feet again and slowly made his way home. It was a long walk to the mud-brick hovel he and his band of men called home. His mind drifted to that day, that Thursday, when Yeshûa was betrayed by Yehuda Iscariot.

That whole period immediately preceding Yeshûa's arrest, judgment, and even the Crucifixion, was heavily mixed up in Shimon's head. Perhaps it was necessary to protect his sanity. Too many things happened too quickly. He, whom Shimon considered invincible, suddenly allowed the lower forces to sweep Him in their current. None of this made sense. At least not then, not at the time. And even when He'd returned for those few days—forty short days during which Shimon saw Him only a few times—did little to alleviate the painful longing he felt for his Master.

Yet now, a few days after He'd left them for the second time, the echoes of judgment returned to Shimon with the force of a howling wind of the desert... The Court of the Gentiles surrounding the Temple was filled to the brim. No, not by the Gentiles. By Jews. By Jews all waiting for the Sanhedrin to pass their judgment.

Shimon had seen a bunch of old men, old tired men and their aspiring assistants, who accomplished little in their lives, pass judgment over a man in the prime of his life, who taught, unflinchingly, the philosophy of love. A man, who'd never hurt a fly. One man against seventy-one. One man, His hands tied behind his back. And they dared to pass judgment?

In the name of what? Tradition?

Even Pontius Pilate absolved Him. Gave Him his dispensation from any wrongdoing. But not they. They demanded His blood.

Yes. That was a true Sanhedrin trial. The trial of death.

Shimon blinked as he saw, again, the image of Yeshûa standing relaxed, almost nonchalant, if perhaps with just a trace of compassion for those who judged Him.

None of this is real...

"None of this is real, *Kepha*. Do not be afraid." The words lingered in his ears, his mind, his heart.

None of this is real? Then why can't I, Shimon, go and face the judges and declare the Truth taught by You, Master?

They know not what they are doing...

Forgive them?

Thursday night and then again on Friday morning. Once wasn't enough. Not to sate their pride, to fill their cups with bitterness that would follow their lives to the end.

"We demand his death. He claims to be the King of Jews. In the name of Rome, you cannot allow this!"

They cried out, and the masses, the dumb, ignorant masses picking up the chant. Death... death... death...

Fools. His kingdom is not of this world.

Shimon shook his head. The images behind his closed eyelids were becoming too real. It was as if he was about to face the same horrors once again. Shimon quickened his pace. He hardly noticed that he left the Sanhedrin far behind. He desperately tried to think. Not to remember—to think. If he were to lead His people, he, Shimon, needed a clear head. He needed to be objective. Logical. Not a bundle of nerves wrapped in pain of memories.

"Let the dead bury the dead," he whispered, through clenched teeth.

He walked slower, his head down, trying to avoid the holes and the loose rocks strewn about the street. This was not the main street. This was where he and those like him tried to avoid the spies of the High Priest, who already seemed to spread their tentacles to pounce on His followers. It wouldn't be long now. They were a jealous bunch.

They wanted power. Power to control peoples' minds, perhaps even their hearts? Though not with love but with fear. But most of all, they wanted to control peoples' purses.

It was getting dark. More dangerous. Not from the priests or the corrupt sages; not from the members of the council. Perhaps, not yet. But from ordinary, honest riff-raff, who couldn't make ends meet. Yet, at the same time, he knew that nothing would happen to him. Not now. Not yet. There were things he had to do first. Only... only he needed courage. And in that very moment, for the first time since Yeshûa had let, he felt, he knew, that that too would come. Soon.

He didn't know how very soon.

***

3

SHEOL
THE DAY BEFORE

Fifty days. Fifty days sustained by slowly waning faith. Yes, He had come to see them on the third day, though it wasn't really He. It was Yeshûa as He'd said He was. It was Yeshûa that seemed to walk through walls. We had been gathered in a small room, scared, all doors tightly shut, locked, and then, without a warning, He was with us. The next moment He was gone. Or it felt as though it was the next moment. When He came, time seemed to have stopped.

The women saw him, too; Mary Magdalene and others. In fact, they saw Him first. Imagine…

"He was with us, He really was," John assured the doubters. "For an instant of eternity, He was with us," he repeated, and then his eyes filled with tears. "He really was…" he was looking at Shimon, apparently begging for confirmation.

John truly loved Yeshûa. We all did, but John was special to Him. He was graced by Yahweh. That's what his name means in Hebrew. Yôhanan—Graced by Yahweh. He must have been. Perhaps we all were.

"We all were," John cut in, evidently reading Shimon's thoughts. Or it could have been the expression on Shimon's face. They all missed Him badly.

And then Didymus came. Later they called him the Doubting Thomas.

Put your finger here... put your hand into my side...
You all know the story. Thomas believed as we all did.
Yeshûa was real. Real and yet...
Perhaps He was more than real?
After all He did say He'd never leave us.
I'll never leave you...
Those words still reverberated in their ears. Words not one of them would ever forget.

In a way, He still was with them in their thoughts, their minds, their hearts... He filled every moment of their waking day; often their dreams. Only it was so hard, so very hard to accept it with one's emotions. They all missed His presence. His physical, presence; the sound of His voice, the look in His eyes. The touch of His hand.

Still... He did come back, if only for a while.

And now, or soon, His spirit would descend on them. So it was prophesied from the time of Moses, so it will remain. Fifty days after departure from Egypt, Moses brought the tablets down from Mount Siam, and now, fifty days after Yeshûa was murdered, He'd send His spirit to them.

It had to be thus. It had to be. "Or we'd all die of sorrow," John whispered. They all thought so.

It had to be thus.

For the Sadducees, Shavuoth, which even then the Greeks called Pentecost, always fell on Yom Ree-Shon, on Sunday, the day after Yom Sha-Bat. The Pharisees celebrated it on various days of the week. They were always different. Superior? They thought so...

The Believers, as most people in Judea, followed the same tradition as the Sadducees. They chose to celebrate this day on Yom Ree-Shon. Jews came to Jerusalem from the farthest corners of Judea, Idumea, Perea, Samaria, and even Galilee and Decapolis—though the journey was hard for many. People would travel for days, on foot, carrying their food and water, to be at the Temple on the Feast of Shavuoth.

It was a national celebration of their glorious past; of the evidence that Yahweh was their One God, One Protector. That Yahweh was that which unified them all.

For Shimon's friends, all ten of them, the last few days felt like living in the antechamber to Sheol—where only the dead found their home. More brothers have disappeared, without any explanation, without a justifiable reason. They were not even active proselytes—hardly ready to take on new responsibilities of the New Teaching yet, it seemed that the powers of Sheol were mobilizing against them.

Sheol—the abode of the dead.

Sheol—where the dead buried the dead, never allowing them to come alive again. So the Master had said. Or at least He warned against the dangers. But some didn't listen. Some didn't believe that none of this world is real. Not even Shimon, though he'd never admit it.

Shimon the Rock, Kepha, would never admit it. But he tried to believe. He tried hard. Shimon found most things hard. Not like rock, but difficult.

There was only one hope. Tomorrow.

"Hope always lies in the future," he told them.

He was trying to cheer them up. They all needed cheering up. The present was not acceptable. It was fraught with danger. If the present continued, the Master's teaching would fall on deaf ears. On the ears of the dead.

We must all wait another day, or really, another night.

Tomorrow the count will be over. The fiftieth day. Since the beginning of time, since the day Yahweh promised Moses that forty-nine days after they'd left Egypt they would be given the Law to live by, the Jews expected a new revelation. These days, they thought they would learn how they could be rid of the Romans. Or any invaders. They wanted to run their own country. And not pay those exorbitant taxes, of course.

Since those early days, generations have counted the days from the Feast of Passover, hoping for a New

Revelation. Tomorrow it will be over. The light will come upon them. The light of Torah. Of Instruction. Of Teaching.

And even as thousands gravitated toward the Temple, so did the one hundred and twenty Believers, intermingling with others. Not many. So far, just one hundred and twenty. It was a start. In the midst of them, moving with the crowd, advanced the disciples led by Shimon, followed closely by his brother Andrew, who never allowed Shimon to stray too far. He really felt protective about Shimon, particularly since Yeshûa's death. Shimon just wasn't the same any more.

Andrew also kept his eye on James, son of Zebadiah, who'd become known as James the Greater. The Greeks, up north, called his father Zebedee. Frankly, they all used Greek names. Everyone spoke Greek. James was much taller than the average Galilean, towering over the crowd surrounding him. Andrew repeatedly motioned him to keep his head down, only to receive a broad, ear-to-ear grin in response. James never accepted that anyone could possibly wish him any harm.

A few steps behind them came Jude also known as Thaddeus, who tried hard to restrain Simon the Zealot. Simon would rather fight the Pharisees than convert them to the New Teaching. When, on that fateful Yom Hah-Mee-Shee, that Thursday, after what became their last meal together, Yeshûa led them to the Garden of Gethsemane, Simon tried to cut off Malchus's ear. He would have succeeded if it hadn't been for Thaddeus restraining him. Even Shimon had to be restrained by the Master Himself from attacking not so much the Roman soldiers, but the treacherous servant of the High Priest.

Thaddeus has been looking out for the young, explosive Simon ever since.

Approaching from another direction, so as not to attract too much attention, came John, brother of James, thus also son of Zebedee and Salome. He led Philip and Bartholomew, and Matthew, and Didymus—yes, the Doubting Thomas.

Finally, as the self-appointed rear guard came James the Less, also known as the Just. He darted here and there, making sure that no unsavory characters, such as the High Priest's spies, would get near any of his friends.

They all walked slowly, mixed in with the crowd, so as not to be indentified. They all knew that danger was lurking, but the spies of the Pharisees couldn't spot them in the darkening day. They all, the masses, looked pretty much the same. Just simple people. Simple, ordinary folks.

Soon after sunset, more than a hundred Believers, mixed with some three thousand travelers—tired, disheveled— converged on the Temple courtyard. As many as could, tight, shoulder-to-shoulder, pressed inside, to spend the night under the Temple roof. They lowered themselves to their heels, crouched, then sat on the stone paving, laying down where there was room to rest. For many it was their first time in the Temple—first time in Jerusalem.

It was a feast everyone wanted to attend, at least once in their life.

Tomorrow thousands more would come. They'd spread across the court of the Gentiles, and even further down the slopes. They all came in the hope of Shavuoth bringing new hope, new revelation, new guidance, as it has done throughout history. Or—at least—many, many years ago. They all needed help. With the Romans around, they needed all the help they could get.

As soon as the sun had set, the protection of darkness emboldened the disciples to press closer together, surrounding Shimon on all sides. When it was definitely night Shimon rose to his feet and recited the ancient blessing:

"Baruch atah A-donai E-loheinu Melekh Ha-olam asher kid'shanu b'mitzvotav v'tzivanu al S'firat Ha-omer."

Not all of his friends understood Hebrew—as some, perhaps many, had been born and raised far north, and seldom, if ever, visited Jerusalem. With a gentle smile Shimon repeated the words in Greek, which most people understood. It was the common language, or the *lingua franca,* even for the Romans. Yes. For some disciples, even such words as Sheol were meaningless. They gave it the Greek name. They called it Hades. The place of those not yet awakened.

"Blessed are You, Lord our God, King of the Universe, Who has sanctified us with His commandments and commanded us to count the Omer."

Some heads looked up even as he spoke. They seem to draw strength from the ancient promise. The words gave them renewed faith in a greater tomorrow. Counting the Omer, they knew, was counting the forty-nine days that brought them to this day. Which brought them to Shavuoth.

For Shimon the night was strangely relaxing. Luckily, there was no moon, but the stars seemed to shine with a particular brightness, as if they, too, awaited the revelation that was to come tomorrow. Was there not a star that led the Three Wise Men to Bethlehem? Did they not bring gold and frankincense and myrrh to the Lord?

Shimon looked at his empty hands. He brought nothing but his aching heart. And hope. An abundance of hope, as they all did. Would that be enough?

Even as Morpheus embraced his tired bones, Shimon's mind seemed to reach back to happier times. His eyes, under his eyelids, drifted back, until he saw vague reflections of a dying fire. Yeshûa was standing in the middle of the circle of His friends, His loose robe swaying a little in the shore-bound wind. It was a warm, balmy night. All His friends, the disciples, often spent the night, outdoors, together, at the sandy shores of the Sea of Galilee.

A smile displaced the almost permanent frown on Shimon's tired face. He felt the gentle breeze on his cheeks; Yeshûa's voice was soft, persuasive, removing all doubt, all worry from his mind.

Shimon was happy. Again.

They sat in a circle, listening to Yeshûa talk. It was very different from the times when the Master talked to the masses of people who, for some time now, were following Yeshûa wherever He went.

When He preached to them, He preached how to live, here, on earth, how to manage their life, how to overcome difficulties that arose between various people. Essentially, He taught them that when they eliminate strife and selfishness, life would become easier. For everyone. For them and for others. He taught them how to live. How to conduct their ordinary, everyday lives.

His teaching was very simple. If you love one another, He'd said, then you eliminate all enemies; you become surrounded by friends; and friends, He said, help one another. What could be simpler?

But when Shimon and the chosen few, the twelve of them, and Yeshûa were alone, away from being overheard by others, He talked of different things. He talked of His Kingdom. Not in parables but... well, His words often sounded strange. He taught that whatever we think of, whatever we feel deeply about, creates an echo in a reality which is akin to a dream. And that is why, He'd said, it is not what we do that matters so much, but what we think and feel. These are the two foundation stones of my Kingdom, He'd said. This is where we become masters of our own domain, where we are truly in the image and likeness of our Father. This is where our will is the most powerful force in the universe. On earth and in heaven. This is where Ye are gods, He repeated, many a time. This is where ye are gods.

None of this is real... He'd repeated often, though only when they were alone. Unless you accept this truth, you cannot enter the Kingdom of Heaven, He'd said. He insisted on that. Heaven is within you. In the Kingdom where we are all gods.

Heaven is within you...

Shimon didn't understand most of His words. That last statement, about heaven, was the hardest to understand. He doubted that his friends understood any better. Not with their mind. But what did happen was a strange feeling that Yeshûa was telling him what he already knew. What he'd always known, deep, in his heart.

A rare smile appeared on Shimon's face. Lately, it did so only when he was alone with his thoughts. His dreams. His memories. Yes, mostly with his memories. He wouldn't let them go.

None of this is real...

As so often, when Yeshûa spoke time seemed to stop. Perhaps He did transport them, if for but fragments of eternity, to a different reality which He called His Kingdom.

The fire was dying now. A spark flew, here and there, Yeshûa's contour dissolved in the ripple of the wavelets of Gennesareth. Gradually the water became lustrous, perfectly still.

And then Shimon heard a great wind rushing at him from above. Yet he didn't wake up, though he could swear that his eyes were wide open. He also felt Yeshûa's Presence. Just as He'd promised.

***

4

THE DAY AFTER

It took **Shimon the whole of the night** to recover. Whatever had happened on Shavuoth, on that southwestern hill of Jerusalem, was not only beyond his expectations, but it didn't make any logical sense. Not with logic as he knew it.

Frankly, his recollection of that day was hazy. Fragments went well beyond real, yet they were as vivid as some of the things Yeshûa had done and said when still amongst them. Others, other things he himself had said, other reactions from the crowds, seemed veiled in a haze of improbability. Yet, again, throngs of people seemed to sway with his every word, as though grasped in a gigantic wave of Truth spilling from his mouth.

In a strange way, in so many ways, it was a humbling experience. There were fragments of events, or recollections, Shimon couldn't quite accept, couldn't quite reconcile with the way he'd always regarded the world.

Just imagine.

Twelve frightened men, deprived of a will of their own, talking to thousands of people coming from different parts of the world; talking to total strangers, in the strangers' own tongues, in their local vernacular, telling them of things which completely upset the usual, accepted norms of behaviour. And the men, those foreigners, seemed to be accepting the new world-view, accepting the new concept of reality; accepting, absorbing, making it their own.

"Does this make any sense?" Shimon looked at his friends, his co-conspirators, who stood throughout the long day, from sunrise till sunset, sharing the Good News.

They'd all been talking, all been expounding, all had been sharing the Good News, which they hardly understood themselves. All twelve of them. That's right, twelve, no longer eleven.

Shimon smiled against his will. There was nothing funny about it—about yesterday. The same semi-smiling, semi-disbelieving expression played havoc with his friends' faces. They kept looking at each other, hoping that someone, anyone of them would offer an explanation. They still couldn't quite accept the reality of what they knew had happened.

"Does any of this make any sense?" Shimon repeated, this time as though talking to himself.

His colleagues all knew what he meant. They all looked just as flabbergasted. Whatever they did yesterday, on that incredible *Yom Ree-Shon*, on Shavuoth unlike any other Shavuoth, was as much beyond their understanding as beyond any logical process that could be explained by the human mind.

"Does this make any…" Shimon stopped short.

To Shimon it didn't. He was a stubborn man. He wouldn't give up his established mindset easily. In that sense, he really was *Kepha*. And he might be persuaded to compromise on any matter, other than on the Master's teaching. On that he was immovable.

Yet, at the same time, it was he, Shimon the Rock, who was no longer afraid, who stood proud in the midst of a hornets' nest, on the broad steps of the Temple itself, steps leading to the Hall of Hewn Stones, to the Sanhedrin, to the Holy of Holies beyond. It was he who had preached to the swaying masses.

He stood and spoke the words Yeshûa put in his mouth, with priests looking on, unable to do anything, unwilling to show their true colours in front of the milling thousands who seemed to hang on his every word.

And not just *his* words.

The same was true of all his friends. Every one of them. They just couldn't reconcile their own memories of that day with the way they regarded reality of everyday life. It was as if the Master had been there, standing amongst them, speaking through their lips.

They hardly slept last night.

And then, with the rising sun, the fire lit their hearts again.

Ignoring the dangers inherent from the priesthood, Shimon and John returned to the Temple. People, hungry for the Word, were already there, waiting. Both he and John, each delivered another sermon. It wasn't quite like yesterday, but the remnants of fire still burned within them. Other disciples went out and preached on the surrounding streets. This time close to five thousand people heard the Word; close to five thousand people accepted the Good News.

Those were the most incredible days. Had someone mentioned them a week ago, not one of the disciples would have believed it.

And yet, Yeshûa had promised it all.

At nightfall, after the second day of preaching, of sharing the Good News, sanity prevailed. Shimon led his men, in small groups of three or four, back to their hiding place. There was no need to tempt the priests and the Pharisees any further. No one knew what the Sadducees would do—they seemed so lost in their books—but the other members of the Sanhedrin? They were jealous of their power over the people. And proud. Very proud.

For now, the News has been announced. It would spread. Those who heard it would go back and pass it on to the others.

Go and teach all nations...

Shimon remembered those words. He had been told by Yeshûa to go to Jerusalem and await the Holy Spirit to descend upon them. At the time, he had no idea what the Master's words meant. Even now it all seemed unreal, although Shimon's concept of reality was undergoing profound changes. And yet not only Yeshûa but also the prophets Isaiah, and Ezekiel, and Joel, they'd all spoken about it. They'd all said that such a day would come. They said so years and years ago. For a moment Shimon wondered what would the Sadducees have to say about it. After all, it was in the books...

The pouring forth of the Spirit...

Teach all nations...

All nations? Well, they came from far and wide. His job was to plant the seed in the minds of people. There, once heard, the News would spread. To all nations. Even as the wind carries the seed to more and more fertile ground, so the thoughts, the ideas, would grow, ripen, and then be transferred to others. To all nations, until they repaired the erroneous mindset.

Andrew, always the cool-headed, the practical one, stood leaning against the mud-brick wall, examining his broken nails. He watched Shimon from the corner of his eye: the completely changed brother, who not only seemed, but was a different man. He became, once again, the brother he once knew, on the shores of Gennesareth. There was no fear in his eyes any more. There was determination. Even confidence. Once again, Shimon was the brother he loved and admired.

Shimon's transformation had begun the day before yesterday, at the Temple, when the priests began morning prayers at sunrise. It was as though his brother was awaking from a dream. The first thing he did was to appoint Matthias to join their motley bunch of Galileans, to make up the holy number of twelve. He'd take the place of Yehuda, of Judas Iscariot. The poor man. He knew not what he'd done… Perhaps that was why, when the Master had appeared to them, He'd forgiven him.

It didn't seem to have helped…

Shimon chose Matthias because worked hard on spreading the Good News. Also, he was present when Yeshûa appeared to them on that day, three days after He was murdered. Matthias saw Him and believed. He was a good man.

As for the rest of the day, Andrew was as uncertain of events as was Shimon. It felt as though some force, some albeit benevolent power, had taken over his very being and his own will, yet willing, indeed more than willing, to be used. It was like bathing in an endless ocean of abundant love and… and he knew not what else. It was euphoric, inexplicable, and yet intensely real.

All he knew was that, by the end of the second day, some eight thousand people would never be the same again. Nor, for that matter, would any of them. Any of the twelve.

Andrew knew that it was time to move. While Shimon was their spiritual leader—the Kepha upon which their faith could lean on—and become strengthened, Andrew felt responsible for their physical wellbeing. He knew that the Pharisees couldn't and wouldn't let them get away with taking over the Temple, the courtyard, and practically the whole of Jerusalem for the day of Shavuoth. Also… the following day. They, the Pharisees, the Sadducees and the priests, always regarded that day as 'their' feast, and, of course, the Temple, as their domain. Not belonging to the people, but theirs.

Thus, it was time to move.

He'd already made some arrangements.

He'd suggested to his brother that all twelve of them should break up and go to different places, to spread the Word. They would all be sent away, become apostles, emissaries, of the Good News. He knew that while Shimon was still their leader, whatever it was that happened yesterday imbued them all with strength, with still incomprehensible yet nevertheless tangible power, with knowledge, and most of all with courage to do their duty. Their duty to Yeshûa. Their duty to Yahweh?

Shimon listened in silence.

Shimon the fisherman. The fisher of man. The newly restored son of Johnah, hailed from the village of Bethsaida in the province of Galilee, as was his brother Andrew. He'd gladly return to his village to preach the Good News, but Andrew and others, thought that even Bethsaida was situated much too close for the far reaching arms of the Pharisees and the priests.

"Not if you want to stay alive long enough to spread the word," Andrew muttered. He didn't like to contradict his older brother, but, well, Shimon was never the practical one in the family.

Shimon nodded. He also respected his brother.

Andrew knew that now that the seed of success had been planted in Jerusalem, and particularly after Shimon's commanding behaviour in the Temple, for the Pharisees, the Sadducees, and the priests, and for all the ungodly traditionalists, the murder of Shimon would be a prize to aim for. And one couldn't travel anywhere in Galilee or in Judaea without coming into contact with their powerful organization. For once the various factions struggling for power in the Sanhedrin would cooperate. The speedy demise of Shimon would become their common goal. Even outside Jerusalem, they were politically as strong as they were religiously uncompromising. And more than anything, they protected their own.

Andrew knew that. That was how they'd already lost Stephen and a number of others. Quietly, at night, their throats cut or their temples smashed with stones... all brethren innocent of transgression other than spreading Yeshûa's teaching. No one, not one of the factions, claimed the responsibility.

Now, persecution would start in earnest.

The group of twelve spent the night talking, often in heated tones, to assign various parts of the world to specific members of their tiny assembly. They'd already made the decision to spread out, and preach the Good News to heathen, not just to Jews born outside of Palestine. Having decided for others in other matters, Shimon listened to his friends' advice, and decided to set out, tomorrow, on foot, to go as far north as Antioch. There was no point delaying his or anyone's departure. For all they knew, assassins hired by the younger members of the Sanhedrin might already be waiting outside their doors even now. Time was of the essence.

When all was agreed, Shimon rose to his feet.

"We must stay," he said. There was a surprised intake of air. "We must stay and preach. Our families must go. Soon. Now. But our duty lies here."

And then Shimon heard muted sobs.

Caught up in their deliberations, the men completely forgot about the women. Till now, they'd taken them for granted. The meals, such as they were, had been prepared. The floors had been swept, their clothes washed. Never did anyone of them hear a single word of complaint. Not a whisper. Yet, here and now, they've made decisions completely ignoring the women's likes or dislikes, their wants, or desires, or aspirations.

True. They were not making plans for their own benefit. They may well have been risking their lives in their projected endeavours. Yet... yet not one of them could imagine living without the women, without 'their' women being around— without their wives', sisters' or even cousins' help. The Master had never ignored the womenfolk. He treated them with the same respect He allotted to every human being that walked this earth.

Shimon felt deeply ashamed.

He stirred heavily, then got up, walked up to his wife and stroked her hair. "I am sorry," he whispered. "I'm very, very sorry. I didn't know what I was doing. Will you forgive me?"

It may well be true, in fact probable, that all the womenfolk would be much safer with the men far away. The priesthood wouldn't bother them. Neither the priests nor the Pharisees had a very high opinion of women in general, and women outside their own household in particular.

Yet, Shimon insisted on the men staying. He stood by his wife, seemingly unable to move.

Other men approached various members of their own families with equally as contrite words. Not one of them realized how much they would all miss their wives, the gentleness of a woman's touch. Suddenly they didn't want to leave. Not one of them.

"Let's all stay and fight, right here," exclaimed Jude the Zealot, rising to his feet and drawing a knife from his belt that looked more suitable for peeling apples than fighting off the priests' assassins, let alone the Roman Legions.

"Later," said Thaddeus. "Later my friend," he promised, pulling Jude back to sit on the floor next to him. Then Thaddeus rose again and walked across the room to make peace with his own wife.

"B-b-but..." suddenly the young Jude's chutzpa evaporated and he sank to the floor. He was the youngest, but living with unrequited emotions tired him more than others. Nevertheless, his heart was in the right place.

Later, much later, they did leave Jerusalem. Most of them. First for Judea and Samaria, then to much more distant parts of the world. Shimon's work did in fact take him as far as Syrian Antioch, though his wife would remain in Bethsaida. There were the children to consider.

At long last, various parts of the civilized world have been allotted to those most suited for each mission. They were each given a task, and a time period for reporting to Shimon of their successes. There was a lot to do.

Shimon, from his base in Antioch, would take on scattered communities of Believers including the Jews, Hebrews who later called themselves Hebrew Christians, in Asia Minor, in Pontus, Cappadocia, Galatia and Bithynia, among others. The remaining eleven had equally as varied assignments to share the Good News; with Scythians and Thracians, and farther out, as well as with the Parthians, the Medes, Persians, Hyrcanians, Bactrians and Margians, all the way to India, and a number of towns in North Africa.

Ultimately, of course, in time, some would return to Jerusalem.

If they survived.

If it was the will of Yahweh.

It was an incredibly taxing assignment, an enormous territory to cover, for just a few simple men. Twelve men with no previous experience of teaching, nor of sharing the Good News, were about to embark on changing the mindset of the world. Virtually, of the whole world known to them.

No experience—except for the day of Shavuoth.

On that day they'd all learned, as though by magic, that single, supreme skill of submitting completely, unreservedly, to the inner voice that used them to perform inhuman, or perhaps superhuman deeds. That single day would last them, each one of them, a lifetime. It was their baptism of the Holy Spirit, which they neither could, nor would, want to forget.

Even if they, most of them, still weren't sure what exactly had happened.

Though unwittingly, there were more tears; quiet, undemanding, yet hard to control. And not just the women's tears. But they all understood. They've all been selected for the job.

And women would have to wait. In spite of mutual sadness, no one suggested any compromise. Men would have to cope without the women—women, without men. Neither had any choice. They'd all been not just called—they'd all been chosen. The select few. Men and women. Both.

***

5

SAUL

S aul wiped the sweat from his face with the edge of the toga slung over his arm. He liked wearing the flowing garment. It made him feel more like a Roman citizen. Like a member of the elite. After all, only Roman citizens were allowed to wear one. It was getting covered with dust, he noticed, with a shrug of disgust. Also, in this sun, it was loosing its color. Everything was getting pasty, dull, like his life of late. His life, his friends, and yes, even his toga. Part of the job, he shrugged, not that it made him feel any better.

He's done a lot of shrugging, lately.

It was all right to be Yehudi, a Jew, he mused, but life was made bearable only thanks to being a Roman citizen. And ridding the countryside of pests and riff-raff, and most of the followers of that carpenter's son who are making all this trouble was all that kept him from being bored to death. That's right, still making trouble, although he's been dead for two years now, yet, well, he was still making trouble.

"I can't stand riff-raff," Saul spat in the sand, muttering the words as though getting rid of something distinctly unpleasant. "Not that the bunch behind me are much better. At least in Tarsus there were people one could talk to. Intelligent, knowledgeable people. Now, even in Jerusalem such were few and far between. Gamaliel? Well, he was an old man now. Kept mostly to himself."

He said none of this out loud, but the words resonated within him, within his frustrated ego. He would never admit it to anyone, but he really enjoyed watching the sticks and stones landing on the backs of the cowards who wouldn't even stand up and fight like men. Or women, for that matter. They were all weaklings that should be expunged from the human race.

He couldn't understand why Gamaliel told him to leave the followers of Yeshûa alone. Why should I listen to him? I'm a Jew, but a Roman citizen, he mused. And proud of it. Not some forgotten Galilean.

Only the Galilean wasn't forgotten. His renown was growing by the day. Could there be something to his teaching?

He spat on the ground, again, narrowly missing his own sandal. He never practiced spitting; not like the centurions. Never had time. They just stood there, on guard, spitting. To kill time, he supposed. Also he never had enough water to waste. Anyway, this was better than tent making. Better than manual labour he had to do in Jerusalem in order to support himself. He was much too old to be supported by his mother. She had some money that continued to come from the domains Paul's father still held in Tarsus, but not much. Barely enough to keep herself in good health.

Saul never forgot that he was a Pharisee. He, like all the Pharisees, stood apart. That made them better than others; better than common people. Only the Pharisees didn't have the money the Sadducees had. The Sadducees turned running the temple into a money making machine.

"Not us," Saul murmured. "Not the Pharisees. We were set apart. Even apart from the money…?"

He spat on the ground again, this time missing his sandal by a good foot. He was getting good at spitting. He was pretty good at whatever he did. Not just tent making. He'd tried many different trades, and always came up tops.

"Just clever," he mused, a judicious smirk crossing his face.

That was before he took on the job of cleaning up the riff-raff from all parts of Galilee, Samaria, and even farther north. He was hoping that soon the whole of Syria would become a Roman Province. That would get rid of riff-raff once and for all.

Saul's thoughts drifted back to the carpenter's son. It was hard to believe that two years have past since the Romans got rid of him.

Kingdom of God—within you?

Saul remembered some of Yeshûa's teaching. What sort of nonsense was that? *Shamahyim* is when Tiberius looks kindly at you. That's real heaven, not some Galilean contrivance. Tiberius Julius Caesar Augustus, the Glorious Emperor of Rome provides you with heaven.

Saul was proud of remembering the Emperor's full title. In time he would be amply rewarded. That would be *Shamayim*, or Kingdom of Roman Elohim, if you will. *Shamayim* is when you get a promotion. *Shamayim* is when people bow to you, low, seeing the Roman insignia. That's *shamayi h'shamayim*. The heaven of heavens.

Even as his thoughts churned with frustrations billowing his ego, his back was straightening up. He was shorter than most men. For years no one had listened to him. No wonder he was frustrated. Surely, he had so much to offer. That was one of the reasons he'd decided to become a Roman Citizen. Of course, in Taurus he was born as one. With Roman insignia he could look down at all men who towered over him. Mostly he did. And they bowed.

"Pick your feet up!" he shouted threateningly, as two of his scouting group drifted too far behind.

He didn't really care about his contingent of men. They were nobodies—a shekel a dozen; well, a denarius anyway. He, Saul of Tarsus, of the stock of Israel... He, Saul, of the tribe of Benjamin, a Hebrew of the Hebrews... A Pharisee, the son of a Pharisee... I, born a Roman citizen, I shall walk in nobody's shadow.

"In nobody's shadow!" he hissed, again, through clenched teeth.

Everyone walked in somebody's shadow. But not he, not Saul of Tarsus.

With every step a little cloud of dust rose on the soles of his sandals, only to fall and settle in the still air. Not a single breath of wind stirred the air. It was hot, like in the Negev desert, but he had a job to do. Those followers of that upstart Yehoshûa had to be kept down from lifting their heads. Who in Mosheh's—I mean in the Divine Tiberius's—name, (he still had them mixed up on occasion), does he think he is.

Did he think he *was*, he corrected himself quickly.

It seemed that one heard a lot more about him now that he was dead. Something didn't feel right. How was that possible? Gamaliel... no. The old man Gamaliel couldn't have been right. Saul had spent some time at Gamaliel's feet learning the Law, but that was long ago. Still, from that day, that peculiar Shavuoth, now two years ago, something strange has happened.

Something very peculiar...

At least he's dead now. Good riddance. King of the Yehudim? That bunch of riff-raff? I could be twice as powerful as any Yehudi. I'm a Roman born and bread.

"By Tiberius's name, I could be an Emperor myself!? He hissed through clenched teeth. And then he looked over both his shoulders to make sure no one heard him. Such thoughts could cost him his life. And yet...

The Divine Tiberius didn't like competition. Saul rubbed his neck. Yeah, one could lose one's head for less then that. Even a Roman citizen.

He shook his head reassuringly.

We have enough trouble with the Yehudim, he thought, a sardonic smile broadening his mouth. There was grim humour in the expression on his face.

Frankly, most of the time, Saul no longer thought of himself as a Jew. His hand drifted up to touch the large brooch he'd treasured since his earliest days. It once belonged to a military style purple cloak worn by a general who'd attempted to make a pass at his mother. Quite openly. His father stood by, helpless. Saul hardly remembered the general, but mother decided to take her son back to Jerusalem. Saul kept the brooch as a token of having a Roman General dine under his parents' roof. And that lead to Gamaliel.

If only his mother had known...

He'd never forgiven his mother. From the shores of the Mediterranean city, the shore washed by the warm waters of the sea, she took him to dry, hot, Jerusalem, where he was surrounded on all sides by suspicion. Since the Romans came, nobody could be trusted. It was too easy to make an extra shekel by spilling some false stories about someone you didn't like. The Romans were counting on it.

Thus, although born in Tarsus, within the boundaries of the Roman Empire, Saul was brought up mostly in Jerusalem. For years he studied at the feet of Gamaliel, a leading authority of the Sanhedrin on the Law. The ancient Law of Israel. The *Imperium Romanum* may have been preceded by what had been the Roman Republic by some 500 years, but that was nothing compared to the history of Israel. Nothing at all.

"One day we shall rise, again... like the Phoenix..." he mused, his eyes searching the road ahead for something to give him and his men some shade.

Still, for some reason Gamaliel warned the whole Sanhedrin to refrain from slaying the disciples of Yehoshûa. Saul never understood why.

"Riff-raff," he sneered under his nose. "Just riff-raff,' he repeated as though to reassure himself. He would not admit it openly, but he'd derived real pleasure from watching Stephen being stoned. Stoned to death, of course.

The sun beat on them mercilessly. It was getting too tough to walk in the punishing heat any farther. Saul wiped his face, again, with his sleeve. As he stopped, the twelve people he led stopped behind him, and immediately lowered themselves onto their haunches.

"In *shamayim*, or the Kingdom of God," Saul mused, "it wouldn't be so hot. Inside of you or outside of you."

"Could we rest for a moment, Master?" the man farthest away asked, looking pointedly at a lone cedar some fifty paces off the road, nestled among some pointed rocks.

There had to be another five leagues to Damascus. His men, lazy though they were, deserved a rest in this heat.

Saul looked at the solitary tree, about three furlongs ahead, and indeed, some fifty paces to the right of the dirt track. There might be just enough shade there to provide some respite for his weary bones. He nodded and quickened his pace towards it. There he picked the best spot for himself. The rest of the men followed and shuffled to get into the shade. There wasn't much of it.

The last thoughts Saul had before dropping off were that the Romans had a lot to learn about what to wear in such heat. Unlike his men, he wore a standard Roman toga. The garb may have looked impressive in *Forum Romanum,* he thought, but here, anything going down to one's ankles could only serve to trip you up, especially when going up hill. On the other hand it did give him an air of authority. And he thought, perhaps hoped, it did make him look taller. If only it weren't quite so bloody hot... Maybe Rome was cooler this time of the year? Ah... let Rome solve their own problems. He had enough of his own.

For no reason at all he was getting angry.

The road was dusty. Weren't they all? Only the Romans had the engineering skills necessary for laying out a half-decent road on which a man of stature could travel. Still, Saul enjoyed his job. It gave him a position people respected. People? Riff-raff, he repeated for the thousandth time; mostly Yehudim who didn't know what was good for them. If they weren't so lazy they, too could have had an empire. Perhaps not as big as Rome, but still, an Empire with a capital E. If Alexander of Macedon could do it, so could a Yehudim. A Hebrew. People with history as old as the world itself. Ah, if I had half a chance... I'd show them...

An empire.

An Empire like the world has never seen...

Rome had their problems, too, but they overcame them. Not we. Not the Jews. Did we not have a splendid history? And look at us now. Nobodies. A bunch of nobodies. If I hadn't been born in Tarsus I'd be just like one of them.

"Well, not if I can help it," he muttered, to no one in particular. Even in his detachment, a mere dozen men, no one would understand his needs. They weren't born free men. Nobodies.

He drew some water from his skin container, rolled it in his mouth, and spat excess into the dust. It didn't taste good. They can't even make good skins, these days, he mused. Actually it sounded more as though he'd snarled. A growling noise emerging from the back of his throat.

There were not many people around he could talk to these days. Not many. There were the Romans, and... and... and even the Romans tended to look down on him. He'd show them, one day. He'd show them...

A vague smile broadened his lips even as he dozed off in full knowledge that at least he, Saul, was one of the people destined for greatness. He felt it in his bones. Images of an empire... a statue of his face and torso, twice his natural size, adorning town squares, his name carved in stone... Tall, tall statue...

An empire like the world has never seen...

An hour later the sun cleared the trunk of the tree and, weaving its ways between the branches, a single ray struck Saul's face with blinding intensity. The rest of his body, even most of his face, remained in partial shadow. He hadn't stirred. He saw himself on the beach in Tarsus. The southern breeze from the Mediterranean was washing over him. He loved that sun. The sun of his youth. Why did his mother ever leave Tarsus? It wasn't fair. Nothing was ever fair in his life. The sun... the glorious sun filling his eyes.

Swish, swish... gentle waves breaking over the pristine sand.

Am I dreaming?

Then he smiled. For a moment he imagined the swishing sounds were the sticks falling on the backs of the cowering traitors to his father's faith.

Then the breakers returned rolling along the sand...

It was as real as any reality. More so. It held him tight in its grip, holding him, embracing him, making him lose all awareness of time. Ah, the caress of the sun of his youth... Not at all like the blinding persistence of heat in Palestine. The words he heard were soft, hardly above a whisper. Mother?

Words? Was someone speaking?

Swish... Saul?

Unbeknownst to him, a centurion in his splendid attire led his small detachment in a measured step along the road. They didn't seem tired at all.

Saul's men tried to melt into the rocks, unsure how the Romans might treat them in the open field. Saul refused to wake up. His mind was miles away, his feet in the balmy water of the Tarsus's shore. Swish, swish, rolled the waves.

Swish... The rhythm of the breakers sounded like a roll of drums; the swish of their metal to metal, of their armour, left-right-left-right... Swish, swish, as though saying Saul, Saul, Saul...

Saul, Saul, Saul, swish, swish...

The Roman scouting party didn't even glance in Saul's direction. They marched past him and his men without giving them a second thought.

Saul...

Saul, Saul...

Swish, swish retreated into the heat of desert.

Saul?

There was more. There was that blinding light telling him something. Telling persistently. Demanding attention. Saul... Saul?

There were other words... for now buried deep in his subconscious. Words made up of light. Of blinding light.

Saul...why persecutest thou me?

He shook his head. The sun continued to blind him.

Saul...tell me... Saul...

He was afraid to recall the other words. Raw fear held him motionless while the sun continued to burn his eyelids. Yet, there was also hope in those words. Wasn't there? If he could only bring them back... *Saul, Saul,* kept ringing in his ears. *Saul, Saul...* There was great pain in those words. Such pain as he'd never known. A soul wrenching pain.

Saul remained motionless. Then he opened his eyes and stared directly into the sun. He still couldn't move. And then, and then... he couldn't see anything. Nothing at all. The sun was filled with darkness.

"Why can't I hear the rest of the words? Why can't I see... Why can't I see?

***

6

THE END OF DARKNESS

Saul raised himself on one elbow, then leaned back, again, collapsing flat on his back. For a while he remained quite motionless. He felt totally spent—more so than usual. After blinking a few times he realized that he couldn't even see his own hand in front of his eyes. My eyes must be tired, he mused. I'll keep them closed for a little while, and the blindness will go away. Must be temporary.

Aren't all things temporary? Even empires. Even Alexander... thirteen years and it was over...

A blink of an eye?

Saul blinked again only to be rewarded, once more, with total blackness. A bit longer, he mused.

Saul has been obsessed by Alexander the Great for some time. Not just because the Macedon's empire was one of the largest empires of the ancient world, but also because he'd established it at such a young age; even if he did die young afterwards. Just thirty-two. About as old as I am now, Saul mused, only I still don't have an empire.

He blinked again.

"Whatever happened to me," he murmured, this time with some unease, "my sight is gone. For now," he added quickly. "For now."

And then he remembered. There were also those words he'd heard. Strange, incomprehensible words. Must have been dreaming? It's amazing what tricks your imagination can play on you, he mused. He remembered how he, as a boy, was pretending to be Alexander himself. He'd raise a stick, high, and command all his imaginary friends to bow low to him. Then his mind returned to the present.

"Why can't I remember what's been said? It sounded important… Why can't I see… Why can't I see?"

And then it hit him. He was blind. Totally, absolutely blind. Not even lifting his head and staring into where he thought the sun ought to be yielded any result. Total, abysmal darkness.

"Could I have slept into the night?" he wondered, a glimmer of hope crossed him mind. "Yahweh knows I was tired enough, but if so, where are the stars?"

And then cold beads of sweat run down his neck.

"Am I dead? Do dead people sweat?"

He didn't say any of this aloud, but the words escaped his lips in a loud whisper.

"You called, Master?"

Saul recognized the voice of one of his men. So, he mused, I am alive. Unless the poor bastard also died, and found himself in Sheol with me.

Saul shrugged, totally baffled. If we're both in Hades, then at least I have one of my men with me. It can't be that bad. He almost smiled realizing that Greek 'Hades' sounded more familiar to him then the Hebrew Sheol. In Tarsus everyone spoke Greek—the language of his childhood.

His thin lips broadened in a forced smile.

"It's all right, Aba'ye, I'll call you when I'm ready," he replied, trying to sound as assuring as he could.

Aba'ye was his number one man. He held the others in marching order. Nevertheless, there was an undisguised tremor in Saul's voice. He wouldn't admit it even to himself, but he was scared. Deadly scared.

Then his mind turned to his bunch of men. In order… he shrugged involuntarily. Some order, he sneered.

He sneered a lot, lately. Sneered and shrugged.

Saul couldn't show any weakness to his men. It wasn't that he didn't trust them not to take advantage of him—his purse was well hidden under his toga—but it would be unseemly. For a moment he was grateful for the abundant folds of his toga as against the short tunics worn by his men. There and then he would have felt naked in one of those. Nevertheless, he couldn't show any weakness.

Impressions are very important to simple folk. What they saw, they believed. They were creatures motivated by their senses, not by their mind.

Saul reached up and felt the cedar trunk behind him. With considerable effort, he pulled himself up to lean against it. He made sure that his face didn't show any fear. Who could tell if anyone was looking at him? People took advantage of the fearful.

Then he closed his eyes.

It wasn't just his vision. There were the words he could swear he'd heard when he stared into the blinding light.

Saul… Saul…

There was more, but it didn't make any sense. Something about persecution? He recalled asking who was speaking. Who…

And than like a wave that swept all other thoughts into oblivion, full recollection filled his mind. He opened his eyes wide, still blind, his mouth ready to scream for help.

I am Yeshûa whom you are persecuting…
I am Yeshûa whom you are persecuting…
I am Yeshûa whom you are persecuting…

The accusation reverberated in his head with repetitive force. No. He hadn't imagined those words. He'd heard them. He was hearing them now, again. There was more but he shut the rest of the words out. He needed silence. He needed to escape from this strange voice…

He stared intensely into the black void, willing the voice to cease.

After another long while he again closed his unseeing eyes. It was too unnerving to have them open and see nothing. With a supreme effort he tried to relax; to slow his pulse down. His heart was racing as though he'd just fought a battle against tremendous odds. At long last his breathing seemed to return to normal.

"What have I done?" he whispered. "In all these years... What have I been doing?"

Saul wondered what time of the day it was. He never realized that without eyesight, time lost its meaning. He might have slept for a long time without knowing it. Was it still daylight?

He realized that as of this moment he became completely dependent on the peasants for whom he had nothing but disdain. Yes, nothing but intense scorn. The group of country yokels he called foot soldiers, a band of only slightly disciplined riff-raff, would now serve as his eyes, as his leaders, possibly his defenders. His short Roman sword, which he wore with such pride, was no better than a stick he could wield against an invisible enemy. Was there an enemy? Had he made any friends among his men? Anywhere? Anywhere in the world? Or did his men have as little regard for him as he had for them.

"Aba'ye?" he called in half tone. He didn't want all of his men to hear. Not yet.

His man must have remained nearby.

"Yes, Master?"

"Something happened to my eyes. You must help me."

"Yes, Master."

There was no animosity in Aba'ye's voice. Maybe they didn't all hate him. Maybe...

What have I done with my life?

Then Saul shrugged, his lips twisted in a lopsided grin.

"It must have been one of those cowards I took a stick to that cast an evil spell on me," he murmured. "You just wait when my sight comes back. I'll show you. I'll show you all! I'll wipe the earth with your miserable carcasses..."

"What was that, Master?" His servant didn't quite hear him.

"Just help me up," Saul growled, shaking his head.

Aba'ye put his arms under Saul's armpits and lifted him up with ease. He was much taller, and all-round bigger than his leader. He was bigger than most men. Lifting Saul off the ground was nothing to him. He carried loads twice Saul's weight for leagues without resting.

"What now, Master?"

Aba'ye's physical strength was not matched by his acumen, although Saul, himself, wasn't sure what to do either.

"You must get me to Damascus," he said flatly. There was nothing else he could think of.

By now other men have seen Saul hanging onto Aba'ye's arm. Standing next to each other they looked like a pair from a traveling motley of actors. Romans loved the theater and most of them saw performances of skits outside the main auditorium. Now, the men weren't sure if they should laugh or expect something peculiar.

There were still about five leagues to go. Saul could still feel sun on his arms and head. Although Saul knew he'd slow the men down, with Aba'ye's help they should make it before sundown. Roman authorities did not recommend traveling at night. Not if you valued your life. Nor would it be healthy for the defenseless Saul. He had no idea if he could rely on his men, if danger threatened, without his leadership. Still, there was little choice.

"Let's go," he said, his voice as commanding as he could master. "Now," he added unnecessarily. The men were all already standing.

The contingent fell into step behind the asymmetrical duo. Aba'ye's large hand firmly held onto Saul's upper arm. He'd be able to lift Saul up off his feet, if necessary. Saul was really small and slight all round. But he was wiry, very fast, and with lightening reflexes. He could make a good account of himself in any scrape. He did many a time in the past.

They walked in silence. In spite of a brief rest, they were all tired. Walking all day in sweltering heat, measuring out just enough water to get to their destination, wasn't easy; neither for Saul, nor for others.

Unable to lead his men, Saul's mind, drifted again to Jerusalem, to the rough-hewn stones of Sanhedrin, where, in the absence of council sessions Gamaliel taught him the principles of the Hebrew Law. People said that his teacher would soon rise to become *Nasi* and *Rabban*, or Master, as the president of the Great Sanhedrin. Saul was lucky to have listened to Gamaliel's lectures. The man, not yet old, already held the reputation of *Mishnah*, of being one of the greatest teachers of all time.

And what have I done with this knowledge?

Saul, hanging onto Aba'ye's powerful hand, was not a happy man. Years of persecution of the nascent Christians were in direct opposition to Gamaliel's teaching. The *Rabban* always advocated tolerance, and reverence, and piety, and, yes, even compassion. He'd make indeed a great *Nasi*. A great leader of the Sanhedrin. Would the younger Pharisees listen to him?

Saul shrugged. He didn't. Not then, not now…

This time he sneered, again, though the confidence, which defined his every move until earlier that day, was rapidly waning.

At the time, in Jerusalem, he didn't know that Gamaliel is the Greek form of the Hebrew name meaning "reward of

God". Funny that, Saul grinned sadly, and I was brought up with the Greek language.

"Where would you have us take you, Master, in Damascus?"

"You'll send two men ahead to find a place to stay. Give them some money." Saul reached under his folds and extracted a few shekels from his leather pouch.

"How much is that?" he asked Aba'ye. He resigned himself to trust his right-hand man.

"Four silver shekels, Master," Aba'ye replied, his eyes wide. He'd never seen more that three shekels at one time.

"Give it to a man you trust most and send him and another ahead. Tell one of them to come back and find us."

They would continue to plod on. At least, on arrival, their meal would be ready. The men would know what to do.

Within a short time Aba'ye was back, smiling at the thought of food that four shekels could buy. He stretched himself leisurely and picked up Saul's arm.

"Are you ready to go on, Master?"

Saul nodded. He had no idea when it would begin turning dark. He had no idea how long he'd rested. Or slept. This was the first time in many years that he had no control over his future. A strange, uncomfortable feeling, he thought.

And then Aba'ye's strong arm lifted him off the ground. He never imagined that relying on someone else could be so easy. Almost relaxing. He wondered who Aba'ye really was. They travelled for two years together, seeking out Christians to give them the benefit of their sticks and, if necessary, his sword, and he never really met the man.

"Are you married, Aba'ye?" he asked.

"Oh, no, Master. I only live to serve you."

What a strange answer, thought Saul. The man has no life of his own. No life at all. A little like me, right now.

For a while they walked on in silence. What could one say to a man who has no life? What could one ask him? Soon one of the men he'd sent ahead would be back and then, soon after, they'd all sit to a hot supper. Saul thought they'd all earned it.

And then…

And then, unless he'd recover his eyesight, he couldn't even go back to tent making. He wondered how much blind beggars made. Probably more than most? More than tent makers?

A moment later he wondered what any of his men were doing before he'd hired them to beat up riff-raff—the so-called Believers. Were any of them tent-makers? Did they have other jobs that paid less? Were any of them married, have children, parents, families?

Who were those men? Those complete strangers?

And then his face twisted with a strange, crooked smile. He'd never thought of his men as someone, as people, who'd earned anything; as worthy of his thought, his concern. He paid them the agreed wage and they obeyed. They were men without life. Riff-raff. Not quite human. And now?

Saul was about to give up on logic. Too many things happened lately that didn't make any sense.

Aba'ye kept a sharp lookout for the road ahead and scanned the bushes on either side of the dirt track. It was beginning to get dark. One could never be too careful. He was paid to beat up some Christians, but not to fight the crooks and robbers who may be on the side of the road, ready to pounce on the unsuspecting latecomers. He knew how hard it was to earn an honest shekel, let alone to feed one's family. That is why he'd long decided to remain single until he saved enough to support a wife and children.

And then he heard footsteps ahead. One of the men they've sent ahead was returning at a slow trot. He waved, excitedly, his face showing happiness and satisfaction.

"They've slaughtered a lamb for us, Master. A large one. I wouldn't let them slaughter a small one. Not me. And the lodging is close by. On Straight Street. Less than half-league ahead."

The man was obviously proud of himself. He also seemed pleased to have served his master well.

Saul detected the tenor of the man's voice. He detected the pleasure. It's amazing how much you can hear when you're blind, he thought. There were a great many things that were amazing. Things he'd never thought of before. It was as though a new life was opening before him. Full of mystery and yet... and yet strangely enticing.

"Good man," he said. It felt good. He'd never praised any of his men before. And he didn't even know the man's name.

***

7

ANANIAS

Waiting was never among Saul's strong points. Even at the feet of Gamaliel, he was the first to arrive, but also the first to depart. Not physically, of course, that wouldn't do, but his attention wandered to do something, anything that required action. His body seemed to have a will of its own, and when he didn't satisfy its needs he'd become frustrated. And now, since their arrival in Damascus, his physical movement was at the highest premium.

On the first day he'd acquired a dozen bruises, a broken finger on his left hand, and a lasting headache following his unwitting attempt to walk through a solid wall. Aba'ye wasn't always there to lead him by the hand, and Saul's impetuous nature did little to restrain his desire to move. To act. To do something. Patience was not his virtue. He discovered that even for men that are blind, time goes on.

Or if it doesn't—it drags on.

He and his men arrived in Damascus just as the last rays of the sun touched the tops of the trees. Almost immediately they reached out for the choicest parts of the lamb, which by the time of their arrival was just about ready to sate their growling stomachs. They hadn't eaten since dawn. After the evening meal they collapsed, totally spent after the whole day's march.

Considering its location, Damascus was still a relatively small town. It had been settled permanently more than two hundred years ago although its history stretched back into antiquity. It is nestled on the Abana River, and is protected by mountains to the west and desert to the east. Yet the river valley is fertile and lush. Also, the town is lying on the main caravan route that stretched from Jerusalem through Shechem, Ramoth-gilead all the way to Hamath, Ebla, Aleppo and finally Haran. It has grown fast, being a natural stop for the traders to replenish their supplies. It picked up the merchants from the whole of Judea, Samaria, all along the Jordan Valley, around Lake Gennesareth all the way to upper Galilee. Less then forty leagues from the port of Tyre, it also picked up trade from eastern shores of the Mediterranean.

Saul knew most of all that—he made a point of learning about the towns or cities he was about to invade, or visit, for whatever reason. But...

But he was blind.

He couldn't enjoy the richness of vegetation after their desert trek. Also, Saul was never a merchant. Although all too often he had to perform manual labour, he considered himself well above such mundane occupations as trading. At least when he worked with his hands, he was producing something. He wasn't just benefiting from the efforts of others.

Whenever possible, as a Pharisee and son of a Pharisee, he aspired to a higher calling, such as protecting the faith of his forefathers; of the long line of prophets and teachers whose knowledge was now being threatened by this unknown upstart. He thought his work noble, even if, of late, he had to resort to wielding sticks and occasional prods with his sword, to enforce the Law, so to speak.

At least that was what he thought until just one day ago. Until those new, strange and persistent words invaded his head, and nagged at his mind, almost continuously, since yesterday.

I am Yeshûa whom you are persecuting...
Why was his mind playing tricks on him?

He thought, again, of Gamaliel. At the time, in Jerusalem, he thought of his Master as a man swept by weakness of age, of the vicissitudes of life itself. He was only a boy, then, for whom everyone fifteen or twenty years older than he looked and sounded like an old man. Privilege of youth? Or weakness of the inexperienced, immature mind.

And now it all seemed so long ago.

On the other hand, perhaps I've grown tired of being the strong arm for those sitting comfortably in their Jerusalem homes, sending such as I to do their dirty work.

Dirty work?

He never thought of it in those terms. His was a noble calling. A calling to protect the faith of...

He's been through all that before. Surely, Gamaliel couldn't have been right. Surely, Yeshûa didn't preach an enhancement of the Hebrew faith, with no intention of destroying it. Could it be that? Could it be that he, Saul, for years now, was persecuting a just man? A man who'd given his life for his beliefs?

And now I am blind. Or, perhaps, I'm just beginning to see...

Ananias left Jerusalem more then two years ago, when the Pharisees, supported by the anger of the High Priest and his underlings, began open warfare against all Believers. He'd lost everything, left all his goods behind. He and his wife took their two children and walked straight north, until the place they arrived in felt right.

He found peace, relative peace, in Damascus. The priests still had their henchmen here, there was an occasional stoning, now and then, but Damascus was a merchants' town. They were not concerned with religion. The Temple and

Sanhedrin were furthest from their minds. Shekels ruled here. Shekels and a good exchange.

Ananias, known to his Hebrew friends as Hananiah, led a quiet life. He shared the Good News with anyone who ventured into his house. He shared his beliefs with his close friends, but he did not brag, publically, of his conversion. He didn't think of Christianity, as it was beginning to be known, as a new religion, but as an implementation of the Law with the New Revelation, which served to strengthen and reestablish the old Mosaic Law.

Ananias was gracious, as his name implied.

All Yeshûa really did, Ananias claimed, was to eliminate impositions and embellishments and superfluities added by the Pharisees and/or Sadducees, not to mentions the priests who, over the years, felt the need to leave their own imprint on the inspired teaching. That, and the teaching of love. Of loving one another. By this you shall be known, said the Master. And this Ananias practiced.

And now, he had a problem.

Yesterday one of his friends came to warn him. He said that a man responsible for more arrests, if not murders, of Believers than just about anybody else, hailed into their town. He arrived in Damascus with a contingent of foot soldiers, directly from Jerusalem, with a mission of cleaning up the "Riff-raff of believers."

So he was told. Not only Pharisees had their spies.

The man was still here, sleeping on the floor. He was waiting for Ananias to tell him if they should all run, or hide.

Ananias was a kind, faithful, honest man. He wasn't particularly brave. On hearing the news, his first reaction was to get his wife and children out of town until Saul of Taurus finishes his hateful mission. He could do nothing by staying behind. He was too old to fight, and sacrificing his life would leave his wife and children without visible means of support. There were not enough brethren around to look after them.

Not yet. Their numbers were growing. In time, they'd get better organized. For now they just kept quiet. And who could tell how many or them would be left after Saul finished his mission?

Ananias was deeply depressed.

People, the new Believers, were looking up to him for guidance. He was, *de facto*, their leader. What would Yeshûa have done, he asked himself? Yeshûa did not have wife and children, his aching heart replied. But he knew that he couldn't use his family as an excuse.

Come... follow me...

He remembered those words. The words meant a great deal more than just following in His footsteps. It meant following His teaching. Of loving your neighbour as yourself. He was one of those who followed. So did his wife. And now?

There was more.

Love your enemies...

There was no greater enemy than Saul. His name was synonymous with fear. Yet there was that enigmatic statement that prayed on his mind.

Love your enemies...

At that moment Ananias knew exactly what he had to do. Just to make sure he asked himself, what would Shimon have done? Shimon remained their spiritual teacher. Knowing what lay ahead, Shimon had left his wife in Bethsaida where they both grew up. She had family there. He, Ananias, couldn't do it. He loved his wife too much. Or had he been just too selfish? Shimon gave up everything, as did the other apostles. Shimon sustained their faith.

Ananias has spent the night in prayer. At first light, he woke the messenger up.

"Where is this Saul you warn me against," he asked the young man.

"Not far, Hananiah," the young man said. "On the street named Straight, in the house of Judah. Why, you want me to take you there?" There was open sarcasm in the young man's voice. Only a fool would enter, willingly, into a lion's den.

It was to be expected of Saul. Straight Street was the main street of Damascus. Only the rich lived there.

"Yes," said Ananias. "Yes," he repeated when he saw disbelief in the messenger's eyes. "Now," he added.

He had to go at once. Had he tarried, he'd lose what little courage he'd mastered. The young man's face grew ashen. But, you didn't deny Hananiah. It would be like denying Yeshûa Himself. He took one more look at his teacher's face, confirmed that the older man was serious, and rose to his feet.

"Yes, Master," he bowed a little. "At once."

And they left.

Ananias knew that his boldness might cost him his life. Only then he remembered his wife and children. It was too late. If he turned now, he'd never muster enough courage to go to Straight Street. Not now, not ever. On the other hand, his spies had told him that Saul was on his way to Damascus to arrest the followers of Yeshûa and take them for trial in Jerusalem. If so, then he'd have another opportunity to bear witness before the Sanhedrin, even if such were followed by his execution. If he did nothing, just waited to be arrested, he would be no better off. At least by going to see Saul, he might be moved by the spirit to accomplish something. He knew that Yeshûa had already performed deeds, through him, that he'd never have accomplished on his own. He looked at some people, and they believed. After a word or two. Well, after a few words.

But these were only his afterthoughts. He'd left his house on an impulse. On a feeling that he must. He'd long learned not to analyze his intuitive urges. He'd learned to obey his inner voice.

Soon they reached the Roman Triumphal Arch leading to the town center. They approached Straight Street from the Roman gate of the Sun. As with many Roman arches, the gateway had a large central arch for horse-drawn carriages, and two smaller arches on either side for people on foot. The house of Judah was about halfway towards the other end.

"When we get there do not tarry. Just point it out to me and go back to my wife. Tell her that I had to go. If she asks, don't tell her where. Tell her it's to see a brother in need. She'll understand."

It wasn't a lie. Saul, Ananias reasoned, must be in greater need than anyone he'd ever met. Even as he spoke, his young companion pointed to a solid door on the other side of the street. It was closed and looked forbidding. It was the house of Judah. A place many travelers stopped by. Those with money, that is. Lots of money.

Ananias waited until the young man put some distance between them. He then crossed the street and knocked on the forbidding door. It seemed a lot more solid than necessary, with wide iron bars holding the heavy boards together; for those who needed extra security. Perhaps they did. They had to protect their money.

The door opened on his third knock. A tall man, about a head taller than he, pulled the door ajar.

"Yes?" It was Aba'ye. From the moment Saul and his men moved in, Aba'ye took over the security of the premises. His size alone would scatter any aspiring crooks away.

For an instant Ananias hesitated. Then he straightened himself, smiled and looked the giant directly into his eyes.

"I am Ananias," he said. "I am here to see Saul of Tarsus."

That's it. That's all he had to say. The rest was in the Lord's hands. His eyes didn't waver under the giant's stare. Surprisingly, at least to Ananias, the giant stepped out of the way and let Ananias in.

"Follow me, Hananiah," he used the Hebrew version of the name. That's all he said.

Ananias followed him inside, but only after Aba'ye shut and barricaded the door. Aba'ye led him with his giant steps into the murky interior. The windows were small, probably to discourage entry. They soon reached quite wide, wooden stairs, which led to the upper floor. They creaked under the giant's weight. Not a word was spoken between them. Evidently Aba'ye did not consider Ananias's frail figure, let alone his gray hair, a threat. Not with him around.

Upstairs they crossed the first room where half a dozen men were lounging around. They hardly moved when they saw Aba'ye, but regarded Ananias with some curiosity. Of course, they had no idea who he was.

And then they entered the inner chamber: larger, better lit, with quite elegant furniture. On a chair wide enough to sleep on, sat a small man, staring straight ahead.

"What is it Aba'ye?" His voice lost a lot of his previous commanding tenor.

"A man has come to see you, Master. His name is Hananiah," Aba'ye replied in hushed tones, as if sharing something confidential with his master.

"Hananiah? I know no Hananiah," Saul said.

Ananias took a step forward.

"Yeshûa told me to see you, Saul. He told me to come."

Saul's face turned pallid.

"But I can't see you," he replied, irony evident in his voice. He then stirred uncomfortably.

"May I approach, sir?" Ananias asked, looking at Aba'ye then at Saul.

A hollow laugh twisted Saul's face. "You can do whatever you like. I can't stop you…"

Ananias took three steps forward and put his hands on Saul's head, his thumbs covering his eyes. He then raised his thoughts to Yeshûa.

You made me come into the lions' den, Lord. May your will be done.

He held onto Saul's head, pressing his thumbs a little harder into the blind man's eyes. Then he stopped and walked back to the door. The giant barred his exit.

"What did you do, old man?" he asked. "Didn't you see the man is blind?"

"I did nothing. The Lord's will came to be," Ananias answered enigmatically.

"Hey," Aba'ye came to life. "You're not one of those believers, are you?"

For a moment there was total silence. Then they both heard stirring on Saul's chair. He got up, shook his head and approached them unassisted.

"You were sent by Yeshûa?" he asked. "The Galilean? Isn't he dead?"

Ananias looked into Saul's eyes. "He just restored your sight," he said simply.

The words reached Saul as though through a thick fog. Then the fog cleared and he nodded, his face an expression of surprise and disbelief.

"He? He restored… Yeshûa?"

…why persecuteth thou me?

The next moment Saul collapsed at their feet. He was out cold. As Aba'ye picked him up as though he were a baby, his body offered no resistance, hanging on Aba'ye arms like a rug. The giant placed him with a strange gentleness on the wide armchair.

Then he stepped back and he and Ananias continued looking at Saul; slight disbelief in Aba'ye's eyes. Slowly, very slowly, a gentle smile widened both their mouths. Then Aba'ye looked at Ananias.

"Yeshûa, you say?" he asked.

Ananias only nodded.

* * *

8

ANTIOCH

Two years have passed since Shimon saw his wife. Or had it been three years? The days here, in Antioch, were all alike. There were no breaks in his routine; no days off. And, frankly, there was no routine, either. He was on call all the time. Whenever and wherever needed.

And it wasn't just his wife. There were the children. The boys must be ready for Bar Mitzvah. Without his father around? They were responsible boys. Ready to assume their duties. Would they look after his wife for him? Look after their mother? And his daughter, sweet Petronilla. She must be a big girl now. He missed her the most. Or as much as her mother.

Knowing, or believing, that he'd done the right thing, that he'd made the right decision, didn't make things any easier. Working in, or rather from, Antioch took him on almost daily journeys; more often that he'd ever imagined. Had his wife come with him, she'd be just as alone, just as lonely, as if she'd remained in Jerusalem. That, in addition to living in one room, sleeping on straw, sharing the kitchen with two other brothers… would not be the way anybody's wife would want to live. Not even for a short while.

At least there, having returned to Bethsaida, on the gentle slopes descending to the beautiful Lake Gennesareth, their real home, she had her own family. Her father had already died some years ago, but her mother, her sisters, and aunts, must have given her a sense of family.

He, Shimon, the Kepha, on the other hand, was alone.

It wasn't easy.

The last few years enabled Shimon to establish contacts with a number of Believers inside and outside Antioch. There was no question of vast crowds, as in Jerusalem on that fateful Shavuoth, but rather a one-on-one contact, preaching to small groups of people who showed even peripheral interest in the Good News. That was how they all called it. Good News. A message of hope, of faith and particularly of charity.

Love one another...

His last words. Shimon would never forget them. Virtually, His only words. Those and love thy enemy. That was it. It was the sum total of his message to the masses. To those that were called.

Only the select few could be told about the next phase of the message. Only the few, perhaps the chosen ones, were ready. And that message was, that nothing on earth was real. Not really. That only thoughts and emotions really mattered. That Yeshûa's Kingdom really was not of this world.

Who would understand such words?

For almost the three years that Shimon had spent with the Master, he hadn't understood them either. And even now only his closest friends accepted the reality of those words. Of words that, in a way, denied reality itself.

My Kingdom is not of this world...

This enigmatic statement still churned in his ears, enveloping the physical reality, the reality of his senses with a haze of uncertainty.

Sometimes, when alone, he imagined himself leaving his body and entering the world of his dreams. Was that the Kingdom the Master had spoken about? Was that the reality in which he could do whatever he wanted, in which nothing was impossible? The Kingdom not of this world?

Recently Shimon entered that reality almost every night. Providing he had time to sleep, of course, which wasn't always. Often the discussions of the Good News took him into the early hours, followed by a quick march to some proselyte in need of his help. But, whenever time permitted, he cherished his escapes into his dreams.

His private Kingdom.

In that Kingdom time didn't exist. Nor did distance. In his dreams he visited his wife, his daughter, his sons; he even met his long dead parents. It was a strange, wondrous Kingdom where the living and the dead rubbed shoulders.

And then, one day, night rather, he'd met the Master. They didn't talk, and yet so much had been said. Perhaps he could have talked, asked questions, but it was as if Yeshûa showed himself only as reassurance. Only to show him that he, Shimon, was on the right track. Was there another heaven beyond the one he'd visited?

I shall never leave you...

He remembered the words also. They all did. All the apostles. Was that what He'd meant? They all felt His presence in times of stress, or weakness, when reassurance was required to carry on their work. Shimon met his old friends periodically. They all worked afar, but there were times when their paths crossed. There was no doubt left in any of them. Not one scrap of doubt.

Until now. But this was different.

Saul of Tarsus announced his conversion. The killer, murderer, Pharisee and son of a Pharisee, announced that he was coming. He'd sent a man to announce himself. To ask permission to see him. And, as so often in the past, Shimon has failed. He didn't have the courage to face the man who'd asked for his help. He refused to see him. At least for now.

Shimon learned later, that following the visit by Ananias, Saul went to Arabia to, as he called it, "to collect his thoughts."

Shimon changed his mind within a few hours, but by then the messenger had already left with his refusal. And a day later it was too late. Saul was gone. Who could tell if they'd ever meet as friends? Could it be that Saul has really forsaken his old ways? That his offer to meet was not some inane subterfuge to murder him, to kill him like he'd killed so many others, among them his closest brothers? Could one trust a man who'd murdered so many times before?

"I have responsibilities to my people…"

Shimon tried hard to justify his decision. But what if he was wrong? What if Saul had really changed his ways?

Now, only time would tell.

That night Shimon looked for the Master in his dreams. He looked and prayed, and woke up next morning exhausted. Yeshûa wouldn't show himself. Not even from afar.

Master, what have I done? Have I failed you again?

Hollow silence greeted his anguish. And then the rooster sang again.

A week later Ananias came to see him. Shimon had forgotten how old and frail Ananias was. He walked with a staff, small steps, his chest wheezing. He told Shimon the whole story. Ananias had no idea if Saul really had a change of heart, but, he said, a whimsical smile brightening his face, "I'm still alive!"

A convincing argument.

They both laughed, even if the laughter of both men was verging on hysterical. Well, perhaps not hysterical, but it certainly was on the nervous side. Saul's reputation had already spread throughout the Roman Empire. At least throughout the segment of the Empire they were both familiar with. Saul was not welcome among the brethren. Among the Believers. Nor was he likely to be—in the foreseeable future.

The two friends sat outside, their backs against the mud-brick wall, enjoying a moment of respite. Ananias was tired. Even on his old nag, it took him nearly a day to get to Antioch from Damascus. Of course, it could have been done quicker, but there were always old friends, some not so old, he felt he ought to visit, just making sure that they remained on the straight and narrow.

"Truth," he often told them, "must be continually rediscovered."

That's why they all needed prayer, he'd said. Not to ask for blessings, but to listen. Just to listen...

The Truth, Shimon knew, was almost whimsical, intangible, yet unchangeable in its Kingdom. It wasn't easy to accept, harder to understand. But once discovered it was intensely real.

The Good News wasn't hard to follow, but only if one submitted totally to its dictates. A half-hearted manner only brought hardship. Most people had to find that out for themselves. Both Shimon and Ananias knew that, yet even so Shimon still had moments of weakness. Although they met rarely, Ananias, older of the two, ended up being the one who'd always cheered him up. Only his body was older.

"It will come, my friend," he'd say when Shimon confessed to his weaknesses. "It will come. Remember, He's always with us."

It was beginning to sound like a mantra. It was a mantra that kept them all going.

"In the meantime, there's work to do," Shimon smiled. "Now that you are here, there's a man I want you to see."

Ananias knew what Shimon meant. They helped each other. Sometimes he got through mindsets Shimon couldn't penetrate, sometimes the other way around. But always they fought for every single soul. There were no exceptions.

At least, not for Ananias. Shimon made an exception for Saul. Of course, he had good reasons.

After a while, they got back to the problem of Saul. Shimon couldn't forgive himself for not allowing a man who'd confessed his conversion from seeing him.

"Even if you did see him, no brother would come near him. They wouldn't trust him after what he'd done for a number of years," Ananias said.

"That may be true, but my job is not to pass judgment but to help…"

Ananias let that ride. Shimon was right, of course, but in this case, even though Ananias took the risk of seeing Saul, he could hardly blame Shimon for refusing.

"You know," Ananias started again, "there was something that troubled me. Saul kept insisting that he heard voices. Before and after he went blind. It could have been his conscience acting up. After all these years…"

He waited for Shimon's reaction. When none came, he continued, studying the younger man's face.

"Anyway, he raved something about being a chosen vessel to bear the Master's name before the Gentiles. When I asked him if he thought that that was his mission, the man answered 'yes'. But also, he'd added, before kings and the children of Israel. What do you make of that?"

"He must carry an enormous baggage of guilt…" Shimon knew well what it meant to feel guilty.

Ananias decided not to tell Shimon that, after some further instruction, he'd actually baptized Saul; Saul and that giant of a man who called himself Aba'ye. Ananias was impressed by the big man's almost childlike gentleness. And, after all, the Lord moves in mysterious ways and chooses many strange vessels.

Shimon yawned. They had talked last night till the early hours. Tonight, they needed to catch up on their sleep.

For a short while, both men retreated into their private kingdoms. They woke up just as the first stars began to shimmer over the vast Syrian sky. The semi-arid climate made them as sharp as diamonds—and as inaccessible to men of their station. And yet kings had to spend fortunes to buy them for their wives and concubines. Shimon and Ananias had an abundance of those heavenly sparklers for free. In the palm of their hands.

About the same time, Saul crossed the outer boundaries of the Land of Edom, also called Idumea, the outskirts of the Arabian dessert. A high, undulating, parched plain, punctured with loosely scattered rocks. He was alone. He left his men, and most of his silver coins, with Aba'ye, trusting him to do the right thing. He refused to give him instructions. When Saul set out on his lonesome way, the giant had tears in his eyes. For a while Saul decided to forego tent making, or any work to keep body and soul together. In a strange way, this very decision gave him a sense of freedom.

Ananias's arrival in Damascus, at Judas's house, left him stunned. Why would a man, no longer young, visibly elderly and tired, come to him knowing his reputation? Weren't those Jews, who call themselves Believers, afraid of anything?

"I would be!" he half hissed, half whispered. "I wouldn't come near me…"

For a brief moment his face twisted in a cruel, almost lascivious grin and then, for the first time in many years, it relaxed in a strange, unfamiliar smile.

What was the mysterious power that those Believers, that Ananias, possessed that was so very strange to him? Who was Yeshûa? Who was he, really?

The Believers called him the Son of God. But he, Saul was a Pharisee. He knew the Law. Did not the Scriptures say that Ye are gods? That we are all sons of the Most High? Did not the Believers merely repeat the long forgotten words?

And if so, why were they condemned by the Sanhedrin?

Though not by Gamaliel…

It's been awhile since Saul was alone; alone anywhere. To do his job, and for his own protection, men have always surrounded him. His indispensible foot-soldiers. His men.

Men he paid to protect him. Riff-raff he called them, but in essence he trusted them with his life. He wouldn't think of falling asleep without two or three of them standing on guard.

And now, for the first time in more years that he could remember, he was alone. There wasn't a single living soul around.

"Don't need protection here," he mused, hardly believing his own thoughts. He was so preoccupied with danger generated by men, including by men like himself, that he never imagined that snakes, serpents and scorpions feast at night.

Even as he'd heard so much more when he was blind, now he saw beauty he'd never seen before—beauty in the contours of the dessert. Mysterious contours emerging from the windswept, moon-enhanced rocks, jutting up at various angles, indifferent to his presence.

"What a strange world we live in..." he muttered to himself.

He was no longer a young man, but only now, for the first time in his life, he was aware of beauty. Beauty and mystery that the dessert kept from him until this day.

"Master, I didn't know what I was doing..." he whispered.

He looked up at a starlit sky, as he used to when still a small boy on the beach in Tarsus. And then, for the second time in the last couple of weeks he lost his sight; only this time, it was because his eyes were filled with tears. Slowly he walked up to the nearest rock, leaned his back against it and began to cry.

***

9

ARABIA

When Saul recovered, the moon was high, casting grotesque shadows all around him. He breathed in the night air of the desert inspiring, for the second time in as many days, an indescribable feeling of freedom. He no longer felt compelled to serve anyone. At least not anyone in Jerusalem or in Rome. He felt free, as he'd never felt before.

Before leaving Damascus, he gave away his Roman toga and other paraphernalia of his rank, and took in exchange a simple Jewish *abayah*. He'd only kept his own undergarments. Also, though with strangely hesitant misgivings, he kept his short Roman sword. He couldn't break with the past completely. At least, not yet. His sword was even more precious to him than the brooch his mother had given him.

The sword defined who he was. Who he had been all these years. Every zealot he'd ever met was jealous of this symbol of power. Of superiority.

The *abayah* consisted of little more than a rectangular piece of woolen cloth. The front and the openings for arms remained unstitched. It was particularly useful to him now, as he could wrap himself in it to keep warm. And that was how he'd spent the first night in the desert.

His head covering, a must for anyone venturing into the desert, was a simple square woven cloth, folded triangularly.

One corner protected the nape of his neck, the other corners crossed under his chin and were held in place by a woolen cord. He looked no different than any wanderer, a vagabond, who'd lost his way in the desert. There were such men, moving from village to village, from town to town, in search of employment. These were hard times in Palestine. Without people helping each other, many would not have survived.

Maybe there is something to this New Teaching, he mused. To the Good News which Ananias tried so hard to impart to him. His head was full of concepts that were completely outside his previous ideas of how the world worked—in spite of having spent years at the feet of Gamaliel. Although seemingly the same as the Hebraic Law, in some indefinable way, it was different. Or was it just Ananias's fault?

"I'll have to visit him again," he thought, a little jealous of the old man's knowledge.

Saul was a man of action, not of philosophizing. "They ought to leave that to the Greeks," he'd often said. "At least they are good at it." Then he'd list a long line of Greek names he remembered from the days he'd spent in Tarsus. Even as a young boy, the Greeks impressed him in many ways. More than anything—they had history. More history than the Romans.

On the other hand, from what he'd heard, those new Believers were a completely disorganized bunch. Right or wrong, they needed a leader who knew how the world works. They had no idea. They were idealists. Dreamers.

"Isn't this what I am becoming? A Believer?" He grinned again. "Or perhaps just a dreamer…"

During the short time he'd spent in the desert, he'd grinned more than he ever had in his life. It seemed natural. Effortless.

"Maybe there was something to it…" he repeated, this time sounding more pensive.

The next morning, he walked ahead, the sun guiding him toward the south-east. By the time the sun was a little past its zenith, quite by accident, he came across an empty shack, probably once inhabited by a hermit or a beggar, who evidently sought solitude.

For once, his short stature came in handy. He could almost stand up straight inside. The shack had a roof of closely laid palm-leaves, and it was enclosed on three sides, protecting him from the prevailing wind. The word shack didn't quite do it justice, it fell short of that, but it was a shelter of sorts. It would do for now. Outside there were remnants of charcoal, the residue of a fire. Someone had lived here, he mused. Someone must have found food that sustained him. He touched the hilt of his sword. It felt good.

It would do, he decided. For now.

And for an inexplicable moment, probably for the first time in his life, he felt grateful. To whom? To Yahweh?

Surely, not to Yeshûa.

And yet…

Saul walked around slowly, nearby, becoming familiar with the dessert. He'd always crossed it by road or a dirt track; he'd never stopped in it for any length of time. By the time the sun travelled halfway towards the western mountains, he began to feel hunger. He tried to remember what animals lived in the semi-arid terrain. He knew of many insect species. In his days of travel, he's also seen many times all sorts of arachnids—creepy things with eight legs; creatures that included spiders and scorpions. One arachnid called a camel spider was almost as much as a span in length, certainly more than a handbreadth, a width of four fingers closely pressed together; and in the past he'd seen scorpions a little shorter than that though, he knew, they only came out of plant cover, or crawled out of their holes, at night. At least the camel spider carried no venom. Not for humans? It was safe to eat if you could catch it. They moved fast along the desert sand. There were also lizards and birds—though catching them would seem even more difficult.

The birds included the grouse, a pigeon-like flier, and the lanner falcon. He wondered if he could trap any of them. He'd never had occasion to try. It would take all his ingenuity.

With a great deal of luck and perseverance, he might even come across an Arabian oryx, or a rodent called jerboa. The latter, a mouse-like creature, jumped from place to place but also only came out at night. Saul hoped for a bright moon, but for now he had to make do with insects. They tasted not bad, if you looked away when putting them in your mouth. He had to resort to such a diet once before, when he and his men were assailed by a bunch of better-armed bandits, who made their living robbing the travelling merchants. His men carried little more than sharpened sticks, pretending they were spires.

Saul seemed satisfied with his knowledge. As for water, he smiled, if animals can find it, then so can I.

"I'm as smart as they are," he said out loud. He needed to hear the sound of a human voice.

Then he snorted with remnants of derision he carried from the old days. From the days before Yeshûa restored his eyesight. By now he was sure that Yeshûa had something to do with it. The alternative would be that Ananias had the magic touch. And that Saul was inclined to believe even less.

Nevertheless, he snorted. There was no room for magic in his scheme of things. He was a practical man. Pragmatic.

"I wonder how many Believers would survive even one week in the desert. Even one week…"

They needed organization, he thought. A lot of organization. They needed him.

At the time, he had no idea how long he'd remain in the desert, but he knew, instinctively, that if he returned to civilization right now, he would be killed even as he killed others, indiscriminately, until so very recently—a slightest suspicion would have been enough for him to take action. Against the innocent? Ananias told him that he who lives by the sword, dies by the sword. Apparently Yeshûa has said it at one time or another. There were a great many things Yeshûa has said, and he needed time to let them sink into his mind. Most things were quite new to him. Ananias seemed to know all Yeshûa's teaching by heart. Perhaps that's where he carried it. In his heart. Would that be the way to learn?

Ah, yes, a very strange man, this Ananias.

Days passed. Only the nights weren't easy. Time and again he'd wake up, sweating, being surrounded by half-dead bodies begging for mercy. Only when he rubbed his eyes, the grotesque corpses dissolved, slowly, in the chimerical shadows of the night.

Corpses don't beg, he reminded himself, yet later the same dreams returned, night after night.

To say that Saul was bitter would be an understatement. Spending evenings at Ananias's feet, learning with all his might, giving up his profession, previous beliefs, money, power, none of those seemed enough. That is why he'd escaped into the desert.

Day after day, sitting propped up, his back against a rock, he'd close his eyes and try to remember. Now and then, as he recalled that day he'd fallen asleep in the shade of the lone cedar tree, he imagined he had seen a figure of light, of a strange eerie light, speaking to him. The words were always the same: Saul, Saul, why dost thou persecute me?

Not any more, he'd answer, clenching his teeth in a feeling of unaccustomed guilt. Not any more…

At times he'd talk to the birds, to passing scorpions, telling them about Yeshûa. No, he didn't go mad. He tried talking to people in Damascus, but his reputation preceded him. They were afraid of his past. No one, with the exception of Ananias and Aba'ye, and perhaps a few of his previous foot soldiers, believed in his sincerity. They've all become

Believers, while he was still struggling. At the same time, he needed to win their hearts in order to organize them. Not just his soldiers. Everyone. Everyone who looked up to Ananias.

He could show them how to become safe, or at least safer, more powerful; how to defend their interests. No, not with sticks and swords, but with guile and cunning. Not with lies, not deceitfulness, but with organized tactics. With strategy. With well-organized communication. With an enhanced messenger system, with means of quick transportation, to avoid and evade mounting attacks by the priesthood. He knew already that his contingent of soldiers had been replaced by other men willing, indeed delighting in arresting, imprisoning and, if necessary, killing the Believers. For a price. There was little most men wouldn't do for a price. Yes, even killing.

These were hard times.

Murdering, he corrected himself. Murdering, not killing. He remembered all too well. Unfortunately, so did the Believers.

Saul felt he could do a great deal for them. But they wouldn't listen. They didn't trust him. They suspected his motives.

He would return to his shack, dejected, depressed, slowly realizing that it would not be by his, but by Yeshûa's power that something might, just might be accomplished. It wasn't an easy realization for a proud man. For a citizen of Rome.

And then he remembered Ananias coming to him when he was still blind. He must have known that he, Saul, would think nothing of having him cast in irons, and, if necessary, decapitated. But Ananias relied on the power of his faith. On the protection of Him who said, I am always with you.

Saul was beginning to understand the meaning of faith. Of moving mountains, of accomplishing the impossible, of serving without any concern for ones own safety.

"I can hardly recognize you, Saul," Ananias had told him just yesterday.

They had a long talk, well into the night. Saul had walked for six hours each way, to and from his shack, to meet Ananias. Once a month he took a pilgrimage to his old teacher, to assure himself that he was on the right track. Once Ananias wasn't at home, yet Saul sat in his room, waiting, feeling that the old man was there, almost hearing his quiet, persuasive voice. Ananias returned just when Saul was leaving, yet, for some strange reason, Saul felt renewed, strengthened, more sure of his way.

Those trips served another purpose, though a much more mundane one. Once a month Saul had a real meal. He paid for it from the little money he's kept for himself. He thought that drinking enough water to sate his thirst completely was in the realm of luxury. Even more so the wine that Ananias offered when he supped with him. Those were very special occasions.

After about a year, Saul changed his name to Paul. He introduced himself to nearby spiders and scorpions. They didn't seem to mind, as though saying, I don't really care who eats me. It wasn't much of a change, but he wanted to leave his past truly behind him; that, and to be less recognizable. Then he walked around, farther afield, introducing himself to sand flies, and birds of the desert. They all seemed to accept his new persona.

Would people?

Finally, he walked into town.

The new name helped a little—not much. But he was determined to try everything in his power. He'd build an empire for Yeshûa yet.

"Will they ever accept me?" he asked his teacher, on his next trip to Damascus.

"It is not for me to say," Ananias replied. "But greater things have been accomplished by lesser men than you. Keep faith, Paul. The Lord works in mysterious ways."

In spite of his powerful faith, Ananias was worried that the Believers might lose a man of Paul's commitment. He could do so much, if only they would forgive him.

Days passed, followed by lonely nights. Hunting for scorpions and spiders did little to make up for lack of human companionship. Saul, or rather Paul, paid dearly for his past.

Then seasons turned into years. Since moving into his shack he re-thatched his roof with palm-leaves three times. He even carried some straw, with him, to make his bed softer. And then, one day, he decided to try his luck elsewhere.

It was a long walk to Jerusalem, but not too far to try his luck. By now, with daily hunting for food and monthly surreptitious visits to Damascus, he was used to walking. He used his time to think, to listen to the voice slowly growing within him. Or, perhaps, the inner voice was always loud enough—only he didn't know how to listen.

He was hoping that, at least there, in Jerusalem, people wouldn't recognize him. His appearance has changed considerably. His beard grew longer, his clothing, even his name, all bespoke of a different man. He needed to share the light that came into his heart since he became a Believer. He needed to share his new convictions with those who were still searching.

He'd travelled light, carrying only water and some fruit which grew in the wild at the first stream he came across. And, of course, his beloved sword. Not that he intended to use it the way he'd used it in the past, but he might have to hunt on the way. From his shack, he intended to cover the distance in less than four days.

He left early, with the first ray of the rising sun. This was Paul embarking on this first journey. There was hardly a trace of the old Saul within him. Not just physically, but his worldview has, by now, taken a diametrically opposite view. This time it was he who was risking his life. If the people he'd persecuted in the past recognized him, it could be his doom. Perhaps, a permanent one.

He remembered Ananias—he had to try.

In spite of years of travelling experience, he felt an unfamiliar disquiet walking along the road he'd passed many times before. Then, in the past, he'd led a contingent of men, ready to pounce on any threatening character. Now, he was alone. More alone than he'd ever felt on his way to Damascus. Even his nook of the desert has already become familiar to him. This, he'd never faced alone.

Yeshûa, are you there?

He smiled at his thoughts. Somehow such a simple question calmed him down. After all, he was not going to Jerusalem for his own glory. With the people in Damascus rejecting him, he hoped to be of some use in Jerusalem. If only people would not recognize him. If only he could remain incognito—a nomad upon whom the light has shone. Wasn't *Yohanan ha-mmatbil*, the man they called John the Baptist, a bit like that?

Of course, he didn't have to remain incognito.

That's what a Roman citizen would say. Incognito.

He remembered the voice that once rang in his head, asking him if he was going to return to Jerusalem to crucify Yeshûa once more. It seemed like ages ago. Long ages. And yet only three years have passed. In three years his world has changed beyond recognition. He hoped he has, likewise.

Even as he examined those last three years, he wondered what precisely has changed his mind; what really changed the way he regarded the world, the way he regarded the

Believers. Had it been those strange voices he'd heard? Was it the restoration of his sight?

He smiled as the truth dawned on him that it was none of those things. It was, it has been, something completely unexpected. It was the single act of courage exhibited by a frail old man coming to help him. Not to heal his eyes, Ananias didn't know about his blindness when he'd knocked on Judas's door. It was the courage he'd shown—courage to come alone to heal his soul.

Paul knew, there and then, that he wanted a share in the source of such power. Of power that enabled an old man to face, to stand fearless, against insurmountable odds.

And then, he mused, and then to emerge victorious.

***

Part Two

35-50 AD

10

ENIGMA

S **himon was not a happy man.** He missed his wife, his children, even the companionship of his friends. It is true that he developed many new contacts, people of great value of character and convictions, but it wasn't the same. Over the three years of being with the Master, twelve of them, now eleven not counting Matthias, have grown a bond that went far beyond friendship. In a way they've become one. One in Messiah—in Christ, the Greeks called it. Shimon now also called it "in Christ". Everyone spoke Greek in Antioch.

And now Shimon felt alone.

The only man with whom he held a closer affinity was Ananias. The old man also knew the secret teaching of Yeshûa, yet Shimon never discovered how he'd acquired that knowledge. Shimon was baffled. They'd spoken so many times together, yet Shimon never learned if Ananias had actually ever met Yeshûa. He always sounded as if he and Yeshûa had spoken just recently—yesterday, or the day before. A strange man, Ananias.

"Perhaps," Shimon murmured, his eyes searching the sky showing the first signs of the coming dawn, "perhaps knowledge such as his comes to some when they are ready."

Shimon spent many an early hour wondering. Yet now, he also had other problems.

He could not reconcile what he taught his aspiring Believers, and what he truly believed was Yeshûa's message. The real essence of His teaching, which Yeshûa shared but with the few of them, was so incredible that no man or woman, no matter how willing, could possibly accept. Not without an act of faith. Thus, by the very nature of human beings, Shimon had to teach them only what a teacher could teach children, leaving the full weight of knowledge for later. Even as the Master had taught the many, he could teach them only how to live here, on earth, in this reality in which dog eats dog to survive.

Frankly, he didn't think that the real essence could be taught. Once witnessed by anyone, as he'd experienced it in what became known among the few as the Transfiguration, the rest had to be experienced from within.

There had been just three of them: James, the son of Zebedee, his brother John, and himself. Yeshûa led them apart, away from the others. Even as they stood waiting for something to happen, the Master's body began to shine with bright rays of shimmering light. The light grew so intense that they had to shield their eyes. All three of them.

Then, even as they looked, squinting, two more figures appeared. Shimon, James and John knew, yet they knew not how, that the other two had been the prophets Moses and Elijah. They too had been clad in light of shining glory.

Neither he, nor James, nor John have ever been the same again. The reality of the Kingdom had been revealed to them. They didn't just believe, they knew that it was real. They witnessed it with their own eyes.

They also knew that no one would believe them.

How could they? After all, what they'd witnessed was not of this world.

Many are called and it seemed that, indeed, only a few were chosen, Shimon thought. And now he had knowledge he could share with no one. Except for his old friends now scattered around the world, and Ananias.

It wasn't easy.

In the meantime, Shimon continued to work on enlarging the numbers of Believers. He was trying hard to revert Jews to the original teaching of the prophets. To the teaching of Moses, so plainly explained by Yeshûa, yet so seemingly difficult to accept for people who have lost their way.

It seemed apparent that, in order to enlarge their own power over people, the priesthood of the Sanhedrin was principally responsible for twisting the essence of the old teaching. To control them, their minds. To collect their tithes? No wonder Yeshûa said the Pharisees were hypocrites. He didn't think much of the Sadducees or the priests, either. They shut up the kingdom of heaven against men, He'd said. The words still rang in Shimon's ears.

...you neither go in yourselves, neither allow you them that are entering to go in.

Strangely enough, the teaching seemed so easy to impart then, on that mysterious day in Jerusalem, during the festival of Shavuoth. Yet, the same facility, the same ease, the same inspiration was never repeated again.

Then, on that day, Yeshûa's Presence was palpable.

After a number of years of conscientious work in the provinces assigned to him, of spreading the word in the areas he'd accepted as his responsibility, Shimon was beginning to run out of steam. He did his best to preach as the Master had preached. Sometimes using the same words. The same phrases, same images. He tried to preach to many. To all who'd listen? What he missed was preaching to the few.

Yet, even then, the Master had protected some of His teaching with a veil of ancient symbolism. Only those people would, or even could, understand it who already had the knowledge, at least some idea, of the true nature of man. If you thought of yourself only as a physical entity, as an animal disposed only to eat, drink and procreate, most of His teaching would have passed you by. Not just ears but your heart had to be open to accept the truth hidden within His words.

No. Even then it wasn't easy.

Thoughts mattered. Thoughts and emotions. The body was just the result...

Love your neighbour...

Love your neighbour. That would be a good start. Ultimately, the rest would follow. This was what kept Shimon going. The need to spread out the love for his fellow men. Just out of love.

Why was even that so difficult?

Weren't they all Jews? Brought up in the teaching of the prophets? Didn't Moses tell us to love our neighbour as ourselves? When did we forget this commandment? Yeshûa just repeated the words. Was He alone who remembered? Is that why they'd murdered Him?

Shimon's work wasn't hard. Not physically. There was plenty of traveling, of course, but once there, once he reached his destination, the brothers looked after him with sincere generosity. He remembered Yeshûa once saying that the Son of man has no place to lay his head. It wasn't that bad. Only that... well, Shimon seldom laid his head in the same place more than one or two nights in a row.

Still. He'd chosen this life.

He'd chosen to spread the Word. He was doing it gladly, only... he was getting tired. The same words repeated to similarly looking people, with the same questions being asked. For years and years. Why couldn't they learn from each other?

And now he was losing the name by which his mother had called him. More and more people called him Cephas. They might as well have been Greeks, not Jews. And he still only preached to his own people. At least, mostly. Wasn't that what the Master had commanded?

People were funny. They went through the whole lexicon of names. It had begun with Shimon—which in Jewish means Jacob's son—and changed it to Simon; then Simeon, Sumeón, and finally Symeon followed in quick succession. Then they gave up.

"Someone told them that the Master had once called me Kepha. That spawned a new attack," Shimon told Ananias, smiling with a quizzical look in his eye.

The two friends were sitting together, reminiscing. It was only the second time this year that Shimon visited his old friend, but he felt the need for renewal. Ananias never failed to restore the fire in his heart.

What followed, Shimon continued, was a new wave of names. Kepha became Cephas, which also means rock in Greek. This was quickly translated into Petros, and subsequently into Latin as Petrus. Obviously the citizens of Rome needed their own piece of rock. There have been echoes of this in the past, already in Jerusalem and in Galilee, but not to such a degree. Shimon was sure that, in time, the Gentiles would find a dozen new names by which to call him. After all, what's in a name? What mattered was what he was teaching. Not who he was.

Still, it wasn't easy.

"What should we do?" Shimon asked, after a pensive silence.

"Change your name to one they'd never recognize, my friend. Something like Pierre, or Peter!" Ananias managed to say that with a straight face.

A woman, much younger than Ananias, came in and placed a tray with two goblets in front of the men.

"Greeting, Adina," Shimon rose to his feet. Contrary to popular belief, he had great respect for women. Perhaps more so since he lost the warmth of his own wife. Ananias married Adina when he became a widower, and Adina's husband was

imprisoned, and then murdered by the Pharisees. Or it could
have been the Zealots. Perhaps they took turns?

Shimon smiled a little wistfully. Most of the time,
Ananias remained in Damascus. He was getting too old to
travel the rough roads. And Adina was everything her name
implied. Gentle, delicate, tender. Perhaps traits more suited to
a girl than a mature woman, but the name suited her. She
carried all three of these qualities. Most Hebrew names had
special meaning. Most of them pleasant ones.

Adina returned his smile, bowed and withdrew. She was
well aware that for both men their moments of collegiality
were rare and precious.

For a while the men sipped wine from the local
vineyards, known for their richness. It was good to relax. It
was good to just talk, even about the weather, without having
to choose ones words carefully.

"I feel you ought to appoint some men," Ananias said,
watching Shimon's reaction over the rim of his goblet. "You
try to do too much yourself, my friend."

That was true. Shimon found it difficult to delegate his
ministries. He covered a vast territory all by himself. Then
Ananias pointed knowingly in the direction in which Adina
has disappeared.

"Perhaps then you could bring your wife over to join
you?"

At this Shimon looked up.

"You think she'd want to? After all these years?"

Shimon suspected that his wife assumed that he'd left
her, possibly for a younger replacement. He only sent
messages to her about twice a year. There weren't that many
people he could trust, going that far south from Antioch. Not
without endangering her life.

Ananias didn't answer. Then he took another sip of wine,
as if drawing courage from it.

"What have you got to lose?" he asked softly.

This time silence extended for a longer time. Shimon's mind drifted to Galilee. He met his wife in his future mother-in-law's house, in Capernaum. His wife's name was Perpetua. Is Perpetua, he corrected quickly his discordant thought. A name of Latin origin. Then, in those early days, he was sure that, as her name implied, they'd never be apart. Their daughter was born within nine months of their wedding. She must be a big girl now, he often mused, then he dismissed the thoughts. They were too painful. But his mind drifted back to the place he'd once called home. Probably as beautiful as her mother, he continued to muse. As beautiful as her mother…

After some heavy sighs escaped Shimon's lips, he looked up with a guilty expression on his face.

"I didn't come here to whine," he said, raising his goblet.

"To whine over wine?" Ananias asked.

They both laughed. The wine did them both good. The whining helped a little, too. Adina had her moments of inspiration. Gentle, delicate, tender, and now inspiring.

"You are a very lucky man, Ananias. May the Lord be with you."

This brought them back to the reason for Shimon's visit.

"We garnered most of the Jews in, what I call, my territory. I spend as much time keeping them in order as I do looking for new converts."

Ananias was about to speak, but Shimon held up his hand. "There is more, my friend, and I don't know what to do."

This time Ananias leaned forward. He was a very good listener.

"I still think," Shimon continued, "that we are tending to concentrate on quantity at the expense of quality. I, or we, teach them the fundamentals of faith, forgetting that faith is only a means to an end. That, ultimately, they must all learn to know. They must achieve, what the Greeks call, Gnosis.

An inner knowingness. A certainty beyond the slightest shadow of a doubt."

For a moment silence enveloped them with a veil of unspoken secrecy. They both knew that there were things that could not be said, that could not be expressed in words. After a little while, it was Ananias who sighed deeply. He opened his mouth to speak then, stopped himself. Instead, he smiled a little sadly.

"Many are called though few are chosen," he said at last. "We can offer them wine, but we cannot make them drink, Shimon. Only Yeshûa can do that."

He said can, not could. For him the Master's presence was very real. As for wine, it always symbolized secret knowledge. Even Yeshûa referred to it as such.

And he is not with us, thought Shimon.

"Yes, He is, Shimon," Ananias corrected. "Always!" He must have read Shimon's thoughts from his facial expression.

This was the first time that Ananias saw weakness in Shimon's faith.

"You must be tired, my friend," he said gently. "You can have my bed tonight." He was as gentle and tender as his wife.

Then he got up and went to see her. She'd already prepared a straw mattress for the both of them in the outer room. It was getting so that she could read her husband's thoughts. Providing they were gentle, delicate and tender.

Usually, they were.

In spite of Ananias's placid, relaxing manner, and the sharing of a cup of wine, Shimon couldn't sleep till the early hours. His mind was filled with turbulent thoughts, his conscience sending signals that he was escaping his responsibilities, that he didn't even resemble a Kepha, let alone act like one.

"I am letting you down, Master. Please, guide me..."

Yet for the first time he wondered if he had any right to expect guidance from Yeshûa. Too many mistakes, he knew. He'd made too many mistakes. Would He have taken refuge in Antioch, leaving the brethren behind? Shimon knew the answer, and beads of cold sweat covered his forehead. Contours of the three crosses silhouetted against the stormy night sky filled his vision. He tried to blink the images away. Then he heard a hammer striking metal. He slid from his bed to his knees. He didn't pray; didn't ask for anything. Not even forgiveness. He just knelt there, waiting for mercy. Waiting for the images and the sounds to go away.

"I am not worthy, Lord... I am not worthy..." his lips formed the words in silence.

Finally, his knees gave way, and he slumped onto the floor. He woke up at first dawn and climbed back to bed. He still had an hour or two left. For some reason, he felt strangely cleansed.

Early the next day, Shimon and his young proselyte climbed into the donkey cart, and his man picked up the reins. Shimon pointed south. The man looked surprised.

"Jerusalem, my friend," he said. "Jerusalem awaits us."

Shimon felt that he was needed there. Such surprising inspirations often formed in his mind after a meeting with Ananias.

He knew not why.

***

11

JERUSALEM

H **is beard served to hide** his well-known features. In the evening of the fourth day, Paul arrived at his destination. He pulled his head-scarf lower over his face, and pushed the door open. It took a moment for his eyes to adjust to the penumbra of the interior.

It was a small inn on the outskirts of Jerusalem where some of his men once stayed, before he hired them to serve as his foot soldiers. He found it hard to believe how much had happened since those days.

He dropped two mites, the smallest Jewish coins, on the heavily scratched surface of, what served as, a reception desk, paying in advance for a single night. After all, he had no idea if the Believers, after the painful rejection he'd experienced in Damascus, would accept him in Jerusalem. A young, scruffy boy, probably the proprietor's son, whisked the money away, and took him to a room upstairs. The room was hardly bigger than his desert shack, but the bed was softer than any bed he'd slept on during the last three years.

Now that he finally arrived, he realized that he was utterly exhausted. No, not his body. It was his mind. He still didn't know how to rely on faith. As a once-Pharisee he knew the theory of teaching, the letter of the Law, so to speak, but not the spirit. Not the spirit of the New Law, as enhanced by the truth of the Master. Yet, even then he didn't resort to prayer. Ananias taught him many things, but, alas, not how to pray.

"Prayer is little more than becoming one with Him that is within you, Paul. Trust Him, and your prayer will succeed."

Easier said than done, he'd murmured at the time.

Not that four days of marching didn't take some reserves out of him. It was a very different story to walking less then twenty leagues from his desert shack to Ananias's house. A trek of four days, sunrise till sunset, with little food or drink to ease his journey, left him exhausted. He still carried some money left over from his "good days", from his previous job, but he didn't know for how long it would have to last. Since he'd resigned from his old profession, he had long learned to be thrifty.

Although he had not eaten since noon, he took a sip of water from a vase on the side-table, and collapsed on the bed, feeling completely spent. He fell asleep immediately.

"Oh, all right, I admit it, I am tired," he said out loud, not caring if anyone would hear him. No one did. The door was already closed.

Apparently, it was not his fate to rest for long.

During the night, he woke up a number of times, feeling that he was being eaten alive. Having acquired a different taste for food during his sojourn in the desert, he managed to find most of the bugs that tried to make a feast of him, and reversed positions. He found even the smallest insects palatable enough to eat. They were quite different from those he found, or that found him, in the desert.

Necessity, he thought, is the mother of invention.

In spite of his nocturnal feast, Paul went downstairs for a real breakfast. With one or two exceptions when he'd stayed overnight at Ananias's house, he hadn't had one since moving into his forlorn shack.

How time flies, he mused.

He downed the food like a man that was starving. He very nearly was. During the last three years, his already small frame seemed to have shrunk, and his face exposed angular contours of his cheekbones. He looked as though he'd just come out from a long stint in prison.

Sated, Paul licked his fingers with satisfaction, and looked up from his plate. Then he froze. Looking straight at him was Aba'ye. He was sitting alone, two tables away, his large body hardly fitting on the bench against the opposite wall. His old friend was watching him. After a silent moment of recognition, Aba'ye smiled.

Paul got up and approached the giant.

"Surprises will never cease," he said, noncommittally.

Aba'ye's smile broadened to a grin.

"Good morning, Master," he replied.

"Paul," the previous Saul corrected. "Please call me Paul." Then he, too, smiled. He'd never used the word 'please' to his ex-servant before. Perhaps I am learning, he mused.

"Yes, M-m-m-Paul," the man replied. Old habits died hard. "This is a dangerous city," he added. "I thought I'd look after you... a little?"

Paul's danger could come from both, the Believers who were still scared of him, and the Pharisees and priesthood whom he'd betrayed. With the Sadducees, one never knew.

"Do you live here now, in Jerusalem?"

"No, M-m-m... I mean, Paul. I'm still in Damascus. But I carry messages for people. I feel safe on the road. Not many people want to attack me," he added with a big grin that seemed to cut his face in half.

Paul kept looking at the old soldier, with widening surprise.

"And how did you know I was here?"

"I followed you."

"All the way from Damascus?"

"Master Ananias told me that you might be in need of help. I was about to leave Jerusalem when I saw you at the gates…"

Paul sat down heavily. Wonders will never cease, he thought. A man he once regarded as riff-raff was now teaching him the meaning of friendship. And then he thought of Ananias. Apart from Aba'ye, Ananias was his only other true friend.

"He told you that I was coming here?"

"He thought you might."

He thought I might. What a strange and wonderful man Ananias is. He seems to rely on his inner senses more than anyone I've ever met, Paul mused. Now the only question is how to get to see Shimon. Assuming Shimon is here. Paul had never discussed Shimon's whereabouts with Ananias.

"He probably wouldn't tell me, just in case," he muttered sadly.

"Shimon is here," Aba'ye said, looking Paul in the eyes. "I can ask around where, if you like?"

Before leaving, Paul made Aba'ye swear not to reveal who he was. And then Aba'ye said something that made Paul marvel, again, about human nature. Aba'ye said that he still held onto virtually all the money Paul had left with him. It was well hidden, he'd said, in Damascus. At least he didn't bring it with him.

Of course, by now, after the sumptuous breakfast, Paul didn't have a shekel to his name.

"I gave each man his due, a little extra, and kept the rest in case you might need it," Aba'ye said, his eyes registering hope of approval. "I got some here for you, if you need it?" He pushed a small leather pouch across the table.

Paul nodded, not knowing what to say. They exchanged a few more words, hardly finding a common language. Paul was always a doer, not a talker and, during the last few years, he'd become a hermit. A taciturn hermit. Hardly enunciating a word. One could but wonder how he intended to preach. As for his apparent wealth, he never imagined it would be so easy. After Aba'ye left the table, Paul followed him with his eyes, asking himself just how did Aba'ye know, before, that he was thinking of Shimon?

But Aba'ye was gone. His heavy footsteps resonated along the hard floor. What a strange man, Paul mused. What a strange and wonderful man. And I didn't even say thank you.

In spite of the donkey and the driver doing all the work, Shimon arrived tired. Of course, being continuously shaken, up and down, and sidewise, on the crude conveyance that took them along the primitive, unpaved road didn't help. Even then, it wasn't really that. His tiredness was not of physical origin. He'd spent half his life travelling. No. What got him tired was living in a constant state of the unknown. There may also have been an element, an undercurrent of fear, which, though well under control, still extracted its dues on his mental and physical constitution. Shimon was not young any more.

But mostly it was the uncertainty.

There was nothing he could count on. Nothing to be really sure of, or about. Nothing he could expect with any degree of confidence. Except for Yeshûa's help. That never failed him. Never. He remembered His words. Thomas had reminded him.

Become passers-by.

That is what He'd said to Thomas after He'd risen. Shimon remembered the instruction, but sometimes just remembering, he was ashamed to admit, it didn't seem quite enough.

Five years have passed since that glorious Shavuoth. Three since Shimon ventured as far as Antioch. He never lost contact with the brothers in Jerusalem, but seldom came to see them in person. They all had their duties. And for

Shimon, specifically, Jerusalem was by far the most dangerous place. In Rome, what little they heard in Antioch, Caligula didn't inspire any trust or reliance in the future evolution of the Roman Empire. The world was becoming a big unknown.

Or had it been always so?

Nothing, nothing was certain. Nothing was permanent.

Become passers-by.

This time, on his way back from Jerusalem, Shimon was hoping to see his wife. He avoided personal contact with her so as not to endanger her and her family, let alone his children. To the Pharisees and the priests, Kepha was a dirty word.

In Jerusalem, Shimon made directly for the house of James the Just. Not the house James had lived in earlier. He had been forced to change his living quarters seven times since Shimon went up north. He had to. His brethren had told him that it wasn't safe to stay in one place for too long a time. A few months, at most.

James was the only one left. He was the only one of the original twelve apostles, that remained in Jerusalem. The others had already spread far and wide, as originally discussed. Throughout the Roman Empire. They visited Jerusalem only now and then, even as Shimon did, which made James the Head of the local Christian community. No apostle ever struggled for, let alone usurped, glory; they already were the chosen ones, but under pressure from Shimon and other apostles who'd left word, James the Just agreed to become the Overseer of Jerusalem. *De facto*, he already was. Has been, for some time. Officially his title was Bishop, a word that had meaning only to the faithful. To the Believers. As of now, at long last, James the Just was recognized for the duties, which he already performed for quite a time.

Next morning Shimon had heard the unwelcome news. James's people reported that Saul, using the name Paul, is asking him, Shimon, for an audience.

Shimon felt a cold wind touching his temples.

Saul, the most guilty of them all, is asking him for an interview. A meeting. Then, Shimon remembered his visit with Ananias. Didn't his old friend say that he'd baptized Saul? What would Ananias have done?

Actually Shimon knew. He knew very well what Ananias would have done. He'd already done it. He'd walked into the lions' den.

"I'll see him," Shimon said, "but not here. Find me a neutral place. A place that will endanger no one."

Was he, Shimon playing for time?

Is this why you've brought me here, Lord?

They waited until dark, and met at another inn, at the other end of town. Paul has been brought there by a circuitous route. Shimon's people took all the precautions. Nevertheless, he arrived punctually. By the time Shimon arrived, Paul had no fingernails left.

As he saw the older man come into the room at the back of the inn, Paul rose and bowed deeply. He knew of Shimon's reputation. He also knew of his power within the growing church.

Shimon returned a weak smile, straightened Paul by his shoulders and pointed to a bench. He did his best to be congenial. Even as Shimon sat down, Paul remained standing. As Shimon was much taller, he only had to look up a little to meet Paul's eyes. He wondered if that was why Paul remained standing—to force him to look up to him?

"What do you want of me, Saul?"

"I seek your acceptance, Master."

"I am not your master, Saul. Why do you seek my acceptance? Did not the Lord accept you already?"

This was the last answer Paul had expected. Did not Ananias tell him that by the act of baptism he was accepted into the church?

"I have been baptized by Ananias, Rabbi."

Shimon found the title Rabbi acceptable. It simply meant teacher or doctor. He nodded.

"And what have you done with your gift of faith?"

Again, Paul was stumped. He took his gift and ran away into the desert. To think things out? Or just to escape from the danger of rejection?

"I seek to learn, and to share my learning," he replied, feeling that he wasn't saying the right words.

"And what is there to stop you, Saul?"

"They don't accept me, Rabbi. I tried hard, but they don't accept me…"

"Who doesn't accept you, Saul? Did not the Lord accept you into His church?"

Paul was quite lost. He expected to be examined for his knowledge of the Law, of the Law as amended or renewed by the teaching of Yeshûa, and instead he was being asked questions about things that never crossed his mind.

"My faith is strong, Rabbi. Truly, my faith is strong…"

"You must prove your faith not by your words, Saul, but by your works."

Until now Paul was standing. Now, he lowered himself to the bench, his back sliding down against the stone wall. He lost all hope that he would be accepted into the community of Jerusalem. He also had little idea what to do, but whatever it was, he realized, he had to do it on his own. Perhaps far away? Somewhere where no one had heard about him. About his past.

Slowly he got to his feet, bowed deeply, and turned towards the door.

"May the Lord be with you, Paul," Shimon whispered loud enough for Paul to hear.

"And with you, Rabbi," he answered. And then he left.

He was beginning to realize that this was not the end.
This was only the beginning. It must be for the best. It
seemed that his talents were needed elsewhere. Among the
gentiles? Was not the truth revealed for the whole world? For
all men?

Even as he walked, his pace quickened. There were
things he had to do. Great things. He had to build an Empire.
An Empire for the Christ. For Yeshûa. For the one Man who
had never rejected him.

And then he froze. He heard footsteps behind him. He
had been warned that there were many, here, in Jerusalem,
who hated him for what he was. For what he'd once been.
Both, Christians and the Pharisees. It wouldn't do any good
to tell them that he was no longer Saul. That no longer was he
a killer or betrayer. He was Paul now—a new man in both,
soul and body.

By an old instinct his hand moved to his hip; and there it
remained. Empty. For once, he didn't carry his sword. He
spun on his heels, descending into a crouch. The next
moment he took a deep breath and smiled.

"You left your sword behind, Paul," said Aba'ye. "I
thought you might need it," he added, handing it over, hilt
first.

Paul took another deep breath.

"You keep it, Aba'ye. I'm sure you can put it to better
use than I ever did."

Aba'ye's face lit up in gratitude. Never in his life did he
imagine that one day he might own an object as beautiful as a
Roman sword.

"Thank you, M-m-m... Paul," was all he could say. He
was totally overwhelmed. His hard, almost brutal features
softened, became almost childlike, full of unexpected
pleasure.

Paul smiled. He wondered if Aba'ye had as much
pleasure from receiving the sword as he had from giving it to
him. And then Paul grew pensive. There was something else

that happened that he'd missed. Just now. Recently. He couldn't put his finger on it.

And then he had it.

Just as he was leaving the inn, Shimon addressed him by his new name. He called him Paul. And for reasons he couldn't possibly explain, this simple fact filled him with inexplicable joy.

***

12

ESCAPE

Caesar Tiberius, the second Emperor of the Roman Empire, known throughout Rome as Tiberius Julius Caesar Augustus, lived to a ripe old age of seventy-eight. He died quietly in his villa at Misenum, a seaport in the south of Italy. There were hints that Caligula dipped his fingers in his demise, but Rome was always full of innuendo, especially after the death of an Emperor.

Tiberius never desired to be an Emperor.

"Only fools would seek it, only Jupiter's son would agree to it," he is known to have said. He was referring to Mars.

Perhaps Jupiter, and particularly Mars, did have something to do with his life. Tiberius's character was such that he would be remembered as one of Rome's greatest generals. If it hadn't been for some jealous senators, he would have been voted divine honours himself. No wonder the senators declined to accord him the elevation to divinity. After all, he considered the senators to be men fit to be slaves. No doubt, the Caesar was referring to their mental acuity.

Farther east, King Aretas IV Philopatris—already recognized by Tiberius's predecessor Augustus, the famed Gaius Julius Caesar Augustus—as the King of Nabataeans, was the most powerful neighbour of Judea. He called himself "Friend of the People", rather than "Friend of Rome", not to mention "Friend of the Emperor". Aretas was a proud and devious man. In time, he took the opportunity of Tiberius's death to take over Damascus. Caligula who, as could well be expected, succeeded Tiberius, grudgingly recognized Aretas's claim, probably in appreciation of the latter's expedition against the Jews some decades ago, and for placing a considerable army at the disposal of a Roman general.

Quid pro quo?

Caligula was different.

Emperor Gaius Caesar Augustus Germanicus was also known as Gaius, although behind him back, they called him "Little Boots". That's what Caligula means in Latin. Little Boots.

Paul long suspected that Caligula wouldn't last long. He didn't. Possibly his need for longevity had been expressed in his determined desire to think of himself as a god. To play safe, he eliminated senatorial power, higher echelons of the armies, and many threatening or otherwise inconvenient lives. Sadly, Paul found the method familiar. Caligula couldn't allow the Senate to have more power than he did. To further assure his own immortality, he had two temples built to his short-lived glory. By AD 40, he was gone.

He probably was a Little Boots after all.

Paul sighed deeply. It was becoming harder and harder to find a role model for his ambitions. He was still determined to build an empire for the Christ, for the Messiah.

For Yeshûa.

And now Claudius.

How time flies when you're having fun, Paul thought. Somewhere, at the very outskirts of his troubled mind, Paul was glad that he wasn't an emperor. Any of the emperors. Ever.

And so, in the fullness of time, Emperors Augustus, Tiberius, and Caligula were followed by Claudius. Tiberius

Claudius Caesar Augustus Germanicus, to give him all his dues. Claudius had his work cut out for him. Caligula messed things up a little. Problems of Rome were problems of the Empire, and Paul, after all, was a citizen of Rome.

Now, Paul had an additional problem. His own.

After his rejection by Shimon in Jerusalem—at least he took Shimon's reaction as rejection of his services—he was hoping to remain in Damascus for a little longer, to learn more from Ananias. After all, no greater friend a man could have than the old man, who risked his life to save him. And Ananias was among the few who trusted Paul not to fall back into his old ways.

As a direct result of the political turmoil, Paul's life in Damascus faced another danger. There were many Believers, recently calling themselves Christians, who still thought that he was only playing a scurrilous game to get back in the good graces of the Pharisees. The priests, for their part, would no longer trust him to carry out any missions on their behalf. They hadn't even approached him. He'd already failed them once. The Pharisees hated him even more. After all he, Paul, or at least his previous alter ego Saul, was a Pharisee himself. A Pharisee, and son of a Pharisee. A double treachery, if you will.

Paul refused to accept a single denarion, or a Greek lepta, or even a lousy kodrante from the temple treasury, or from any of the brethren, in exchange for his proselytizing services. Apparently, the fact that he was willing to carry out any manual labour, day or night, to keep himself, and not to be a burden to others, to the brethren, wasn't enough.

And now he had to dodge the new King of Damascus, well known for his anti-Jewish disposition.

Paul has been told that since King Aretas took over, there were guards at all the gates leading to and from the city. After all, long before the Romans took over, Damascus had already been a walled city. Paul did not relish being scrutinized by any of the parties, be they the Romans, or the Pharisees or the priests, and now the armed guards of Aretas, who probably all kept their spies in close proximity to the city gates.

A closed prison? In the past, walls had been intended to keep people out, and now? Now they kept people within.

And within its walls, Paul was hated by many.

What saved Paul's life was the Saturnalia. To be more accurate, Saturnalia and Hanukkah. A strange double act to say the least.

Saturnalia was an ancient Roman festival. It was celebrated with a sacrifice at the Temple of Saturn at the Roman Forum, although the theme of the festival was fun, fun, fun. An orgy or two wouldn't hurt either, if an opportunity presented itself. Outside Rome, throughout the Empire, ordinary citizens took part in the festivities with private gift-giving, continual partying, and a carnival wherever the numbers warranted. In Damascus the number of Romans was scarce, but they made up for it by drinking wine in wild abandon. The local merchants made a lot of money on them. Each day the price of wine went up, as if by magic.

"Shortage," vintners assured the buyers. "Must bring it from far and wide."

Actually they only had to bring it from their cellars, usually a few steps down below the houses they lived in. They saved large quantities for just such occasions. They all knew that the festival was celebrated on December 17th, but it was unofficially extended through the 25th. That's a lot of wine…

And this is where fate, at long last, turned in Paul's favour. Fate was seldom kind to Paul, but he always tried to turn her wiles to his advantage. And so it was with Hanukkah.

Hanukkah is the Jewish Festival of Lights, an eight-day and eight-night festival commemorating the rededication of the Holy Temple. Although, according to the Hebrew calendar, it begins on the 25th day of the month of *Kislev*, according Roman reckoning, it may occur at any time from late November to late December. After all, the Roman calendar changed its form a few times between the founding of Rome and the present era. And this year, the Festival of Lights, coincided with Saturnalia, the ancient Roman festival of the god Saturn.

Paul made his plans.

By the middle of December the city of Damascus was already getting ready for festivities. Jews and Romans, alike, seemed in a frenzy of activity. A question of one-upmanship? To take part in Saturnalia you didn't have to be Roman—you just had to like Romans. Or at least like Rome. Or even just the Emperor? You had to like having fun! Of course, to take par in the Festival of Lights it helped if you were Jewish.

Taking great care not to raise suspicion, Paul learned that, at least for now, the only places that directly threatened his wellbeing were the city gates. Apparently King Aretas didn't trust anybody. Not even during the festival, although he did allow the outsiders to take part in the celebrations. For a small fee, of course. The Romans were bribed, likewise. Or their bribes were accepted, depending on the case in point.

Paul, Ananias and Aba'ye spent the last Yom Sha-Bat, in other words at least one evening of Hanukkah, together. Not as boisterously as the citizens outside, but with abundant love.

"Where will you go, Paul? What will you do?" Ananias sounded worried.

Paul didn't discuss his plans with Ananias, nor with anyone else. Not because he didn't trust his old friend, but because he didn't want his own reputation, good or bad, to precede him. He wanted to start with a clean slate. Now, that he was leaving, he felt free to share some of his plans.

"I shall go home," he said simply.

"I thought this is your home, my friend?" Ananias replied. Adina smiled warmly while Aba'ye nodded vigorously.

It was true. Paul had spent more time in Ananias's house than anywhere else, lately. Except, until recently, in his desert shack, of course.

"I shall go to the home of my childhood... to the place where my mother raised me." His voice sounded dreamy, and then his face darkened. He didn't even know if his mother was still alive. He'd asked about her in Jerusalem but to no avail. Who could tell, perhaps she's gone back to Tarsus? "Do you know," I haven't visited Tarsus for many years?"

"I think you're wise," Ananias said, after some moments of thought. "You need to go where you'll be accepted for what you are, not for what you once were."

"I hope that's a complement, old friend?" Paul said, a smile twinkling in his eye.

"Yes, my young friend. It was intended as such."

Yet there was sadness in his voice. He was going to miss one of the brightest students he ever had. Perhaps the brightest.

Finally, well after midnight, Aba'ye and Paul said goodbye, and left quietly through the rear door, which lead to the garden. It would be foolish to venture into the street full of revelers.

They made an odd couple. Paul looked like a short but very fat man. Under his loose *abayah* he had a thick rope coiled around his middle. Aba'ye, on the other hand, was tall and lanky, huge by comparison to Paul. He carried a basket in one hand, his other resting on the hilt of the sword Paul had given him. He wouldn't use it, of course, except in dire need in defense of his old Master. He called him Paul, but the old respect remained. He also loved Paul as one would an older brother.

They didn't have far to go.

After only some hundred paces Aba'ye pointed to a stretch of wall, completely unguarded, and on the side where the moon cast a shadow. In fact, as far as they could see by the moon that was playing hide and seek with the clouds, the wall was not guarded at all. The builders must have relied on its inherent inapproachability. Which it probably was—from outside. And from inside if one didn't have a long rope and a strong basket. Paul and Aba'ye had both.

They chose a spot that remained in shadow. Aba'ye put the basket down, and reached out to unwind the rope from around Paul's waist. He held onto one end, while Paul spun on his heels. They practically laughed as they prepared for Paul's illegal, stealthy departure.

Once or twice the sounds of the street grew nearer, but they retreated as fast. Aba'ye wound the rope twice around his own waist, then lifted Paul with ease and placed him in the basket. The other end of the rope was already well tied to the handle.

"Goodbye, my friend," Paul said. "I'll miss you."

He meant it. Aba'ye taught him as much about friendship as anyone. Even his Master Ananias. They both risked their life on his behalf. And he'd done nothing to earn their generosity. That was one of the reasons why he had to go.

At the last moment, Aba'ye couldn't resist an act of rare familiarity. He reached out for Paul, already in the basket, and put both his arms around the precious cargo he was about to lower over the wall.

After holding him for a while, he asked, his voice that of a youngster asking his father for permission to do something naughty.

"May I come and see you, Paul? May I?"

Paul needed time to replenish his lungs after having air squeezed out of them.

"I thought you'd never ask," he replied. "I thought you would never ask..." and two great tears rolled down his cheeks. He was glad the moon found this moment to hide behind a cloud.

"Goodbye, Master," Aba'ye said, and lifted, then lowered the basket, over the edge into total darkness. A moment later he felt a tug on the end of the rope. He hoisted the basket up. It was empty.

The ground was solid and reasonably level. Paul was grateful for the time he'd spent hunting in the desert. Walking at night over unknown terrain was child's play for him. He moved like a desert fox, a creature of the night, darting from shadow to shadow. There was no need to tempt the guards who may or may not have been keeping an eye on the outside. Soon he was out of sight.

For a while he still heard sounds of revelers milling in the streets. The Jews would remain mostly in their homes, but the Romans and they friends would have taken to the streets in throngs. Paul was glad he was outside again. Like during those three years he'd spent out there, alone.

Paul traveled lightly. He carried some water, and enough food for two or three light meals. He felt no need for more. This time, at Aba'ye's insistence, he took a few silver coins, enough to take him along in greater comfort compared to what he'd enjoyed for the last few years.

The journey would take him through Antioch, which Paul recognized as Shimon's territory. He was determined to remain there incognito. Shimon had told him what he must do, and he was determined to do it.

"By my deeds they shall know me," he repeated, thoughtfully, to himself. Morning and night. "By my deeds they shall know me."

He expected the journey to Tarsus to take a little more than a week. It measured about seventy-two leagues. Unless he stopped for a few days in Antioch, in hiding, just to see what Shimon had accomplished. But only if he could remain invisible. He knew that he had a great deal to learn. The apostles, as people called them, had spent three years walking with Yeshûa. Day and night, learning from the Master. What magnificent time it must have been. He'd give his right hand for such a privilege. For the honour of being among the chosen.

But it was not to be. While the Master was walking this earth, he, Saul, had been busy destroying His people, as best he could. Yes, Saul. Not Paul.

At least that they must allow me, he mused bitterly. Whatever I do, I do the best I can.

And then he saw the first rays of the sun. He turned and took a long look at Damascus only just visible in the rare morning fog. The place of his rebirth. The home of Ananias. And Aba'ye. The only two friends he had in the whole wide world.

And now?

A new day, a new life. Away from everyone.

Paul was always a loner. Not in the physical sense, but in the way his mind worked. In the way he put everything he had, all the effort, into his every endeavour.

He knew, or at least felt that once he started doing exactly what he was intended to do Yeshûa would be with him. His powers would be multiplied, even as Shimon's have been on that day of Shavuoth, in Jerusalem.

My day will come, he repeated, looking up into the sky. But... but let it be Thy will, he whispered.

And, unbeknownst to him, at that moment he became one of the chosen ones.

***

13

CORNELIUS

Having **met the growing assembly** of brethren in Jerusalem, and officially elevated James to the position of Bishop, Shimon was free to return to Antioch. He decided to use the opportunity to veer a little from his way, and visit Philip, an apostle like himself, who lived in Caesarea, a mere day's journey from Jerusalem for his trusty ass.

As his donkey plodded along, the reins in the hands of a young acolyte, Shimon couldn't help but wonder if he'd told Paul the right things. The problem with being a leader, particularly a leader by appointment not by choice, was that everything you said was taken as an irrevocable truth. He was not allowed to be wrong. To change his mind. Perhaps that was why Shimon never allowed himself time to think things out. He replied immediately, relying on his intuition to speak through him. His responses, or decisions, came out unobstructed and uncoloured by his own predilections. By his own, personal, likes or dislikes. It was as though he was only reacting to something, or someone, to a will that was not really his own. After all, the decisions he was called to rule upon, usually, if not always, concerned areas that were heretofore unexplored; realms that exposed and crossed new territories—uncharted and unexamined.

Unfortunately, this method, probably the only method he could use, invariably resulted in mental *post mortems*, in later analyses of his conscious mind, which, surely, was but a fraction of the totality of his mind. A mere fraction.

At least, he hoped so.

He truly hoped that his words to Paul would serve the new, regenerated Paul, to serve the Lord in the best way possible. He had to trust in that. As always.

Caesarea wasn't far now. It was a port on the Mediterranean, an important meeting place for travelers from afar. It kept Philip busy with newcomers, who would, Philip hoped, take the Good News with them to their own parts of the world. Also, Philip could hardly move around with the same facility as Shimon did. He had sired four daughters. He was, one might say, anchored in the Port of Caesarea. Attached to a single location. And his were not ordinary daughters. All four of them seemed to have visions of what might be. They all prophesied.

Shimon had long learned to live in the present, to leave the future to Yahweh, but each time he passed this way his curiosity pulled him to Philip's house.

He sighed remembering that Philip they called the Evangelist was not the Philip of his youth; was not Philip the apostle. With him Shimon went way back, to Bethsaida, on the shores of Gennesareth. They played as boys together. For Shimon, visiting Philip would be like going back in time. To carefree days of yore.

But this was duty.

As Joppa was little more than a two-hour ride, they left late. Shimon didn't want to impose on Philip, and decided to stop for the night just before entering the city.

Soon after they'd stopped, Shimon's thoughts returned to Paul. He continued to struggle with mixed thoughts, or perhaps feelings, about him. He had no doubt that Paul was a good man. After all, Ananias had already befriended him, and Shimon would trust Ananias with his life. There was a barrier, however, between him and Paul, which Shimon couldn't quite overcome.

Shimon was always a simple man. Brought up to be a fisherman; he took life as it came, with few complaints, but also without a broader outlook of the world. For many years he had been content to stay in his village, until Andrew pointed out Yeshûa to him, and henceforth Shimon was taken under His wing. He had been, he remembered, so overwhelmed by Yeshûa's presence, that he left his home, his work, his loves and habits, and followed the Master ever since. He never questioned His teaching, seldom asked questions. He assumed that Yeshûa would tell him all that he needed to know, in His own, good time.

But, at some deep, subliminal level, he always missed his village. He missed the simple life that gave him inner peace; that did not warrant decisions that were affecting many others.

Perhaps that was why wherever he travelled, from Jerusalem all the way to Antioch and beyond, he always gravitated to his own people. To Jews. He never befriended any of the Gentiles, never felt the need to share the Good News with them. Surely, didn't the Master come to right the ways of His own people?

And Paul, he had been told, didn't seem to mind mixing with the unclean. Ananias had told him that, in the desert, Paul had actually eaten unclean food. Shimon could never do that. It was forbidden by the Law. Paul, a Pharisee, ought to have known better. He remembered that Yeshûa didn't particularly like the Pharisees, but surely, they knew the Law, even if often they fell short of practicing it.

What if there was no other food in the desert? Then Paul shouldn't have gone there. He ought to have found other ways, other means to absorb the Master's teaching. Didn't they all? Yet no one went into the desert. Why, even eggs of unclean birds were not to be eaten, not to mention the birds of pray themselves.

On the other hand, the Law allowed eating locust while forbidding other insects. Didn't Paul know that? Wasn't he a Pharisee? Perhaps there was no locust there…

Shimon shrugged.

Why would Paul have to go into the desert? Well, the Master did so for forty days, they say. But… but that was different. He was the Master.

And yet…

Shimon struggled with his thoughts from the moment he'd heard, in Jerusalem, that Paul had asked to see him. The same thoughts filled his waking hours ever since. Even now, sitting relaxed on the two-wheeled cart heading for Caesarea.

"Will I have time to drop in to Bethsaida?" he wondered. He more or less promised his wife he would; through a messenger, already some time ago. On the other hand, she hadn't replied to his message. Perhaps no one had travelled his way…

He dismissed the thought. He had other problems.

Shimon gazed at John, his driver. The young man, a recent acolyte, seemed lost in thoughts of his own. Did he know about all the clean and unclean animals? Did he think that the Gentiles were as clean as he or I? As any of the Jews? The chosen people?

Are we really the chosen people?

He gazed at the donkey grazing on the side of the road. He saved Shimon having to walk vast distances. A faithful animal, which didn't do anyone any harm. Why was a horse or a donkey unclean? And doesn't it say in the Torah that during the great famine in Samaria, they sold an ass's head for fourscore pieces of silver? And ate it?

Did not the Lord ride a donkey into Jerusalem?

Poor donkey. It served the Master so well. Perhaps better than I ever did. And… and it was faithful, he added, with a deep sigh. And it was always faithful…

Shimon did not sleep well that night. He dreamed of birds of prey flying so close he could touch them, then of a donkey laughing at him as he tried to pull the cart himself...

He tossed and turned on the narrow bench of the cart. They laid down the back support, flat, and both stretched on the seat, their legs hanging over the side. At least the height above ground kept the sand-bugs away from their skin. The unclean sand-bugs, he remembered thinking, not sure if he was still dreaming or already awake. Did the insects know that they were unclean? They ought to keep away from him. On the other hand, did not the same Yahweh make all the insects that abound on this earth?

By the time the moon rose over the horizon, Shimon was exhausted. His companion slipped onto the cart floor, leaving the whole bench for him alone. Shimon stretched in greater comfort. He closed his eyes. And then he heard a wind coming at him from above.

He sat up and saw a great sheet, a platform, filled with many animals. He peered at it in amazement. And then a voice said: Kill and eat, Shimon. He cringed in amazement.

Kill and eat!

Those were words of command. Words to be obeyed. He woke up startled. Kill and eat? What was the command in his dream? Why would the voice command him kill and eat that which is unclean?

"That which was created by the same Yahweh," he repeated his previous musings. This time he said them aloud.

When those thoughts first crossed his mind it was just a reaction to a half-guilty suspicion. Now he'd repeated the words with conviction. His own words sounded convincing to himself. Could it be that Paul was right? Paul the killer, the murderer... Paul the convert, friend of his own friend, Ananias?

And if animals were all created by the same Yahweh, what of people?

Next morning, soon after sunrise, the cart—yes, and the kindly and clean donkey—pulled up in front of Philip's house. The daughters run out to greet them, soon followed by Philip himself. They'd met a few times before.

Shimon and Philip had many ideas to share, problems to discuss, but most of all the four daughters soon prepared a splendid breakfast. The young man, the driver, ate voraciously, though his eyes followed the daughters' every move, until Shimon sent him out to look after the donkey. Shimon never imagined that he could develop such concern, such friendship towards an animal which, until that very night, he had considered unclean.

"Feed him well, John," Shimon commanded. "And make sure he gets enough water."

He needn't have worried. John always regarded the donkey as clean as he was just after he'd washed him. He liked all animals. Often more so than people. He returned to the table nodding his satisfaction.

They were finishing breakfast when a messenger knocked on Philip's door. The man stretched his arm, palm down, fingers pressed together, in a Roman salute, and asked to see Shimon.

"Cornelius, the Centurion, has sent me. He's asking you to grace his house with your presence," was his cryptic message.

Shimon had heard about Cornelius. He was a man in charge of one hundred men. The reason his name became known was because people talked of his generosity. He was a Roman officer, a soldier, yet he was known for giving generous alms to the poor, of praying—even in public, and of setting a good example for his household. Shimon wished that some of his own people were as good servants of the Lord as Cornelius appeared to be.

"And just how did your Master know that I am here?" Shimon asked?

"He'd dreamt he saw an angel, Sir. The angel told him…" The man was obviously embarrassed. Soldiers don't speak of angels. It's not manly.

Shimon raised his hand. Slowly the pennies dropped into their allotted places. The unclean donkey, the animals he'd dreamt of, which he was to eat without discrimination, and now, he was asked to visit a house of a Gentile.

"Will you show me the way?" he asked gently.

The man saluted again, smacking his right arm across his chest. "As you command, Sir."

The man was polite, indeed obedient, but his eyes already began to oscillate between the uneaten food on the table, and the four maidens peeking from the open door to the kitchen.

"There is a condition, though…" Shimon said, winking at Philip at his side.

The man looked instantly worried.

"The condition is that you first eat a hearty breakfast!"

A salvo of laughter emerged from the kitchen, even as the soldier's cheeks turned bright red. He was a very young messenger.

They arrived in Caesarea a little after midday. Cornelius, in his splendid uniform of a Centurion, waited for them outside. His men have been told to keep a keen lookout for the last hour or two. He couldn't be sure that Shimon would come, but he trusted the Lord that his prayers would be heard. He was a man of great faith.

Shimon waved his arms from afar.

From some distance Cornelius looked taller. Only when their cart got closer did Shimon realize that the men on Centurion's either side were shorter than he was. Also, Cornelius stood on a rock, to see farther out. What he may have lacked in height, he made up for in the enormous width of his shoulders.

Once Shimon and John dismounted from their humble conveyance, the Centurion came a few steps closer and prostrated himself before Shimon. He obviously knew, or guessed, who Shimon was. Shimon was embarrassed by this show of abject obeisance, and rushed to lift the man to his feet.

"Come, Cornelius, I am only a man. Just like you."

Shimon listened to his own words in vague surprise. Just like you, he'd said. In the eyes of Yahweh are we not all the same. No one is born superior to another. Be it in Rome, Jerusalem, or in Bethsaida. We are all children of the Most High.

Why didn't I see it before?

That very afternoon Shimon baptized Cornelius, as he did his whole household. Not since the day of that splendid Shavuoth... not since that wondrous day was Shimon so happy. And his joy was contagious. They all laughed and cried tears of joy.

As for Shimon, a whole new world seemed to have opened to him. Thousands upon thousands of souls. None were unclean. None were unworthy. Only their deeds would speak of their merit. And no ones' deeds spoke louder than those of Cornelius. A Roman soldier. A Centurion. A man born to fight. As of now he'd fight openly for the souls of others.

At long last, looking at Cornelius, Shimon realized that none were as worthy as his Roman host.

On their return, Philip invited Shimon and John to spend the night in his house. Shimon accepted gladly. While in Jerusalem, every day, every waking moment, he'd spent time in discussions, arguments, on matters of organizations, responsibilities and even having to clarify a number of items of faith in which James needed his support. In Jerusalem he had to be Kepha. Here in Philip's house, he was an honored guest. A friend who came from afar, to spend a quiet evening. To share old stories, even memories.

Shimon didn't realize how much he needed just such an evening. The last time he enjoyed an atmosphere as warm and as congenial, was in the house of his friend Ananias, and that felt like ages ago.

Just before retiring, Shimon remembered that he must contact Paul and offer him his apologies. At the time Shimon didn't know that it was much too late. That Paul would have already gone his own way, at least for a while, and if he ever returned, he'd come with deeds instead of words. Somehow, Shimon felt guilty about Paul. He felt guilty so often in his life, he was getting used to it.

Maybe it's just part of being Jewish, he mused, his mouth lopsided in a quizzical smile.

Just before he fell asleep in a soft comfortable bed, he sat up in horror. He suddenly realized, belatedly, that John and four virgins slept under the same roof.

"May your will be done, Lord," he whispered. Then he looked up, blinked a few times and collapsed. It was too much for one day. He hoped that John thought likewise.

***

14

BARNABAS

He had to do it. Even if it did bring danger to her, to her household, and to his mother-in-law's household. And to his children. Surely, the Lord would look after them?

It's been so long, so very long...

Even the donkey seemed tired. John barely held onto the reins, allowing him to plod his way along the road. Not much of a road. Once the Romans took over Judea, they stopped maintaining it. There wasn't enough gold around; nor silver; nor any precious commodities. People here, they said, were more preoccupied with intangible things. Like Yahweh, and Torah, and now, for some years now, with Yeshûa's teaching. A good man, by all accounts, but he never made any money, they said. He wouldn't do well in Rome. Religion was fine, it had its place. Rome had many fine temples for dozens of gods and goddesses, but you couldn't make any money out of that. Except for the priests. They managed to squeeze the last penny, nay, the last farthing out of the people. The simple people, of course. Just the simple people. While the rich got richer...

Shimon had never been to Rome, but he heard people talk. Temples, they said, magnificent temples to false gods... And goddesses, of course. Lots of them.

The donkey kept plodding along, as though encouraging idle thought. You had to kill time. Poor donkey.

"I wonder what he's thinking," Shimon murmured.

"What was that, Rabbi?"

Shimon looked at John who was stifling a yawn. "It was nothing," he replied, dismissing the matter with a wave of his hand. "It was nothing."

It was a little boring, but the road was good enough for the two-wheel cart Shimon had been given, last year, by his brethren in Antioch.

"So that you can come back to us sooner," they smiled, as though enjoying their little joke.

In fact it was to ease his journeys. He wasn't old, not yet, but he wasn't getting any younger, either. He carried a lot on his shoulders. By now, the trip to Jerusalem on foot would have been too much for him.

It was even a good stretch from Joppa to Antioch, but not that far, nor too much out of the way, to Bethsaida. Shimon and young John made their way back again towards the north, but just before reaching Caesarea, Shimon pulled on the reins, and the cart veered northeast towards Nazareth, and onto Tiberias. John didn't say anything, although he did look a mite surprised. The Rabbi just smiled.

Shimon couldn't believe his eyes how the town had grown. In his day it was hardly more than a village.

In my day... he chuckled. In another lifetime?

As they approached the shores of Lake Gennesareth, Shimon's heart quickened. He forgot how many years have past since he last visited its shores. So many memories of Yeshûa, of his dearest friends and, most of all, the purpose of this particular digression from the road to Antioch, his wife, all rushed into his awareness seemingly at once.

His wife, Perpetua, now a total stranger. In his mind she still was a young, beautiful maiden.

He couldn't tell her that he was coming. It was too dangerous. She might have shared the news with others—

with her friends. And, well, women like to talk. Like to share the good news. Who could blame them? Years have past since he held her in his arms. He felt, now, as though he'd never been married. Perhaps, he mused, perhaps now that the children were all in their teens, perhaps she could join him in Antioch; although there, too, he hardly spent more than a few days at a time. He was a man without a home.

It has been ten years since he left his home. Thirteen since he began to follow the Master. At least then, during those first few years, he'd visited her, now and then. And now, he even didn't attend his son's Bar Mitzvah.

"What sort of a father am I?" he asked himself bitterly.

Shimon recognized his old house from afar. His family home of so many years. His father and mother lived there before him. Before *them*. It stood there as if nothing had happened. As if he'd left it only yesterday.

So many years…

He pulled on the reins and told John to let the donkey graze. He didn't need much time. It wouldn't be safe to stay long—but a moment or two with memories…

He walked the rest of the way.

And then he froze. A maiden, perhaps seventeen or eighteen years old, was coming towards him. She'd just left his house and approached him as though in a hurry. He caught his breath. He waited until she reached him, and then went passed him.

"Petronilla?" he whispered, not believing his eyes. The girl was beauty incarnate. A spitting image of his wife.

The girl who had just passed him slowed down, turned slowly, but didn't approach him.

"How do you know my name?" she asked. She spoke with a trace of a Galilean accent. There was no fear in her voice, just curiosity.

"I s-s-saw you coming out of… that h-h-house," he said. He almost said 'my' house. He'd never stammered before, not even when facing large crowds.

"Yes?" she asked, obviously finding his answer inadequate.

He was trying to think fast. "I wondered if Perpetua was in…"

"You know my mother?" the girl asked.

"I knew her once. She told me about ah, her daughter. You remind me of her."

"I remind you of her daughter?"

"Forgive me. You remind me of *her*. Of Perpetua." Shimon was trying hard to keep the tremour out of his voice. "Is she in?" There, I said it. He let the air out of his lungs slowly, so as not to sound nervous.

The girl smiled.

"She doesn't live here right now. She's there, out yonder." Petronilla pointed to the road leading along the edge of the lake towards Capernaum. "She's looking after grandma. Her mother is sick of late. Can I help you?"

"No… n-n-no. You already did. Thank you. Please, give your mother my love."

With that he turned and walked quickly away towards the place where John was waiting for him with the cart and donkey. So my mother-in-law is sick. I wonder if I could help… probably would do more harm just by being there, he mused.

Another deep sigh escaped his lips.

Some distance away he turned and looked at the girl he left behind. She was still there, unmoving, waving her head from side to side, as though trying to remember something.

"And the boys," he whispered to himself. "Tell the boys…" his voice was caught in his throat. "Next time," Shimon whispered. "Next time, my love."

She was much too far to hear his words.

Even as he spoke two tears rolled down his cheeks. He waved the last goodbye, and turned quickly.

It was the Lord's will, he thought. It was the Lord's will.

He didn't dare stay in the vicinity of both Bethsaida and Capernaum any longer. Someone was bound to recognize him, and the Pharisees were quite unforgiving. They would tell the priests and they would find someone to do their dirty work. The brethren lost two disciples only last week—just for saying that we ought to love one another.

"We don't care who you love, just pay your tithes," they replied.

"But we have no money..." they pleaded.

"Then we'll put you out of your misery," was their glib answer. The sticks fell, followed by the stones. As an example. As always. To discourage others from being poor.

Without a second thought the priests or the Pharisees would use his wife, his family, to shut him up.

"Or else," they would say. "Or else...tell him to stop turning people against us." At the moment there was nothing to connect him to his old village. He stayed as far away from it as he could.

He didn't dare to look back again until he was a good distance away. The girl was gone. With her, his dreams. Perhaps one day... he mused, but he refused to formulate the thought. It was too painful.

"It is the Lord's will," he repeated to himself, though it didn't sound easy.

Soon the donkey, the clean donkey, the gift of Yahweh, took him far along the road to Antioch.

On Yom She-Nee, two days after Yom Sha-Bat they arrived in Antioch. They were both greeted like heroes coming home, victorious, from a war. By then Shimon was reconciled to his fate. He knew, or at least hoped, that if Petronilla described him to her mother, then Perpetua would have recognized him. She would know that he was there, that he'd visited their old home, almost, and that he still cares. She'd also explain to his daughter why he didn't introduce himself properly. There would have been a long scene in the middle of the village, with tears and laughter, with people looking and, perhaps, soon applauding. He felt like a prodigal father but it couldn't be helped. He loved his family too much to risk their lives.

The next day, at sunrise, people were waiting for him to make decisions. Many decisions. The church was spreading, even in his absence. Strange, he thought. The farther we are from Jerusalem, the more brethren join us.

He started working before breakfast. By noon he was exhausted. And so it was day after day. Inside or outside of his house. The church was growing, and Shimon has not yet learned the art of delegating responsibility. Before the week was out, he called Barnabas.

"You've got to get him to help us," he said, still lost in his thoughts. "We may not agree on all things, but his heart is in the right place. And, I feel, he knows how to organize people." There was news coming often from Tarsus.

Barnabas was used to listening to Shimon thinking aloud. He waited until Shimon finished before asking.

"Who, Rabbi, whom shall I get to help you?"

Shimon looked up. "Why didn't I tell you? Paul. Paul of Tarsus. Tell him we need his help."

"I'll leave at once, Rabbi," Barnabas said, than turned on his heal.

"Yes, yes, tell him that we need him," Shimon repeated.

He had a strange feeling that Barnabas will deliver the news of great joy to Paul. If Ananias was even half-right, then Paul is exactly what the church in Antioch needed. His youth, his energy, his total commitment. Isn't that what Ananias had said? Total commitment?

Barnabas had already met Paul in Jerusalem, and the big Aba'ye in Antioch. They had become friends. Aba'ye visited Paul in Tarsus, and stayed with him for a while. Later Paul became too busy. Within a short time he had created a congregation worthy of the name Church of Tarsus. The news had spread. Paul was a man of action. Barnabas had heard all that from Aba'ye. He thought he'd help Paul, and for the rest of the day he run from house to house, announcing that Paul was coming to spread the Good News. Telling everyone that Paul performed incredible feats of apostleship, that he'd spread the Good News to the very ends of the Roman Empire.

Barnabas didn't think that a little exaggeration would hurt. From what Aba'ye had told him, Paul was going to need all the help he could get. To be accepted, that is. Here. In Antioch. This was just the first step.

Barnabas's was born in Cyprus of Hellenic Levites. His parents named him Joseph. When he ultimately inherited some land in Cyprus, he'd sold it, and gave all the proceeds to the apostles in Jerusalem. That is how he got his name. In Greek the name Barnabas means "son of consolation", or "son of encouragement". His gift to the church in Jerusalem was certainly a great consolation, and his behaviour in Antioch attested to his capacity to encourage brethren.

He was one of the first teachers in Antioch, and probably the hardest working brother under Shimon's guidance. He was delighted that the Rabbi had asked him to get Paul to come and help them. He and Aba'ye left at first light, and, though on foot, they covered the distance in three days. Paul welcomed them with open arms, and when told of Shimon's request, he embraced them like newfound brothers. Actually, he embarrassed one of them. Barnabas. Aba'ye presented a problem. Though, not for long.

Paul, with great speed and alacrity, pulled a chair within easy reach of Aba'ye. Then, with his usual agility he jumped on it, and launched himself at Aba'ye with total abandon. He caught him, as intended, around Aba'ye's upper chest, a destination he would not have reached had he attempted the assault standing on his feet.

Once there, however, he performed a two-handed hug on his old friend, quite unabashedly, and with great gusto. So much so that Aba'ye, although virtually twice Paul's size, lost his footing, and toppled backwards on top of Barnabas, who was standing behind him. The next moment there were three bodies lying on the floor, in various and unusual angles of disarray.

"I have been praying for Shimon to accept me since I met him in Jerusalem," Paul declared, trying to extricate himself from arms and legs that didn't belong to him. "And now?" he concluded, "and now my prayers have been answered."

His facial expression suggested that he might want to use the advantage he held over his friends still being on the floor, by embracing them for the second time. Instead, on brief consideration, wisely, he raised his eyes to the ceiling and expressed his gratitude directly to Yahweh.

All that remained was for the three of them to perform a short but joyful Jewish dance, usually reserved for wedding ceremonies. While Barnabas was the first to give up, the ridiculous duo continued spinning on their heals until they gasped for air. No one, however, seems to have minded.

Within two days Paul transferred his duties to his deacons. He had already appointed three of them, in case he was called upon to leave on short notice. It was always his intention to travel, so as to spread the Word far and wide amongst the Gentiles. At the time, that was how he differed with Shimon, and to this day with a number of other Believers. He was definitely well organized.

Three days later they arrived in Antioch. Barnabas knocked on Shimon's door and let Paul come in. Shimon rose to embrace him, but Paul dodged his arms and put his own arms around Shimon's knees.

"Please rise, Paul," Shimon bend down to lift him. "Your deeds precede you."

Paul rose to his feet, an unusually shy smile on his lips. Shimon embraced him with both arms.

"Forgive me," Shimon said softly. "I was not afraid for myself."

Paul nodded. He knew even then. And they both smiled. As of that moment, they became one in Christ.

***

15

AGABUS

"**D**ifferent people are endowed with different gifts," Barnabas said, his eyes defying anyone to contradict him.

He was in good company. A year has passed since Barnabas and Aba'ye brought Paul back from Tarsus. To Paul's disbelieving though extremely joyful surprise, the whole community of Believers has accepted him with open arms. He had no idea, of course, that Barnabas and Aba'ye took the elevation of his popularity as their own personal challenge. As a matter of fact, once brethren heard about Paul's accomplishments in Tarsus, there was hardly any convincing necessary. As so often in the past, the advice Shimon gave Paul in Jerusalem has proven to be right.

Paul's dreams have come true.

Shimon, Paul, Barnabas, and a newcomer named Agabus were sitting outside, behind Shimon's dwelling, in a tiny courtyard smelling of flowers and corn growing on the other side of the stone fence. It was an intimate place, shaded from the midday sun, and protected from the hot wind blowing from the desert. They all felt relaxed, a luxury not often shared.

Paul and Agabus have just engaged in a discussion, with Shimon looking on, silently, but keeping a keen eye on both younger men. They discussed the gifts of healing, prophecy, and even restoring dead men to life, if such were indeed possible for anyone other than the Master.

"And just how did He do it?" Paul challenged passionately.

Paul was a very practical man. Even his own visions, way back on the way to Damascus, were still troubling him. He'd accepted them emotionally, he needed them to have been real to be able to rationalize his own life, but from the intellectual point of view he had problems accepting their logic. Tarsus was among the foremost centers of Greek thought, and logic was an integral part of Greek philosophy. Aristotelian logic and mathematics were the mainstays of Greek thought, and both were deeply imbedded in Paul's psyche. He has virtually reconciled himself to live with this apparent duality, with the disparity between his emotions and his mind, when Agabus's arrival from Jerusalem stirred things again.

Agabus was the last man who'd want to cause trouble. A man quiet by nature, yet one who refused to keep quiet about matters that he felt have been revealed to him. He wasn't alone. There was a whole group of prophets who stuck together and compared notes. On this occasion they claimed, practically in unison, that the new Emperor of Rome, Claudius, whose full title, according to Paul, was Tiberius Claudius Caesar Augustus Germanicus, was in some way connected to the oncoming famine in Jerusalem. No one, however, volunteered to say how or why.

"I could get hungry just reciting his name," Paul murmured under his nose. Barnabas heard him and burst out laughing.

"What say you to that, Agabus?"

"Actually they just take on the names of their predecessors and add a few new ones so that we might be able to tell them apart."

"Now that makes it all perfectly clear," Barnabas butted in, again, raising more chuckles.

"Doesn't Claudius mean lame, or crippled, or something like that in Latin?" Agabus decided to show off his knowledge.

"As a matter of fact, Claudius was afflicted by both, a limp and slight deafness, due to sickness at a young age. If it hadn't been for the Praetorian Guard, he'd have been long assassinated by his nephew Caligula. Fortunately for him, it was Caligula who was assassinated himself. That... and the fact that he was the last male member of the family line, elevated him to be the next emperor."

Paul recited all this from memory. His new calling notwithstanding, he considered keeping up with knowledge about potential enemies a must. And, after all, he still was a citizen or Rome.

"Nevertheless..." Agabus began, but Paul, always a practical man interrupted.

"So what are we going to do about this famine?" Paul sounded as if he didn't give much credence to Agabus visions in particular, and to other prophets in general.

Agabus looked at him with wide eyes. "By the grace of Yahweh, I am a prophet, not a caterer." There was hurt in his voice. He still wasn't sure if anyone was taking him seriously.

Paul felt a little sorry for the frail young man. He looked at his new friend with compassion.

"If we assume that you are right, we must decide if, and if so how, we can help our brethren in Jerusalem. They, thanks to the priesthood and the Pharisees, will suffer the most."

This simple statement from the ever-practical Paul was followed by a long silence. His fellow Believers, Christians as they began calling themselves, dealt with the soul, not with body. Also, most of the time they were quite penniless. They've all experienced many a time hunger but, in a way, they took it in their stride; as did Paul in Arabia.

This was different. They were talking about ordinary people who might not have been blessed with faith strong enough to take them through the hard times.

Shimon, his back resting against the mud-brick wall, who until now just listened, stirred in his place. All eyes immediately turned towards him. But he didn't speak. His eyes travelled over the small group as though waiting to hear something that would touch on his domain. His concern, even more so than those present, dealt with matters of spirit, and spirit alone.

Agabus who felt responsible for the prophecy cleared his throat. "I suppose they'll have to take up their cross and bear it?"

"You want them to suffer?" Shimon spoke, at last, his tone hardly above a whisper.

Once again, all eyes turned towards him.

"Yahweh didn't create their woes. Nor did our Master," Shimon added, his voice neutral, noncommittal.

This simple statement left them speechless. Paul stirred, Barnabas looked lost, and Agabus looked like a man scorned for being a messenger.

"If an obese man is deprived of food, is this not a blessing? And if people refuse to accept the teaching of the Master, should they not be shown that that spirit is stronger than the body?"

Paul was the first to react.

"You mean, Rabbi, that under pressure they might turn to… to the right way?"

"I mean that no one has been created to suffer. Not even here, on earth."

Agabus eyes turned upwards. "Many people will die…" he said, his voice apologetic.

"And is there not a fate worse than leaving our body to enter the Kingdom of Heaven?" Shimon spoke very softly.

"*Mens sana in corpore sano,*" Paul quoted an old saying. He preferred the Latin version of a quip by Greek philosopher Thales. Although he spoke Greek fluently, Latin influences were becoming progressively stronger. Paul thought that Thales saying was much more then a quip.

"Healthy mind in a healthy body," he repeated when the other three looked up. "A healthy soul…"

"I think we get the idea," Barnabas smiled. "The question is, which comes first?"

Shimon looked at Barnabas with approval. The young man was a good teacher. A good Rabbi of the Good News. Barnabas put his finger on the heart of the matter.

"We all create our reality. Or realities, if you prefer. This is true of both individuals and groups. It may not sound fair, but it is hard not to get your sandals soiled when walking through mud."

Paul opened his mouth to speak only to close it again. For him, his body was the temple for the spirit. It was a necessary part. A *sine qua non*, he thought, again in Latin. His body was, so to speak, a matter that is indispensible. A *nec plus ultra*. Body and soul were one, to him. There was nothing beyond. Without body the soul was… he didn't quite work that out, as yet, what did happen to his soul when it would, irrevocably, one day, leave his body. Can it exist autonomously? In full consciousness, in full awareness of self? Or did it just hang around, suspended beyond time, in limbo, waiting to enter another body.

As he looked up he noticed that Shimon's eyes were on him. He felt a little uncomfortable.

"This reality is not real," Shimon said, staring into Paul's eyes. "It is not real," he repeated.

Paul heard Shimon saying that before, some years ago. He didn't quite understand it then, he didn't quite understand it now.

Paul had never met the Master. Yeshûa didn't convey His inner knowledge to the masses. And even the future apostles had problems accepting the teaching, prompting Yeshûa to cry out, repeatedly, "Why can't you understand my words?"

Most people just wouldn't, or couldn't, accept it. For Yeshûa, is seems, His reality, His Kingdom, was not of this world. Shimon wondered if Paul would ever understand that. Such knowledge, he knew, could come only from within. Only Yeshûa could transmit it directly, on a one-on-one basis. Words alone could not explain it.

Nevertheless, Paul did his best. His dichotomy was exacerbated by Greek, Roman and Pharisaic backgrounds. The Christian teaching was the fourth change in the direction of the path he travelled. But while his heart found peace in the teaching of Christ, his mind continued to rise in rebellion.

Then Shimon spoke to him directly. Paul had a feeling that no one else could hear the Rabbi. It was just between him and Shimon.

"My body is what I use, not what defines me," Shimon said, though his lips did not seem to be moving.

"Shall I only achieve my potential, shall I only emerge in full, when I eliminate my body?"

"Not your body, Paul. Your ego."

"B-b-but I am me…"

"No, you are what is within you."

"Then what am I?"

"The answer, Paul, will only come to you when you stop searching for it. That is the real meaning of "let it be Thy will".

"But how… how…?"

"Remember his words: 'My peace I give unto you.' Only in total peace, in total relaxation, if you will, the I AM, the real you, can do Its works?"

"Relaxation?"

"Yes. Only when you give up, forsake all your attachments, you'll achieve that for which you're searching."

"What are you two talking about?" Barnabas asked. "I can't hear a word you're saying."

Shimon smiled.

"You will, my friend. You will when you're ready."

Paul shook his head, not sure if he really heard Shimon talking, or just imagined it. He was sure of only one thing. It had something to do with ego. With his ego. With his opinions of his self-worth. He remembered, vaguely, from so very long ago, what shock he felt when he was still sitting at the feet of Gamaliel, and the Rabbi repeated the words of the psalmist. He thought that Yahweh would strike them both with lightening. Yet the words still reverberated somewhere deep in his memory. "Ye are gods", he'd said. "Ye are gods…" Even now he winced when he remember them. Did Gamaliel blaspheme? Paul remembered he'd later looked up the words in the Torah. Gamaliel was right, yet…

"None of this is real, Paul," Shimon's voice seemed to be reaching him from afar. "You are what is within you."

A moment later Paul became aware of the other two men who were looking at him with quizzical expressions.

"I am all right," he assured them. "Sometimes my mind wanders… I'm all right."

And then he looked at Shimon. The old man's face was full of light. Light heightened by a broad smile. He merely nodded.

"So what of the famine?" Barnabas asked, looking alternatively at Shimon and Agabus.

When the young prophet remained silent, he turned his eyes to Shimon, evidently expecting a decision of some sort. Shimon always made it. It was his job. The older man, smiled, and remained silent. Then he looked at Paul, as though encouraging him to speak.

"There are different kinds of famine, caused by different kinds of hunger. And of these, the hunger for spirit is the hardest to contain," Paul said, looking down at his feet. "It is also the hardest thirst to quench."

His sandals have covered a lot of ground trying to sate his thirst. A great deal of ground. "Shall I ever learn?" he asked himself. And then he looked up, again, at Shimon's smiling face. He'd never seen the Rabbi so happy. It seemed as though he was about to get up and dance.

Then, to his further surprise, he noticed that not just Shimon, but all three men were looking at him.

"What did I say?" he asked, surprised at their staring glare. "What have I said?" he repeated.

But all three men remained silent. Slowly all three got up, and each in turn came to Paul and, without a single word, embraced him.

Early the next day Paul and Barnabas began to make plans for a journey to Jerusalem. Paul decided, with Shimon's blessing, to take Barnabas with him. Apparently the illustrious, if slightly lame, Claudius would not contribute much to sating the spiritual truth people sought. It was up to the two of them.

The famine was indeed getting worse. Even the acolytes were slipping into their old ways. The priesthood and the Pharisees and the Sadducees were winning, while the Roman pipers played the tune to which no one would dance. Those who have come into life were dying again.

Coming from Antioch, neither Paul nor Barnabas, nor even the community of Believers, the Christians as they were now calling themselves throughout the northern provinces, could supply their brothers in Jerusalem with material goods. The prophecy for material assistance could only be passed on to Romans, perhaps to some obese priests, but hardly to the apostles. They've already given up all to serve—to spread the Good News.

Soon after Paul and Barnabas left town about one league behind them, they saw a solitary man following them. For the first time in a long while Paul regretted having given up his sword. The roads were still as dangerous as ever. Neither he nor Barnabas had anything worth stealing, but the possible assailant wouldn't know that, and he might be well armed. As the man's long strides brought him closer Paul recognized his massive frame.

"Can I come, too?" Aba'ye asked.

Paul smiled, then looked at his old friend with love in his eyes. "I thought you'd never ask," he replied.

And the three of them quickened their pace.

The moment Paul had left, Shimon put his secret plan into action. He felt that at long last he could leave his church in Antioch in capable hands. Paul may be young, he thought, but he was fully committed to the work for the Lord. Shimon no longer had any doubts about that. The trip to Jerusalem would strengthen him further, and give him extra authority. He would be back, soon, and take over the reins of the work in Antioch. In the meantime, Shimon could carry out his own plan.

He was already packed, and had a few silver shekels sewn into the hem of his coat. His brethren, the closest friends, knowing of his intentions, insisted that he take the money. Whatever happened, he'd have to pay for the ship. He would walk the rest of the way. But it was a long journey. It could be at least a year before he'd get back. Lord willing.

Surely, Shimon thought, my miraculous escape from prison in Jerusalem also made it advisable to leave my present environs. Paul was different. He could fight, physically if necessary, for his own safety. Shimon lost that privilege having witnessed Yeshûa restoring the ear of the guard. The ear Shimon had cut off in the Garden of Gethsemane.

Imagine, I drew my sword, he mused. I, Shimon, carrying a sword...

It was a different era. A different time. Things change.

There was little time. The priests and the Pharisees had just murdered James. James the Greater, they called him. The brother of John. He'd gone to build a Christian foundation in

Iberia. And then felt he needed to come back and help his brothers in Judea. He was captured almost on his arrival. Herod the Agrippa murdered him, to please Jewish leaders who were furious at how rapidly the church was growing.

They beheaded him.

Shimon would probably have been next.

Three days after Paul's departure, Shimon quietly set out for Seleucia, the port of Antioch. A few hours walk brought him there, but he had to wait another three days before a Roman officer took pity on him and, for just two silver shekels allowed him to board. Shimon had the ability to look destitute and distinguished at the same time. The officer was probably thinking of his own father...

The ship looked huge.

The large square sail just aft of amidships and a smaller, also a square one, closer to the high raised bow, looked impressive. Compared to the fishing boats Shimon had been used to in his far, far distant past, this ship looked enormous. If for no other reason that it was about five times longer, had a much wider beam, and it took a ladder to climb aboard.

He was told that below the raised deck, there were a number of slaves, used to work the oars. Shimon was also told that he'd never see any of them. They were not allowed on deck. They worked, ate, and slept below. Shimon hated the idea, but there was nothing he could do about it. While sails were used for general travel, all Roman ships had at least one level of oarsmen, in case of dropping wind, or the necessity of fight or flight against or from an enemy. Also they provided more control when docking.

At the stern, two large sweep oars, one on each side, were used for steering the ship.

The soldiers, and on occasion some passengers, were clustered on deck, exposed to all aspects of often-inclement weather. Merchants carrying gold or silver invariably tried to buy a passage on a naval ship. It offered much greater protection. As for comfort, only the Roman officers could hide under a tent-like shelter. Even then, the ship offered more security than merchant ships which invariably overloaded their capacity in the hope of maximizing the profits.

The ship took more than a season to get Shimon to Rome. Why Rome? Rome was the center of the world; the center of the Empire; the center of civilization. It was where the church had to leave its mark. Immediately.

On an otherwise crowded ship Shimon was completely alone. He took no one with him. Not even to carry his water. There were no other Jews on deck. Yet, by the time they came ashore, every man on board was a Christian. Yes. Even those below the deck. Shimon had that power of persuasion.

"It is not I," he always corrected. "It is the Lord's power."

Shimon stayed in Rome a lot longer than he planned, but by the time Claudius issued a decree that all Jews must leave Rome, the church was well established. Only Shimon could have achieved that.

Or… the Lord, as he'd say.

Yet, even on his departure from Rome, various disciples who travelled to and from Syria or Galilee, advised Shimon to keep his whereabouts secret. He was too valuable to the church they said. You are the Kepha, they reminded him. Yes, even in the relatively short time he became known in Rome as Petrus. Petrus the Rock. Or Kepha. The man who never wavered.

Shimon only smiled. How little did they know, he mused. How little did they know?

***

16

FAMINE

It was a very different story travelling in a group of
three, than covering long stretches of road all alone. Paul
was used to loneliness. He suffered from it practically all
his life. After a while, he stopped missing people. In time he
found it difficult to spend any length of time in the company
of others without becoming mentally and emotionally
exhausted. He probably thought he'd become drained of
ideas.

And then he began preaching.

It was only during the years he'd spent in Tarsus, after
his rejection in both Damascus and Jerusalem that he began
to overcome his reticence towards sharing his time, let alone
his most intimate thoughts, with other people, more so, with
total strangers. Now, on this journey, he was no longer
taciturn. He even joked at the slightest provocation.

While Aba'ye was hardly an intellectual giant his parents
endowed him with a good dose of humour. He exhibited it
mostly by describing the expressions on people's faces when
Shimon was teaching. He had Paul and Barnabas doubled up
in laughter, which slowed them down, but they all agreed, it
was worth it. By contrast, yet in a strangely complementary
fashion, Paul found Aba'ye's imperturbable stoicism under
changing circumstances, be it regarding the weather, or heat,
or even in the face of suspected or approaching danger, to be
also bordering on comical. Nothing, absolutely nothing
appeared to upset the giant, with the possible exception of

having to put any physical distance between Paul and himself. Aba'ye was Paul's clinging shadow, often in the literal sense, by allowing Paul to use his bulk to provide the welcome shade.

Barnabas, on the other hand, was a veritable font of information. He kept up to date on all knowledge pertaining to the expansion of the church, of the converts to the Good News. His head was like an abacus, summing up all the faithful and their activities from far and wide. The Christian church was growing, though not nearly as fast as Paul would like.

"An Empire," Paul said. "We must create an Empire for Christ."

Barnabas looked at him with a mixture of surprise and admiration. He wondered what exactly did Paul have in mind. He didn't have to wait long to learn. Paul, seeing a willing ear, began to expound on his vision.

"We'll start by voyaging to far away places. We'll use ships that travel as far as the horizon... and then beyond. I see us sailing to Cyprus, to Attalia and Perga... Then on land to Pisida, and Phrygia, and Galatia... all the way to the cities in the north." His eyes turned dreamy. "I see the Good News sweeping the Empire... I see the Good News as a fire that is spreading... that is consuming the world."

Paul caught himself, feeling slightly embarrassed. It was more than evident that Paul had been studying the maps of the Roman Empire with great interest. Perhaps that was what he had been doing in Tarsus. They say Tarsus is a great center of knowledge.

"It's just a dream I had," he added, not meeting Barnabas's eyes. "I have," he corrected himself.

And what of the 'Kingdom not of this World', Barnabas eyes, rising to the snippets of clouds drifting overhead, seemed to ask? What of Shimon's vision? But he didn't say it out loud. Paul's vision was, to a young man, much more exciting. Also, it was much more likely to succeed. After all, they were here, on earth, this is where they had their being. As for Shimon... wasn't the Rabbi growing old?

"And what of the money?" Barnabas reasoned that sea voyages would not be cheap.

"Money will come to us..." The dreamy quality of his voice was returning.

"From where?"

"From wherever it is now..." Paul answered, and this time his eyes were smiling. He was on his own turf now. He found a listener and he was determined to convince him. It was like preaching only on the means, rather than the end.

"From brethren?" Barnabas asked. He was about to point out that the spiritual famine, which Agabus prophesied for Jerusalem, might have a physical component.

Paul looked at him, his smile implying that he was well ahead of his friend.

"I have some funds in Tarsus. My parents have a property there. Soon it will be mine. Perhaps, it already is. I can't think of a better use for it than to spread the Good News."

"Rather than feed hungry brethren?"

Paul looked irritated. "Didn't you listen to Shimon? It is spiritual famine that is about to overcome them. Didn't you hear him?"

Barnabas heard him well enough. Only it was Paul who had advanced this theory, not Shimon. On the other hand, Shimon certainly approved it. Barnabas realized that he had to make a decision—either to follow the explosive fire that Paul intended to spread, or the inner fire of Shimon, which bewitched only in moments when he and the Rabbi were alone. It seemed to emanate from him. From deep within him. Shimon was like a dormant volcano that rumbled only on special occasions. Yet both visions seemed as strong as the sun that beat on their heads. Even the snippets of clouds were slow in approaching.

Barnabas was young. In broad daylight, Paul's vision seemed by far the more attractive.

Aba'ye was carrying the food and water for all three of them. When the sun was directly overhead, he asked, shyly, if it was time for some food.

"It isn't the weight I am carrying," he hastened to assure the two men, "but my stomach is growling something awful."

Both Paul and Barnabas heard it. They had to agree that it was rather awful. No wonder. It had a lot of body to support.

Paul nodded, pointing to a small knoll with bushes atop that might provide a little shade.

Paul hoped to arrive in Jerusalem on Yom Sha-Bat, to inspire the people who were, presumably, congregating in the Synagogue. He was hoping that sufficient years have passed for the masses not to recognize him. Since he would also appear as Paul, and not Saul, his health should not suffer unduly. At any rate, he was prepared to take the risk.

He had to—sometimes. He had to even before his diametric change of heart.

Nevertheless, he glanced sideways at Aba'ye. He deserved a rest. The giant looked as carefree as a baby. Some ten paces away he was already stretching himself on a patch of skimpy grass, leaving the shaded spots to Barnabas and Paul. Aba'ye was like that. Also, Paul thought, quite indubitably Aba'ye was without a care in the world.

And why not? Aren't we all supposed to put our faith in the Lord? Who more so than he, Paul, who aspired to become one of the apostles? Didn't the Master tell them not to worry about tomorrow? Ananias said He did. And then Paul chuckled. He also remembered the rest of that sentence: "for the morrow shall take thought of things of itself." Shall take, Paul wondered? Will it? Tomorrow, or in a day or two, we shall be in Jerusalem and... shall tomorrow also have "sufficient evil thereof." Just how much evil will tomorrow bring?

Questions.

Paul always had plenty of questions, although the answers, too, had given him abundant problems. Answers like those dealing with the Kingdom of Heaven. What had Shimon really been talking about? He seemed to have been implying that heaven is not a destination after death, well perhaps for the masses... But he was as firm in suggesting that heaven was a state of mind. That it is a condition of a man's consciousness—a state, or condition, to which we can aspire while still here, on earth.

While alive and kicking!

Shimon was quite serious about that, but only when the few, those nearest to him, were alone. As if this knowledge was not to be divulged to the masses. To ordinary people? Weren't we all ordinary?

Shimon also talked a great deal about the real knowledge in the Torah being hidden under a veil of symbolism. Was this concept of heaven, here and now, only of symbolic value?

What did Shimon mean by ordinary people?

Again Paul looked at Aba'ye. Wasn't he in heaven? Right now? Most of the time? Was Aba'ye ordinary? Or is he the best friend I ever had?

Wasn't Aba'ye in heaven of his own making? Is heaven always of one's own making? For all of us?

Or, at least, most of the time?

The sun moved to the west of the midday. It was time to go.

After almost two weeks they arrived in Jerusalem. The day following their arrival Paul was beaten up by people who recognized him in spite of the passing years, of his long beard, and even of a different name. Of course, he'd insisted on going alone, without Aba'ye at his side.

To be honest, they tried to kill him. Stones were flying. Aba'ye, who refused to stay far behind, ran up and pulled him out of the crowd just in time. Yet Paul was not easily discouraged. He went back the next day, to the same spot, on the steps of the Temple.

This time, John Mark, the evangelist known and respected by the people of Jerusalem, stood first and told people a few words about Paul.

Having been told that Paul is under Roman protection, the crowd held back their wrath. And later, when he spoke to them in Aramaic, they listened.

The following words Paul read aloud from a letter he'd written earlier that day. He decided he must coordinate his thoughts, put them in writing, to make sure he left out nothing that would be of importance to the people.

"Brethren and fathers, hear my defense before you now. I am indeed a Jew, born in Tarsus of Cilicia, but brought up in this city at the feet of Gamaliel, taught according to the strictness of our fathers' law, and was zealous toward God as you all are today."

About then Barnabas saw Paul take a deep breath, while Aba'ye, at his side, tensed all over.

"I persecuted this Way to the death, binding and delivering into prisons both men and women, as also the high priest bears me witness, and all the council of the elders, from whom I also received letters to the brethren, and went to Damascus to bring in chains even those who were there, in Jerusalem to be punished."

Paul spoke to them, reading slowly from his letter, as though sharing that which he'd never shared with anyone before. The people must have felt it. They also felt his contrition. It was real, or seemed real. With Paul, one couldn't be sure. Barnabas thought that for Paul, his purpose, his dream, his Grand Scheme took precedence over minor details of his life.

Wasn't he building an Empire for the Christ?

Paul told the people a great deal more. He described to them all that had happened from the moment he'd fallen asleep on the way to Damascus. They listened, fascinated, at the dedication of Ananias and later at Paul's own commitment to spread the word.

At long last he stopped. He bowed slightly, nodded to the crowd, and walked down the steps towards Barnabas and Aba'ye. Nobody tried to stop him.

This time Paul did not suffer any harm. He did not, as yet, become the crowds' favourite but, though grudgingly, they decided to give him another chance. All in all, their faith was strengthened, their thirst and famine a little less pronounced.

"If Paul could pull himself up from the pit of Sheol, so can we," they whispered.

A few walked up to him to touch his hand, or placed their hand on his shoulder. Two or three, embraced him. And the rest let him go, unscathed.

Paul was not inclined to stay in Jerusalem any longer than necessary. He'd made his mark, perhaps laid ground for future visits. He was no longer a villain from a foreign land. He also showed people that the Good News had the power to save him, to save his own soul, to lift him from the abysmal pit of Sheol. He's done his job.

The next day the three of them plus a new companion, John Mark who had already helped Paul, set out on the return trip to Antioch. Paul was in a hurry. It seemed that, at least in his head, his plans were approaching fruition. For the first league or two, he walked faster then anyone else. Even Aba'ye had trouble keeping up with him.

Paul, the sinner of the past, was on fire.

They slept on the side of the read, ate just fruit, stopped at wells for a drink of water, and arrived in Antioch exhausted. Paul was surprised that Shimon wasn't there. He wanted to share his impression with the Rabbi. For some reason, no one told him where Shimon went.

Still, Paul had his own plans. His own calling.

Time went by…

Some years later, on his return from Rome, Shimon was preaching to a group of seekers, certainly more than two hundred but less then twice that number, who gathered on the square outside the Antioch Synagogue to hear him speak. Shimon didn't announce his return. He slipped into his old dwelling as though nothing had happened, as though he'd never left. Yet, somehow, people heard. A few of them were locals, but most came from outside. Shimon's name brought them here. They'd already heard about the Good News from Christians dispersed over a large area, but came to hear the news from the source. That's what they thought of him. The Source. From the source, or as close to the source as they could get.

Shimon stood still and waited until silence spread over the men and women farthest away. Then he raised his arms and greeted them.

"Grace be unto you, and peace be multiplied."

A slight wave rippled over the crowd.

"And with you…" they replied.

"Blessed be Yahweh, the Father of Yeshûa, our Lord, which according to His abundant mercy has begotten us, again, to a new life, through His blood and resurrection."

Not many understood the words; those who studied Torah had some idea, the others just listened. Most of them were Gentiles, and their knowledge of any religion was less then elementary. Both Greeks and Romans had too many gods to make heads or tails of any of them. Most may have heard about Zeus, or Jupiter, but that was as far as their knowledge went. These were simple folks.

In that Shimon found an advantage.

Do not put fresh wine into old skins... he remembered the Master's words. The skins that faced him were as fresh as they could be. The meaning of his words would reach them later, perhaps in their sleep, perhaps in moments of rest from the vicissitudes and worries of everyday life.

When they came here, to the square, people had little idea of what to expect. They heard about eternal life that those strange Christians promised, an offer they found very hard to resist; or, at the very least, they wanted to find out more about it. The snippets they heard whetted their appetite, particularly since right now, right here on earth, their life did not inspire them to sit on their laurels. It was all right for some Greeks to put a wreath around their temples and smile, but most simple folks expected a little more. They needed more.

Shimon knew these people. Until not so long ago, he was one of them. He knew that if he could plant the seed of understanding, to literally whet their appetite, they would come back. And next time, he'd get down to real teaching. He would get down to practical matters such as prayer, and contemplation, and changing their view of the world. To matters of a new reality. To the question of who they were—who they really were.

"...to an inheritance incorruptible, and undefiled that fades not away, reserved in heaven for you."

His voice droned, yet there was a persuasive ring to it that kept people listening.

***

17

THE FIRST JOURNEY

They only just got back to Antioch. Even Aba'ye was exhausted. Paul, however, was on fire. Though they only returned on Yom Shee-Shee, the next day being Yom Sha-Bat, with Shimon's approval, Paul and Barnabas went to the local synagogue where Paul preached a powerful message.

To repeat, Paul was on fire.

After the Jews left the house of worship, the gentiles, all proselytes, asked Paul to preach, again, the next Yom Sha-Bat. Then, both Jews and proselytes followed Paul and Barnabas, asking to hear more of the Good News.

Paul and Barnabas became an inseparable duo supporting each other, reading each other's thoughts. They shared Paul's attitude toward the gentiles, which Paul found necessary for his vision of the Empire of his dreams. It paid dividends. On the next Yom Sha-Bat virtually the entire city came out to hear Paul preach.

Paul's fame was growing exponentially.

In late spring that year, the brethren ordained Paul and Barnabas as apostles. Thus strengthened, Paul decided it was time to put his plan into action. Soon after the ordination, Paul, Barnabas, and John Mark—the young man they'd brought from Jerusalem, packed their meager belongings, and set out on their first missionary journey. Barnabas, being

John Mark's uncle, was disposed to look after him, though the young man was doing well on his own.

None of them would ever forget that first night.

After spending the last day and afternoon with close friends, the three left early that evening. Although Paul had ample experience of the joys and tribulations of traveling himself, he was determined to set the tone for the journey, and spend the first night outdoors.

After walking for two hours, they arrived in the middle of nowhere. They wanted to be close to the port, but far enough from Antioch to enjoy the mystery of the night in the desert. Silence spread all around them; not even bugs disturbing their peace. The starlit sky served as the only ceiling over their heads. They sat by the fire, telling stories of their past, sharing their dreams. Even though the campfire was meager—not much dry wood along the path they'd taken—their aspirations, their desire to serve Yeshûa, were as great and as lofty as the sky above them.

Paul talked of kingdoms, of an empire he'd build for the Messiah.

"Not just in Judea and Syria, not even just in Phrygia and Macedonia, but the world over." His hand pointed to the sky. "As wide as the sky, as far as the farthest sea, as strong as Kepha on which Yeshûa said He'd build his church…"

Barnabas listened, amazed. He agreed that they should venture outside their own homes to share the Word with the Gentiles but, he wondered… the world over?

John Mark listened; his eyes closing, slowly, his imagination taking over his waken awareness. Soon new dreams, new images filled his mind. He saw endless crowds of people, stretching all the way to the horizon, all acclaiming the Christ.

The last embers were slowly dying. Silence replaced excited voices, and soon ruled supreme.

They slept until dawn.

Next morning they were within a stone's throw from Seleucia. Once there, Barnabas and John-Mark waited while Paul walked around, looking for a ship. Using a few of his accumulated shekels, the most of which he'd again left with Aba'ye—a man he trusted with his life and with all his worldly possession—Paul bought three places on the ship. He sighed at the memory of having to leave Aba'ye behind. Yesterday, for the first and only time, he'd seen a big man cry.

"You cannot come with us, my friend," Paul had told him. "Who else could I trust to look after my fortune?"

A fortune it was not but, even so, that question Aba'ye could not answer. Paul thought it only fair that the money he'd saved while working for the Pharisees and the priests would ultimately pay for his voyages—for food and drink, for roof over their heads, and particularly for sea crossings. He found it amusing that, in a way, the Sanhedrin was financing his apostleship. He could imagine their long-bearded faces, gaping, amazed, terrified, had they ever learned of his plans.

Whatever the justice of the enterprise, Paul couldn't preach far and wide, and continue to make tents, at the same time. He lived humbly but everything had to be paid for. Aba'ye understood. With tears in his eyes, the giant remained in Antioch.

Paul beckoned his friends to go aboard.

It wasn't a proper ship, not such as the Roman navy would be proud of, but, initially, they only wanted to get as far as Cyprus. The boat was a merchant vessel, ready to leave port within hours. It looked a little precarious. The timbers seemed on the verge of rotting, the sail was in bad need of repair with patches giving it that well-used look, the deck heeled a little to starboard, but... well, it was cheap.

Even so, getting a place on board wasn't easy. Merchants were always waiting for cheap crossings, virtually to anywhere. They had to travel to make money—to exchange their goods for other produce, at a good price. And the boat was neither fast nor comfortable. It took weeks to get anywhere, but it was still faster than going by land while carrying one's merchandize.

Paul made sure that they all carried enough water and food to last them for the trip. They also needed some form of bedding, or at least an overcoat to take them through the nights.

Thanks to Pompey, the Roman noble, better known as Pompey the Great, most pirates in the Mediterranean had been eliminated some time ago with the usual Roman efficiency. Pompey, however, could do little about the numerous rats that seemed bent on attacking, and usually eating, the food that inexperienced travelers brought with them. In addition, the ships were invariably overcrowded, adding considerably to the discomfort of the passengers, particularly at night. All things considered, only the hardiest could tolerate the ship's conditions.

Obviously, none of the above would deter Paul or his friends. They were truly determined.

Thus, from Seleucia, Paul, Barnabas and John Mark sailed to Salamis, the principle city on the island of Cyprus. Barnabas was particularly grateful to Paul for the itinerary of the first journey. Cyprus was where he was born and raised.

Soon after arrival, they preached the Good News in several synagogues. After a short rest, they walked the whole length of the island, all the way to the western coast, to preach at Paphos. Here Paul took charge of the expedition in earnest. Partially thanks to having mentioned his Roman citizenship, Paul and Barnabas have been invited to see the Roman Proconsul, one Sergius Paulus. There was a slight problem.

Accompanying the Proconsul to the meeting was a false prophet, a supposed magician name Elymas. He was making things difficult for Paul and his friend, ridiculing the Good

News. Paul looked directly into the sorcerer's eyes and spoke intensely to him as though inspired.

"O full of all deceit and all fraud you son of the devil, you enemy of all righteousness, will you not cease perverting the straight ways of the Lord? And now, indeed, the hand of the Lord is upon you, and you shall be blind, not seeing the sun for a time."

To everyone's utter amazement, Elymas immediately went blind, while the Sergius Paulus, his master, went pale as a freshly washed sheet. Almost immediately, possibly playing it safe, or out of abject fear, he became a Believer. A few days later, with the Proconsul's approval, perhaps even recommendation, Paul and his party took sail northward, to the coast of Asia Minor, landing in Perga in Pamphylia. By then Elymas, the false prophet, has already regained his sight, but he never again tried to dissuade anyone from being baptized.

The hardships of the journey must have been too much for young John Mark. A little disenchanted, perhaps also afraid, or perhaps disillusioned by the stress that Paul appeared to have placed on preaching mostly to the Gentiles, notably the Roman Proconsul, the young man has decided, a little sheepishly, to return to Jerusalem.

Left on their own in Pisidian Antioch, Paul and Barnabas continued to place their attention principally on the Gentiles. This, needless to say, brought immediate opposition from the leading Jews of the city. Men and women virtually chased them out to the outskirts of town. Not for being ignored, only they assumed that Paul was preaching just another form of Judaism, and thus they had, so to speak, the right of first refusal. Paul never excluded any Jews, he just didn't give them exclusive rights to hear the Word. He merely made himself available to everyone and that obviously included many Gentiles.

"Preach ye all nations..." he repeated the Master's words he'd heard from Ananias. "All nations," he repeated, raising his voice.

Shimon wasn't around to explain to him that in Yeshûa's vernacular, in the Master's speech replete with symbolism, 'nations' symbolized thoughts; 'all nations' meaning the whole mindset; although, admittedly, not to the exclusion of other interpretations.

Nevertheless, Paul's didactic generosity of spirit often resulted in grave consequences.

There were dangers inherent in the work of the apostles. After all, the whole of the teaching was subject to faith. The listeners had to believe in what they have not seen. What they have not experienced with their physical senses.

"...faith," he told them, "is the substance of things hoped for, the evidence of things not seen."

Paul knew from his own past that such is the nature of faith. He knew that he had to convince his listeners that what he was saying was the truth. The potential of faith manifesting in some people was much stronger than in others. Paul soon learned that in some people it was a powerful force that seemed dormant, waiting to be released. In others, it was buried so deep that only time might open their hearts.

Paul also remembered Shimon telling him those three enigmatic words: "Nothing is real". Paul never understood this statement, not fully, but he decided to put it to a test. He also recalled Shimon telling him that we all create our reality with our thoughts and emotions. What if faith was the ignition, the necessary spark, the trigger that activated this creative process?

Soon he had an opportunity to test his theory.

It came to him with a man in Lystra. The man was born crippled. He was never able to walk. As Paul was speaking to the people, his eyes travelling over the crowd, he saw the man; he perceived faith fulminating within him.

After the sermon Paul walked over to the man and, gathering his own courage, he commanded him to get up and walk. All the man needed were the words that enabled his faith to heal him. He immediately jumped to his feet.

Yet, not all was as it seemed…

The gentiles, speaking in Lycaonian language, managed to misunderstand all that transpired.

"The gods had come down to us in the likeness of men!" they exclaimed.

They took Barnabas, the taller one, to be Zeus, and Paul, the speaker, as Zeus's son, Hermes, the messenger of the gods. Almost immediately the priest, in front of whose temple of Zeus, Paul delivered his sermon, brought oxen and garlands, intending to sacrifice them to the two gods who visited them.

The reaction of the Jewish community of Lystra was predictable.

While the younger Barnabas managed to escape, the irate Jews stoned Paul with great perseverance, then dragged him out of town, and left him for dead. Jews liked stoning people, especially those who offended their religious sensibilities. Roadside rocks were their favourite missiles—handy and easy to conceal.

Paul's recovery was nothing short of miraculous. In addition, as was so often seen in the apostles' work, rewards followed quickly the times of tribulations. In Derbe, the next town on their route, a great many have believed. And thus, in spite of many setbacks, in time, the four churches in the southern Roman Province of Galatia, Psidian Antioch, Iconium, Lystra and Derbe, became the foundations of the Church that Paul was building in that part of the Roman Empire.

It was a brilliant start.

With a little trepidation, lots of prayers, and a great deal of courage, Paul and Barnabas traced their steps back to Perga, and this time caught a ship in Attalia to return home, to Antioch in Syria.

Both, Paul and Barnabas needed a rest. They'd earned it.

Some days later, they met, again, in Shimon's backyard, the place they enjoyed most for their intimate discussions. Shimon was greatly impressed by the work done by Paul and Barnabas. He listened to their stories, their trials and tribulations. He praised them for their total commitment to their work. He praised Paul for his dedication that almost had cost him his life. And then, when all had been said and done, and the men were washed, sated and relaxed, he asked gently.

"And did you tell them about the Kingdom of God?"

"Of course, Rabbi," Barnabas replied hotly, as though the question were redundant.

"The Kingdom they'd go to after death, or the Kingdom within us. The Kingdom here and now?" Shimon persisted.

Paul looked away while Barnabas opened and closed his mouth in quick succession, yet saying nothing. Then his eyes went down to his sandals.

"You remind me of my youth," Shimon said, smiling.

Barnabas looked up.

"I was a fisherman," Shimon explained. "The fish I caught also opened and closed their mouth without saying a thing." Then, seeing Barnabas's face going red, he added. "Silence is golden, my friend. I wish more people would practice it."

Paul stirred in his seat.

"We've been kind of busy, Rabbi." There was a touch of bitterness in his voice.

"And you have almost gave your life…" Shimon said softy. "No one would hold it against you, even if you hadn't risked your life, considering the wonderful work you have done for the Christ."

"There is a 'but', Rabbi, isn't there?"

Shimon smiled a little sadly.

"Many are called, but only few are chosen. Both of you, my friends, have been chosen."

Paul seemed content with the response, yet he felt that more had to be said.

"I don't feel chosen, Rabbi," he said, looking Shimon in the eyes. "How does one know if one is chosen?"

"By spreading the Word to people. Need you have a greater reward?"

Barnabas's eyes were growing larger. It is only when Shimon and Paul met that such subjects were discussed. Although he, too, has been named an apostle, he didn't feel equal to his two elder colleagues. Perhaps one day... he thought. He knew that Paul had a high opinion of him, but Shimon never failed to amaze him with his perception of the Teaching.

"Master," he looked at Shimon, "tell us about the Kingdom..."

"Don't call me master, Barnabas, we are all children of the Most High. That is honour enough for me. For all of us. As for the Kingdom, *the* Master, Yeshûa, told many parables about the Kingdom. People will write them down for generations to come..."

Shimon's eyes drifted to another place, another time. He felt the wind caressing his face, heard the whisper of the ripple of water washing over the shore.

...the kingdom of heaven is like a net that was thrown into the sea and gathered fish of every kind...

How could he tell them about the Kingdom? Even the Master spoke in parables... there were no words to describe it in any tongue.

"It is not a place, nor a thing, Barnabas. It is neither here nor there, yet it is everywhere. It is wherever you find it—in heaven and on earth, in the air, and in the depth of the sea. And when you find it you cherish it above all other."

Paul stirred uncomfortably.

"Is it a state of mind then, Master, ah, I mean, Rabbi?"

They were all rabbis; after all they were all teaching, yet it was only Shimon they addressed as Rabbi. He was the only one who really knew. He was Kepha. How else could they build His church?

Suddenly Paul's dream of an Empire didn't seem so important. Masses and masses of Believers would add to His glory, to the Master's glory, but… but they wouldn't get him, Paul, any closer to heaven. Not the heaven here and now. Although, when Barnabas found him lying on the side of the road to Lystra, stoned, hardly breathing, he felt strangely alive. As though his real self was taking over, raising him above the worries of earthly life. Yes, he felt truly alive then.

As he lifted his eyes, he saw Shimon looking at him. A gentle smile, like that of a father regarding his favourite son, was playing about his lips.

"It is neither here, nor there, yet it is everywhere," the Rabbi repeated.

Paul hardly knew why, but he nodded. It was as though he'd understood. Only he didn't. He didn't. Not yet.

The silence extended. After a while Barnabas asked a question that had to be asked. "How can we teach of Heaven on Earth if we, ourselves, don't understand it either?"

"You plant the seed and hope it will fall on fertile soil. And when it does, the seed will be multiplied. And then, one day, a chosen one will come forth and speak of heaven on earth…"

Shimon's voice was dreamy. It seemed as though he was speaking of one who was no longer with us, yet who had never left us.

"Just plant the seed. But always, always keep your eyes open."

Barnabas didn't dare to ask, for what, exactly, he was to keep his eyes open, while Paul thought he knew, just didn't want to admit that to him planting seed was more important than reaping. I'm a sower, he thought. Let others collect the fruit of my labours. I'm just a sower...

And then he looked up at Shimon and was surprised. The Rabbi's eyes were telling him that he was more. That he must be more than that. That there were just a few of them and they had to find more men to plant the seed. To show them the kingdom.

Right here. On earth. Now.

Paul felt like taking time off and escaping into the desert. Arabian, or any desert. Even a diet of insects with an occasional rat or a trapped bird seemed easier than trying to fathom Shimon's words. It was easy for him. He'd heard them from Yeshûa, directly from the Master, not from Shimon, even if he was, has been, His right-hand-man.

Isn't my revelation of equal value? Does not my understanding come from a higher place? From within? And talking of heaven, didn't the Master say that heaven is within you? Is not heaven my source?

Then why can't I rely on my own cognizance? Am I not an apostle? Have the brethren not ordained me? Even Shimon was there. He approved. Didn't say a word against them. Or me.

Then why do I feel so lost? So inadequate? I am filled with confidence amongst the non-believers. I feel confident when I'm spreading the Good News. And yet, yes, and yet here, in Antioch, I feel lost without Shimon. What does he want of me? I cannot give more that my life, can I?

And yet when Shimon and Barnabas and I, and sometimes one or two others get together, it is as though a spirit, or an intangible something, is hovering in the air, touching each one of us, caressing, coaxing—as though we were so much more than just a few weak men trying their best to serve. Sometimes it felt as though we were all one, a single entity, more powerful than the Roman Empire. More powerful that the storms that wash over land and sea, than...

...than anything that could ever stand in our way.

Ye are gods, comes to mind, he mused, and we are all children of the Most High. And at the same time we are all one. Inseparable. Indivisible. United in Christ? And He is with us, every step of the way. Through all time. Everywhere.

...and we were all gathered into a net thrown into the sea, all of us, of every kind into a single net...

And we became as one?

How is that possible?

***

18

CIRCUMCISION

They **arrived in Antioch** in late summer, like a regiment of soldiers, though clad in long religious garb, with blue fringes placed at corners of their mantles, as the Law of Moses commanded. On their foreheads, instead of helmets, they wore broad phylacteries fastened to their heads with straps. These boxes contained passages of Scriptures referring to the Passover and the redemption of the first, from Egypt. Now, presumably, they intended to redeem the circumcised from the uncircumcised.

People on the streets cleared out of their way, not risking the wrath of men who, they remembered, had the power to destroy the strongest among them. Not physically, but by sending others, surreptitiously, to do their work.

Their unclean, ignominious, work.

Confident, they marched, though not in step, their heads held high, their beards hanging low. They were the Pharisees of Jerusalem, the younger members of the Sanhedrin, or at least appointed by them. They were determined to fight for their way.

The old way. The way of the Torah.

Or so they thought. Believed?

They came alone. The Sadducees would not demean themselves by leaving their beloved books. They sent the

Pharisees to do their dirty work. Dirty? No work was cleaner in their eyes. Clean and holy. Like circumcision.

They were determined to Judaize the Jews.

They demanded a hearing. The synagogues were not that full. The people didn't take kindly to the old ways any more. Not so far away from the bastions of their power. From Jerusalem.

"You must be circumcised to be saved," they proclaimed. Practically in unison.

And we will collect the money, they almost added.

"It is not a question of money they assured," looking high over peoples' heads.

"You can be saved for five silver shekels," one Pharisee cried. "Surely, no one has ever given you a better offer... have they?" Towards the end, scanning people nearest him, he wasn't that sure.

People were stunned. Or appeared to be.

Just five shekels for salvation? It's not a bad deal, some thought. And that's only for a baby? For adults... the men's hands travelled protectively to their crotches.

Just for a baby, the blue-fringed Pharisees assured.

Most converts were adults. Most all of them. How could they be circumcised? A man gets a penny, a silver denarius, for a day's work. A man would have to work for twenty days to pay for circumcision. What would he eat in the meantime? What would his family eat? His children? What did those priests do with all that money?

What? They are not even priests?

"The penalty for refusal is *kareth*!" they announced threateningly, raising their beards as though exposing their necks. People had no idea what *kareth* was. "You will be excised from the people..."

"What people?"

Anyway, they had no idea what 'excised' meant either.

Gradually men sidled out of the synagogue. The old ways were too expensive. Paul told them that faith in God, not circumcision, buys you salvation. Having heard the Pharisees, Paul was beginning to make a lot more sense.

Just faith—and good deeds, of course.

Soon the Pharisees were preaching to an empty synagogue. This wasn't good for business, they thought. We have to have a conference, they added. In Jerusalem. There are more of us there. More power to us.

By late fall, Shimon decided to send Paul, Barnabas, Titus and some other brethren to Jerusalem, to discuss the matter of circumcision, and some other problems, with the apostles, evangelists, and other Believers. But mostly, it was the vital matter of relationship between circumcision and salvation. Titus was a relatively new companion of Paul, previously a Gentile, whom Paul refused to circumcise. Paul firmly believed that Christ's gospel clearly absolved Christians from the requirement of *Miswoth*, of being circumcised.

Paul put his foot down and no one in Antioch objected. Least of all Titus.

"There are great many commandments in Torah," Paul said. "Most are for priests, and very few indeed for women. But Christ brought salvation for all, not just the few."

By then the summer heat was waning, and the group set out on their way in good spirits. Paul didn't share all his views with his fellow travelers—not at this stage—but he thought the matter was ridiculous. Five shekels for salvation? Ha! His previous colleagues, the Pharisees, were making a farce out of religion.

With dangers still lurking along the way, they made Aba'ye happy by allowing him to come with them. His sheer bulk not only provided added security, but he was willing to carry more than his share of food and water. He was by far the nicest mule Paul ever met—he meant it in the nicest possible way. Aba'ye was the best friend Paul ever had. Sometimes, he thought, the only one. Although, of late, he saw amity in the eyes of many. It seemed to grow in direct proportion to the friendship he extended to those people. They were like a mirror. A mirror of his heart, his feelings.

As for the conference in Jerusalem, it wasn't just a question of circumcision, but also of authority. Before they left Antioch, Paul and other conference attendees had discussed the subject with Shimon in some detail. Sometime ago, Shimon and Paul did not see eye to eye on this and a number of other subjects. Although Paul had been a Pharisee, apparently Shimon was more steeped in tradition than Paul was.

Paul used his considerable powers of persuasion to convince Shimon that circumcision was not *sine qua non* for salvation. That following the teaching of Christ was the condition, and not a surgical procedure for the benefit of tradition.

"I will not accept that a bit of foreskin is the essence of Christ's teaching," Paul added, with a twinkle in his eye.

Finally, Paul argued that circumcision had been practiced in Hellenistic times by many Gentiles, also by various priestly castes in Egypt, as well as by some Nabataean Arabs, and who knew what other peoples of antiquity. And thus, it was most certainly not just the domain of the Jews.

Paul was surprised how easily Shimon agreed with him. It was only later that it came to him, that Shimon was concerned only with the substance of the teaching; with the very quintessence that would, ultimately, open man's eyes to the Truth. The Truth that Paul wasn't sure he understood himself.

On arrival in Jerusalem, to Paul's considerable if well veiled surprise, he as well as his colleagues were greeted with open arms. The number of Believers had grown. Evidently, the evangelists were still risking their lives in Jerusalem, but continued to work hard to spread the Good News. They were somewhat safer now. There is always strength in numbers. This was Paul's conviction.

"An Empire," he mused. It was becoming his obsession. "An Empire united in Christ."

Seeing the smiling faces turned towards him and his friends, he'd almost said it out loud. Even the blue sky above them promised a day of friendship and agreement.

Paul wasn't disappointed.

The conference was hardly more than a formality. Paul read out Shimon's statement, then, after little more than perfunctory discussion, James read out his judgment that the apostles and elders and the whole church agreed that the Gentiles need not be circumcised in order to become believers and attain salvation.

He further instructed Silas, together with Judas, also known as Barsabas, to travel with Paul and Barnabas to Antioch to deliver the letter written by himself; a letter which summarized what transpired in Jerusalem at the conference. Sending his most trusted men would add to the weight of the decision. It would further strengthen the ties and cement the unity of all Believers. Also, both Silas and Judas wanted to extend their proselytizing experience by venturing outside Jerusalem.

So far, so good, thought Paul.

For him, the conference had a much wider meaning. He came here to establish his authority of what and how he preached in the territories under his influence. No one questioned his motives, but for the first time they also didn't question his philosophy. The apostles received their knowledge directly from Yeshûa; he, Paul, claimed to have received his by direct revelation. He expected serious objections to his thesis. He heard none. He was prepared for a battle—he found only acquiescence.

"I've arrived," he murmured, hardly believing his good fortune.

Barnabas walking on his right overheard him.

"You have, my brother, as you should have and did," he agreed, with this rather complex declaration.

Those, however, were the last amicable words they shared for some time.

Soon after their return to Antioch, having reported on the Conference and its conclusions to Shimon, Paul set about preparing for his next apostolic journey.

What roiled the water between him and Barnabas was the latter's nephew, John Mark, who was keen to make up for his transgressions of the first voyage. On that occasion, the young man had travelled with them to Perga, only to stop there, and to return to Jerusalem. John Mark not only didn't help them with their apostolic work, but hardly offered any explanation why he'd chosen to leave them. Under the circumstances, Paul, not surprisingly, found the young man irresponsible and most certainly unreliable. As a consequence he refused to take him on the next voyage he was planning later that autumn.

The discussion between Paul and his friend became so heated, with Barnabas presumably feeling responsible for his nephew, that he and Paul parted company. Barnabas and John Mark took sail to Cyprus, no doubt returning to their family home to lick their wounds. In the meantime, Paul found in Silas, already a leading member of the Christian community, a wonderful replacement for Barnabas. Together they soon set out for Tarsus.

From there they would travel to Derbe and Lystra, to visit the churches Paul had initiated on his previous trip. In Lystra Paul met Timothy, who'd become a frequent travelling companion on his many journeys. Timothy has also proven a great help in spreading the Word. Like Paul, he found solace in sleeping under the open skies, weaving dreams in front of an open fire, and waking at first rays of the sun peeking over mountain tops.

Sometimes, they were lucky enough to find a spot for the night by a brook, or a river. Though with considerable effort, they often managed to catch a fish in a small net Silas always carried with him, for just such occasions. They'd bake it over the fire, and give thanks for their good fortune.

There was an event, however, that in retrospect, surprised even Paul.

The decision to circumcise Timothy was a contradiction of everything that Paul seemingly believed in. Timothy lived in Lystra. His mother was a Jewess, his father a Greek. While in theory a child of mixed marriage could choose his or her heritage, according to Jewish oral tradition, the oldest codified normative definition used by Jews was that a person is matrilineally a Jew by birth, or else becomes one through conversion to Judaism.

Thus, at least in theory, Timothy could have claimed to be a Gentile, and avoid even the miniscule bodily mutilation. He evidently chose otherwise, since Paul had him circumcised. Either that, or Paul's inner needs were showing. After all, he'd been raised to be a Pharisee. Old habits die hard? Or it could have been that Timothy or his mother had insisted out of Paul's hearing.

However, hopefully, no grievous harm was done.

Shimon was in deep thought. His best friends and the most talented apostles were journeying, doing work for Yeshûa. He felt alone, deserted, spending time in prayer, asking for the protection for his beloved disciples.

He still preached, travelled in close vicinity to Antioch, but couldn't match the energy and enthusiasm of the younger men. He spent a lot of time remembering.

"I like fishing," he whispered, often, remembering the day he'd arrived in Antioch. "I like fishing," he said, again; then smiled at his thoughts.

"Still do," he murmured, his memories taking him to the days of yore.

I shall make you fisher of men...

He was standing some steps away, smiling, seemingly without a care in the world. He was usually like that. Seemingly without a care. Yet, didn't He carry the whole world on His shoulders?

Come, follow me...

Follow me He said. I never asked where. I just went. I am still willing to follow, but his feet leave no more prints in the sand.

Shimon was ready to follow Him anywhere. He didn't have to understand His words. He'd just go, and Shimon would follow. Why could He not understand that I am not the Kepha He imagined I was? Paul has twice the courage that I have. Twice the energy.

"Paul listens to Your voice," Shimon mused, "I just remember."

When can I join You, Master? When will You take me home?

Do others struggle even as I do? Does Andrew, my younger brother? He was the first to recognize You as Saviour. As Messiah. I haven't seen Andrew for years. He wanders along the shores of the Black Sea, along settlements of people who have little contact with the outside world... Where else will you take him, Master? Shall I ever see Andrew again? Shall I ever again see my little brother? Shall I ever see him, Lord?

And what of James, son of Zebedee, and James the Just, as they call him. Master told him never to judge anyone, that justice must be always tempered with compassion... And John? Were they not all my friends?

The wind swirled over the low wall and touched Shimon's cheek. He looked up towards the sky.

"I miss fishing, oh, Lord. I miss fishing..."

Then his mind turned to inquire about Philip, wandering the planes and hills of Greece, and Syria, and Phrygia… such a vast land, so many people waiting to hear the Good News. It had been Philip who'd introduced Bartholomew to the Master. And what of him now? Is he still alive? Does he still spread the Word? He was raised next door to me, in Cana. And where is he now? The last I heard he was in Armenia. It's such a vast world… He was so young when I first saw him… Yes, I remember, they also called him Nathanael, the Gift of God. To whom have you given him Lord?

Shimon closed his eyes. For a moment he thought he felt Yeshûa patting him on the shoulder. He wanted to save that moment, commit it to his memory. And then he felt the breeze touching his face, again.

"I miss fishing," he whispered.

By the time Paul, Silas, and Timothy reached Phrygia, the three had become best friends. Journeys tend to bring people together. They share the toils, the hardships; they have to protect and rely on each other. In Iconium and Antioch, the Pisidian Antioch, Paul delivered the conclusions rendered by the Jerusalem Conference. They were welcomed as friends, and now they were treated to cheers.

"So we are real Christians," they said, their faces beaming with deep satisfaction. Most still thought of Christians as a Jewish sect.

"Indeed you are," Paul assured them. "And don't let anyone tell you otherwise," he added, as pleased as they were with the news he'd delivered.

Suddenly all the hardships of the journey seemed worthwhile. Just seeing the joy that permeated those people was reward enough. Silas and Timothy were in awe. They never realized how great peoples' thirst was. How much they needed the Good News. It was like Greek's ambrosia. It quenched the thirst that was so deep that some people forgot that is could be sated.

For the first time in years Paul seemed satisfied. He realized that whatever it was that he was doing, it brought joy to people. No wonder they called it the Good News. It seemed that in a few months time, people began to suspect that they really were immortal. That the Kingdom of Heaven was real. Here, or there, or now or later, but it was real. They believed that the source of joy and love were within them, not granted by someone sitting on a large horse, looking at them with a degree of pity and disdain.

"You are all children of the Most High," Paul told them. And they believed.

***

Part Three
50 - 68 AD

19

SECOND JOURNEY

No matter how inured they became to walking, after ten days on the road their feet hurt. For Luke the pain sometimes radiated to calves, knees and even hips. Even the youngster, Timothy, regarded his older colleagues with anguish poorly hidden in his eyes. He was beginning to have doubts about being born unto the image of Yahweh.

"Aren't we spiritual beings? Shouldn't I be able to fly?" he wondered aloud, his voice sounding at least half-serious.

As they continued on their way, he thought of the animals he spotted lurking here and there, on the side of the road.

"No wonder," he murmured, "they are smart. Most of them spend most of their time lying down."

Every time they had a chance to sit down, Silas and Timothy collapsed in unison, as though on command.

Paul did not share this luxury. Regardless of how many leagues they'd crossed, he alone remained standing, preaching whenever he found a willing ear. Always on his feet. Perhaps his short stature had something to do with it. He had less bodyweight to carry. On the other hand, standing and walking was his way of life. He seemed to have sat down only to write his letters. Lots of letters. Or at least to make notes for future ones.

From Pisidian Antioch, they took the mountain road to Troas in Mysia on the north side of the Aegean Sea.

"We must conquer new lands, bring new people to Christ…" Paul was adamant. Images of an Empire never left the forefront of his mind.

A single herd and a single Shepherd, the Master had said. Paul was repeating this promise a*d nauseam*. It was his passion. Seemingly, the only purpose in his life. His only dream.

Troas was a city in Mysia dating back to Antigonus, whom Paul remembered as the successor of Alexander. There was very little that Paul didn't know about Alexander the Great.

Alexander was born in Pella, the Greek city that Paul was hoping to visit. Aristotle, one of Paul's early heroes, had tutored young Alexander. By the age of thirty Alexander had created one of the largest empires the world has ever known. It stretched from the Ionian Sea all the way to the feet of the Himalayas. Paul thought that if Alexander could do it for his own glory, than he, Paul, could do it for the Christ.

Then Paul smiled thinking of what transpired with Alexander's empire.

"Alas," he mused sadly, recounting the story to Timothy, "*sic transit gloria mundi.*"

Timothy picked up enough Latin to understand most basic phrases.

But not my empire, Paul thought, grinding his teeth. Mine will not pass. "It will last forever," he mused. "For ever," he repeated, as though to reassure himself. He almost said that aloud.

Paul needed heroes. He was determined to style himself after them. Not in military might, but in creating something that would last for generations. For ever? Paul yearned immortality.

They arrived in Troas on Yom Re-Ve-ee, at noon, and had two and a half days of rest before them. In new places, they only preached on Yom Sha-Bat. The rest of the days, as on all though rare occasions that they were not travelling, Paul would study the Torah and/or make notes for his letters, Silas would share with Timothy his knowledge, but most of the time they would just rest. Sometimes one or more of them would pick up some paid labour, which would result in a rare hot supper. Often they would also have to spend a little time repairing their clothing, which tended to get caught on twigs or dry branches projecting over the narrow paths they often travelled. They avoided the main roads for safety if not for comfort. There were still unsavoury characters prowling around, determined to rob an unsuspecting traveler. Luckily, on narrow side roads and footpaths, there was not enough traffic to make it worth their while. Nevertheless, the last villain that attempted to rob them, Paul converted to Christianity. He gave them all the money he had on him, and apologized for not having any more to give.

Paul would have made a most excellent salesman.

Yom Sha-Bat was the only time that people gathered in the vicinity of a synagogue, or some temple of a Roman god. The latter was a risky place to impose a new religion on people, but it couldn't be helped. Paul always thought of himself as a Jew, and Christianity of an extension, or renewed Judaism. Certainly not as a new religion.

He preached, however, everywhere.

For once, Timothy found a reasonably priced inn, and Paul ordered a few days of rest. Though the journey had hardly begun they were already exhausted. Nevertheless, Paul was restless. After sitting with others over their first decent meal in a month, he took a stroll around the city. As always, his two friends followed.

But not for long. They soon sat down on a stone parapet wall, just to take the weight off their feet.

As a boy in Taurus, Paul was well tutored. He told his friends that it has been Octavian, later known as Caesar Augustus, who transformed Troas into a Roman colony. It now served as an important seaport for those crossing the sea between Asia Minor and Macedonia.

"Wasn't he the Caesar who ordered the census that took Joseph and Mary to Bethlehem, almost by accident?"

Young Timothy stirred, proud of his knowledge.

"The very same, Timothy, the very same," Silas said, reaching back to his own childhood.

"There are no accidents," Paul corrected sternly. "It had been prophesized."

The two men nodded gravely, amazed at Paul's knowledge and wisdom. They forgot that, once, their leader was a Pharisee.

On the day before Yom Sha-Bat, a man by the name of Luke has joined them. He was no longer a young man but looked healthy; a physician by trade, he took delight in writing down items of interest on the parchment he always carried with him. By the time he met Paul and his party, he had already earned a reputation as an evangelist. He inspired the local Christians to open their hearts to Paul.

He was a shy man. Compared to Paul, his love and perhaps his talents, tended towards writing, not speaking.

On Yom Sha-Bat Paul spoke at length about the heritage that the Jewish people can bring to Gentiles. The crowds listened spellbound. Seeing their reaction, Paul realized that there was a great need to spread the Word in Mysia and Bithynia. Yet, as he was about to change their plans that would delay their departure across the sea, he felt a strong need to board the ship. He felt an almost physical pull to go to Macedonia, as though people there were begging him for help. He had premonitions like that before, but never quite as strong.

Mysia and Bithynia would have to wait.

And so, by the time they boarded the ship, there were four of them. Paul, Silas, Timothy, and now Luke. The contact with each other increased their fervour. Paul had power to inspire them all. They boarded the ship with great expectation of things to come.

The sea was friendly. A southeastern wind filled the square sails with a gentle breeze. They sailed overnight by the island of Samothrace, and by late afternoon arrived in Neapolis. For the first time not one of Paul's party got seasick. This fact alone was reason to celebrate. They walked enjoying the feel of solid ground under their feet.

Having rested on board, they took to the road immediately, and by morning of the next day they arrived in Philippi. The full moon illuminated their way with a filigree of shadows, and the cool air made walking easier than in daylight.

"No wonder the Greeks and the Romans made the moon into a goddess..." Timothy marveled, receiving a stern stare from Paul and paternal smile from Luke.

For his part, Silas often found Artemis a source of inspiration without any of her divine traits. He often thought that while the sun might symbolize the power of consciousness, surely, the moon could stand well for the unconscious, for what the Torah called *nephesh*, or animal soul. Nevertheless, he kept his thoughts to himself.

Soon the rising sun dispersed their musings.

On arrival, with but little rest, Paul was keen to preach to the gathering crowd. He had to. It was the day of Shavuoth. A woman, shy and inconspicuous, heard him speak. She said her name was Lydia, which she evidently thought was reason enough to invite all four of them to her home. She offered them food, and Paul, while travelling, was not known for refusing a hot meal.

Later that same day Paul baptized Lydia and her entire household.

It was a great Shavuoth indeed.

Whether it was the good food, or the day of Shavuoth, by the evening Paul gave an impression of being strangely inspired. Walking the streets, he saw a slave-girl, tense and cringing, her eyes darting like those of a trapped animal. He stopped in front of her and put his hand on her head. She seemed possessed by a demon. Even as Paul looked at the girl, she appeared to relax, her breathing returning to normal.

But not so her master's.

Angry at having lost the chance to make money out of his slave's demonic divinations, he spread the word in the city that Paul and his party were the emissaries of the devil. It is true that in some cultures, the devil is said to possess powerful supernatural powers, but in Greek, a devil is a slanderer or an accuser, of which Paul was neither. He never said the girl was possessed. He merely calmed her down.

But people like scandal.

By nightfall, Paul and Silas were assaulted by a group of people. The Jews, for such they were, had beaten them with sticks, and thrown them into jail. But not for long. The devil, or... it could have been his counterpart, must have been angry at the castigating venom of the judgmental people. An earthquake shook the wall of the prison, throwing the doors open. In the meantime, Paul, as always, did not miss the chance to tell other prisoners that the Master has set them free.

Who else had the power to tumble walls?

Our heroes and all the prisoners left the prison praising God. Amazed, and perhaps a little scared, the prison guards joined them. They became Believers. All of them.

"Never a dull moment?" Timothy said when they met outside. Luke gave him a surreptitious elbow to the ribcage. Timothy winced but said nothing.

"They've been beaten up, remember?" he whispered.

Paul and his group didn't dally. With few exceptions, people in this town didn't prove very friendly. Under the cover of night they hurried towards and through Amphipolis and Apollonia without stopping. After a twenty-four-hour, nonstop march, they arrived in Thessalonica. All four collapsed on a heap of straw by the side of the road.

No one disturbed them till the sun was well past midday. Still, on this occasion they needed a longer rest.

Once again, Timothy found a cozy place, just outside town. They stayed there for two weeks. The place was a hollow in a rock, almost a cave under a partial overhung, with floor covered by wind-blown leaves.

Timothy was very proud of himself.

"The Lord provideth," Luke said, a broad smile on his kindly face.

The others nodded in agreement. They lay down on the soft cover, luxuriating in unexpected comfort. The next day they spent most of their time looking for food, which nature disposed all around them. Paul had ample experience of survival in conditions a lot worse than these.

After two weeks of comfort on nature's lap, a local Christian, Jason, invited them to join him in his house. He had been a believer for some time. He felt honoured to have their company.

This time the Lord went all the way: real beds, real food, real roof over their heads.

As always, every Yom Sha-Bat Paul went out to preach in the local synagogue. He was determined to explain how the Torah prophesied that Yeshûa was to become the Messiah. The Saviour of mankind. Even Luke, Silas, and Timothy listened in admiration. Paul was both, a scholar and an inspired preacher. All he needed was an audience.

But, as always, things were never easy. The green monster of envy raised its ugly head. It seemed that every success had its price.

Some Jews, jealous of Paul's success, started a riot. In order to protect Jason and his family, Paul and his friends left their host's house immediately. It didn't help. The rioting Jews, enraged at not finding the apostles in Jason house, dragged him out, together with some acolytes who came to hear Paul talk, and took them all to the civil magistrate. There they accused them of some imaginary wrongdoings.

In total absence of evidence against Jason or his friends, they were all soon released, while Paul and his party were well on their way to the city of Berea.

They heard the news some days later.

"I told you, Timothy, it is never easy. Not just for us, but for our friends," said Luke, who took it upon himself to educate the young man. He also made careful notes of the events to rewrite them later into a more comprehensive form. Luke filled his notes with the emotions he felt at the time.

Though the Jews in Bera listened to Paul's teaching and accepted the Good News, the Jews from Thessalonica, still irate and annoyed, followed Paul to the city, determined to make trouble for him. Since apparently Paul was the only man they were really after, he left at once for Achaia, a seaport southward of Bera, hoping to find a passage for all of them to Athens.

Timothy, trying to hide a vaguely supercilious smile, muttered under his breath: "He who runs away, lives to fight another day…"

This cost the youngster another elbow in the ribs from Luke. "He is doing it to protect us," Luke said, in a way of explanation. "If he stayed behind, we'd all get the wrong ends of the Jewish sticks. Or worse…" he added after a momentary hesitation. And then his tone got even more serious. "I've never heard of Paul running away from anything."

Timothy massaged his ribcage.

Alas, the Jews had again detained Paul's friends. No harm came to them, but Paul, having already booked his own passage, set sail for the new destination. He left the promissory notes for the passage for his friends with a man, a good Christian, who showed him the way to the ship. By going ahead, Paul was hoping to lay preliminary ground for their work. He believed that the Lord would provide for his friends.

For once, Paul had time to spare. It would take a good few days for the men he'd left behind to join him in Athens. For once, he had time on his hands.

Well before Paul landed in Athens, the Romans had long plundered everything that they could carry away with them. Nevertheless, walking through the ancient city, he noticed that there appeared to be more gods here than men.

The city was given over to idols.

He'd landed in the Piraeus harbour. Proceeding north, he bypassed the cemetery and entered Athens by the Double Gate, on the west side of the city. He was immediately overwhelmed by a multitude of gods and goddesses. He went by the Temple of Demeter, the goddess of harvest, admiring the statues of the goddess and her daughter. Next he saw the striking image of Poseidon with his impressive trident. After that there was a whole procession of sculptures, including those of Zeus, Apollo and Hermes standing by the Sanctuary of Dionysus, at the foot of the Acropolis.

Paul was amazed. Nothing in his travels prepared him for such an exuberant splendour as he faced in the first hour.

There was no end to the homage the Greeks paid to their gods and goddesses. For Paul, a devout Jew and Christian, this was more than he could ever imagine. He was depressed and amazed—simultaneously.

At last he chanced upon a synagogue. There, for a while, he reasoned with the Jews and the Gentile worshipers, yet with little success. Later he tried to preach to some people there in the marketplace. He was looking for groups. He found little interest.

He walked on.

Strolling alone, like in the old days, his eyes wide with admiration, he meandered around the city. Athens was one of the oldest cities of the world. He wondered if anyone could render such powerful gods as Athens displayed to become helpless when facing the teaching of Christ.

The temple of Zeus was imposing. Paul walked slowly, enjoying rare moments of unhurried leisure. He amused himself by counting the columns—one hundred and four. More than any temple he had ever seen. The statue of Zeus on his throne was indeed a colossus, yet... it had no power over him. If Paul were taller, much, much taller, he'd look Zeus in the eye.

It had no power over him at all.

He wondered why. Why Yeshûa, whom he'd never met, held so much more of his respect, his admiration, even love, than this huge, seemingly divine statue that was intended to inspire just those feelings.

My Kingdom is not of this world... he mused, his eyes following the contours of the temple. *My Kingdom...* he repeated, remembering Shimon's words and, purportedly, His.

But why? Why was it that this mysterious trait of the Kingdom drew him so strongly towards its discovery? Perhaps Shimon was right. He could not look for it. He had to live in hope that, when ready, it would reveal itself to him.

Will I ever be ready?

Paul sat down, alone, and prayed.

Nevertheless, Paul was a man of action. Disenchanted with his attempts to reach larger groups, he stopped on the steps of the temple of Zeus, and began preaching to anyone who would listen. Athenians were used to various men advocating their visions of reality. Some who stopped to listen were Jews, pious Jews, devout people. Others were followers of

Epicurus who sought pleasures of life. Still others were Stoics, content with their lot in life.

"Lucretius wouldn't agree with you..." was the first salvo from a man looking old enough to be Paul's father. "Zeno's view is that the law of nature is divine, and that its function is to command what is right and to forbid what is wrong," the old man concluded. Then he hopped onto the parapet wall opposite Paul like a young man of twenty.

"But Yahweh..." Paul began; they had already established the assumed divine nature of Yahweh.

"I deny divine providence over human affairs," another man said, sporting a great and confident smile.

"You stand before the temple of Zeus," a still younger man interjected. Pray tell me, what power of mental vision enabled your master, Yahweh, you say, to descry the vast and elaborate architectural process which, the deity adopted in building the structure of the universe?"

"Surely, Pythagoras did not deny the human soul, did he?" Paul tried an attack from the rear.

"If the soul of man is divine, why is it not omniscient?" another man countered the previous argument. "Moreover, if the Pythagorean god is pure soul, how is he implanted in, or diffused throughout, the world?"

Paul had been a Pharisee for many years. In a way, he still was. But he never had to face an Athenian in his attempt to teach the Good News. Nevertheless, Paul did the best he could. He was facing the intellectual progeny of Plato and Socrates, all smiling, carefree, before him—Socrates, Plato and many, many others giants of philosophy and debate.

No, this is no synagogue by any measure, Paul mused, a little overwhelmed. He wished he had someone with whom he could share his thoughts—like Silas or even Timothy. He wondered how would Shimon react.

And the Athenians weren't biased. His listeners engaged in discussion, in arguments for and against Paul's thesis. While Epicureans insisted on their pleasure being here and now, Stoics were prepared to reach happiness by bringing themselves, gradually, into a state of harmony with the universe.

Paul could talk, but he also had to listen. He passed the test. The Athenians were, after all, really intelligent, educated, and most of all probing people. They never missed a chance of a good debate. After listening carefully to Paul's arguments, they invited him to Areopagus for further discussion. The Athenians were truly a curious lot.

An awful lot of very curious seekers.

And then Paul realized the fundamental difference between the Athenians and all other men he'd encountered on his travels to date. With all men, he appealed to their hearts. The Athenian relied on their minds.

∗∗∗

20

PERPETUA

The messenger came late at night. Aba'ye, who was staying with Shimon since Paul had left on his last trip, opened the door a trifle. As Aba'ye peeked outside from his considerable height, only his head appeared under the ceiling through the slot. The rest of his body remained protected by the solid wood. It was unsafe to open the door wide after dark. There were people around, even in Antioch, who still did not appreciate the work Shimon and his friends were doing.

"Yes?" he inquired in his deep basso.

The messenger cringed. The voice came from above. There was no one in front of him. Then he looked up and cringed even more. Aba'ye smiled and opened the door wide, his bulk silhouetted against the less dim interior.

The messenger moved a few steps back before he realized that the shape in front of him was human after all. Colossal, but human. He asked for Shimon the Rabbi.

"And just who are you," Aba'ye wanted to know.

"I have a message from his wife," the man answered.

Aba'ye opened the door wider and let the man in.

Shimon had been expecting a message from his wife for sometime. In a way, he had been waiting for it for years. He was longing for it to arrive. The news was brief, written in Greek.

"All children left home."

That was all. Shimon took a deep breath. At last, he thought. The message didn't say where they went, what they were doing. Just that they had left home. Good, it was safer that way. Safer for them. And she was wise to write so little. Even a cryptic message could have fallen into the wrong hands. There were people who'd think nothing of kidnapping one of his children to force him, Shimon, to stop spreading the Word. Since Paul had set out on his travels to preach to the Gentiles, the Jewish brethren became his, almost exclusive, care. Of late, there were certain people in and around Jerusalem, in Judea and Galilee, who thought of themselves as the elite, and who in recent years were losing their influence. They could have been getting desperate.

Shimon's head was awash with various scenarios.

Would she still recognize him? Would she want to? He took a piece of parchment to write a short message. Then he remembered. His wife couldn't read. After all, he'd only learned how to read long after he'd left home. She had no reason to. At least, not that he knew of.

He called Aba'ye to his side and told him what to tell his wife. He told him that he must help his wife sell their house, and come to Antioch.

"I want you to bring her to me." He looked up at Aba'ye's face and saw concern in his eyes. Shimon smiled. "Only if she wants to come, of course," he added.

Aba'ye still looked worried.

"What is it Aba'ye? What is troubling you?"

"It's Paul, Rabbi. He told me to look after his money."

"And what did you do when you went to Jerusalem?"

"I hid it, Rabbi." And his face lightened; worry dissipating as though it was never there.

Shimon smiled. Aba'ye knew what to do. He'd hide it again. "You can use my house or the yard, if you like?" he offered.

It wasn't his house, but he was living there. For now.

"Thank you, Rabbi, I will."

So that was that. Shimon knew very well where the money was hidden, but it wouldn't do to tell Aba'ye that. His thoughts turned to his family. Or what was left of it.

So the children have all left the house in which he and Perpetua lived. How time flies. I wonder where they went? Perhaps she'll tell me when she comes. When Aba'ye brings her. Soon.

So many years...

Shimon would go and fetch her himself but it would only endanger her. Also, his knees were acting up again. Sleeping on the floor must have done it. It had been a while before he got to a sleep on a bed. Even longer before he had a room of his own. If she sells the house, he mused, we could buy something here, in Antioch.

Our own house... with her... like in the old days...

Shimon slipped to his knees to give thanks.

It had been a long while since Shimon left his house in Bethsaida. He recalled his last, unsuccessful visit. This time all has been planned ahead of her journey, taking greater care to make sure that his wife would be there to see Aba'ye deliver his message. She would not be away on some chore for neighbours, or her family, like the last time.

Then Shimon remembered about the messenger. He rose, wearily, gave him some food, and sent him to the loft, up a ladder, to get some rest.

Aba'ye was back within a short time.

"Where can I put it, Rabbi?" He was carrying a leather sack that appeared to have considerable weight. Moments earlier he'd walked out with it, pretending to be carrying nothing. He thought he was being wily. The sack looked heavy enough, although in Aba'ye hands it was hard to tell. Probably gold or silver, Shimon thought. What else could it be? Shimon knew that Paul had recently sold all his family holdings in Tarsus. It could have been a considerable estate. He'd never asked. Aba'ye must have dug the treasure out from its hiding place in the garden, only to put it there again.

"You mustn't tell me, Aba'ye. Just hide it wherever you want to." Then Shimon saw the problem. "I shall leave the house for a while and you let me know when you finish hiding it."

"Yes, Rabbi," Aba'ye didn't know if he'd said something to make Shimon think that he didn't trust him. No matter. He'd hide it well. It was a small room, or a small garden for that matter, but he'd find a place no one would think of looking.

Shimon didn't like going out at night, but Aba'ye's peace of mind was important to him.

There was a time when Shimon had travelled a lot more. Not only to Jerusalem but he'd visited Lydda and Joppe and Caesarea; and, of course, Seleucia and Issus to the north. From the rest of Syria, people came to see him; to hear him speak. And now that Paul was away most of the time, he had to look after all the converts from the various religions the Gentiles belonged to. Now, there were already more converts of non-Jewish origin than from among the Jews. Perhaps their needs were greater?

But then, some years ago, the spirit was strong in him. He remembered curing the palsied Eneas, raising Tabitha from the dead. Or it seemed so.

And now? Perhaps Perpetua will renew me. Perhaps…

He hardly noticed that Aba'ye was standing in front or him.

"I am ready to go, Rabbi. Please remind me exactly where your wife lives?" He was already wearing his travelling sandals.

Shimon told him exactly where to go, and described the house in detail. Every part of it was etched in his memory. The house and the shore, where he was fishing. He could describe every stone, every rock.

"Tell my wife to leave the sale of the house to our children, and if they're gone, to our cousins, and to come with you at once. They can send the money later," he added.

Now, that it seemed possible, he couldn't wait to see Perpetua. Not a day longer...

Aba'ye left immediately. He carried no food, just some water. His left hand moved periodically to rest on the hilt of the short Roman sword, hanging on his left hip from a thick leather belt. He felt quite safe. He always did. Since Paul changed his orientation, Aba'ye seldom expected anyone to want to do him harm. Nor would he hurt a fly, unless to protect Paul. Or even Shimon. Or any of his friends.

He thought of himself as the protector of the brethren.

Paul didn't stay long in Athens. Athenians' philosophy and beliefs seemed to fulminate only on mental problems. Paul moved on. Silas and Timothy finally caught up with him in Corinth, while Luke decided to take a shortcut to Antioch. He needed time to put his notes in order. He had a great deal to write about.

In Corinth, Paul met Aquila and his wife Priscilla, who'd recently arrived from Italy.

"Claudius has ordered all Jews to leave Rome," they said in unison.

They often spoke as though reading each other's thoughts. The couple has proven to be great evangelists, explaining, even to Paul, the finer points of Christ's teaching.

Paul was pleased to stay with Aquila and Priscilla for another reason. He discovered that both of them practiced his old profession of tent making. Whenever possible, Paul supported himself by offering his services to local tentmakers. This was one such opportunity.

The three of them stayed in Corinth for some time, with Paul preaching the Good News in the synagogue. Eventually the synagogue split into a number of churches. Silas and Timothy found their own places to preach. So many were willing to hear the Word that Paul stayed in Corinth for a year and a half.

Finally, the churches well established, Paul moved on to the city of Cenchrea. From there he sailed with Aquila and Priscilla across the Aegean Sea to Ephesus. There he preached again, and once accepted in the synagogue, he left his new friends to continue, while he sailed on to Caesarea. Palestine was almost like being home. From the harbour, he walked to Jerusalem to celebrate the Feast of the Tabernacles.

After keeping the Feast, he took the long walk to Antioch. This time he was greeted with open arms. By everyone. He was glad he'd hurried, yet he got back only just in time...

For the first time in years Shimon was nervous. Not on account of the possible wrath of other Jewish sects, of the Pharisees, or Sadducees, or any other disgruntled religious faction, but, on account of his forthcoming meeting with his wife. He had no idea how Perpetua would react to both, his invitation and, if she came, to himself. Surely, she wasn't expecting him to go and fetch her himself?

It's been a long, long time.

He wondered if he ought to prepare the house for her homecoming. He soon realized, that whatever he did, it would not come close to her, albeit humble, house in Bethsaida. Neither in space, nor in the view it offered, nor even in the garden filled with flowers and fresh vegetables. So many years have past, yet he remembered even the smallest details.

For some reason he, literally, forgot to pray. Usually when he raised his consciousness to the Most High he felt an easing of tension, a relaxation of his wrought nerves. Not this time. For the rest of the night and the following day, his mind was only on his forthcoming meeting. On her homecoming. Actually, it wasn't even that. It was more like home-leaving, for her. Here, he didn't really have a home. Just a place to rest.

Towards the evening of the third day since the messenger delivered the message, there was a knock on his door. Aba'ye was not there to answer. Shimon was a generous, trusting man. He often had visitors who came to ask him for advice in matters of faith.

He opened the door wide.

Two men in long coats, their heads wrapped in turbans that covered most of their faces, pushed him back inside and closed the door. One held a knife to Shimon's throat, the other looked around for possible opposition.

They were alone.

The man holding the knife kept it at Shimon's throat, and pushed him into a chair. Then the other man walked in front of him, forced his head back, and stuffed a rug into his mouths. With another piece of cloth he wrapped it tight and tied it at the back on Shimon's head.

Then, a sinister smile on his face, he looked deep into Shimon's eyes.

"If you want to see your wife alive, you will come with us. Quietly. Now." He smiled again. "Nod if you understand, old man?"

Shimon nodded.

"Now, not a single sound from you, old man!" the man hissed.

Both men took Shimon's arms and led him to the door. There one of the men holding him stopped, while his companion put his head outside to check the traffic. The street was empty. They pushed Shimon out, closing the door quietly.

They walked some two hundred steps and turned into a side street. There they bodily lifted Shimon into a small cart, threw a large sheet of something, perhaps an old carpet, over him, and smacked the donkey to move forwards. Soon they cleared the limits of the city and turned south.

Shimon could hardly breathe. His nose dried up in the arid, desert-like air, and filled with dust. Each breath he took was painful. He offered his suffering for the safety of his wife.

The journey continued for some time. It was still dark when the cart turned off the main road into a side lane. After another league or so, the donkey came to a stop.

Shimon felt being pulled by the legs towards the open end at the back of the cart. Moments later his head emerged from under the cover, and he saw stars above him.

They dropped him to his feet.

"This way," one of the men said, pushing him forward.

Shimon, staggered, recovered his balance, and walked towards a house, nestled within a small orchard. It was a serene sight in the light of the twinkling stars. The moon offered only about half of its face to witness the night's escapade. The atmosphere was eerie.

"Why don't they just kill me?" he wondered.

The two men pushed Shimon into a shed and threw him to the ground. A moment later he heard the sound of some planks barricading the door from the outside. He didn't sleep for the rest of the night. He couldn't. He tried praying but his thoughts kept returning to his wife.

"Why don't they just kill me?" he asked himself, again. In spite of longing to see Perpetua, his voice was almost wistful.

The following day, around noon, the same two men came and gave him some water. The only good thing was that they had to remove the cloth from his mouth. At long last Shimon could take a deep breath. After two gulps of water, he smiled his gratitude.

"Praise the Lord for your generosity," he said.

One of the man sneered. "We'll see how much will your god help you..." He didn't finish. The beginning of his sentence was ominous enough.

The men left, but not before they tied Shimon's arms and legs. At least they left the cloth out of his mouth. The house must have been far enough away from the beaten track that should he scream no one would hear him. Not that he'd try. He'd do nothing to endanger his wife. Not now. Not after all these years. Also—he almost smiled—his throat was too painful.

After it got dark again Shimon heard noise outside. A group of people was evidently arriving at the forlorn house. Shimon still had no idea where he'd been taken. It could have been in any direction, north or south, or anywhere. He also had no idea why, except for the original threat of not seeing his wife.

And then the door opened and someone was pushed into his room. Soon enough it was slammed shut again, and Shimon heard someone blocking it from the outside. He took a deep breath. It was too dark to see anything, but he detected a familiar aroma. A scent of Jasmine? These last few days he remembered everything about her. Jewish women were forbidden to wear scent, but his wife planted night blooming Jasmine in her garden. Yes, he remembered. Jasmine opened its flowers only at night. Perpetua had it in her garden. When he'd left her side with the Master, she had said that he'd have her scent to remember her by. The scent of Jasmine often lingered on her for days. Now... after all this time...

"Perpetua?" he whispered, "Perpetua...."

It couldn't be, surely after all these years?

"Shimon?" the voice was as quiet as his.

Her hands weren't tied. She moved toward Shimon and felt his presence. Slowly, in total silence, she freed him from his tethers. Then his arms closed around her. At last, finally, they were together.

Neither of them needed words. They spent the next hour in a wondrous embrace. Only Perpetua's occasional sobs of happiness interrupted the bucolic silence.

And then the doors opened.

It was still dark-gray outside. Must have been long past midnight, perhaps approaching the early hours. The sky

towards the east was beginning to lighten. Two men grabbed
Shimon by both arms and pulled him outside. They tied him
to a tree, one of many spread about the orchard. Then they
went back to fetch Perpetua. In short order they had her tied
to another tree, little more than ten steps away. Four or five
other men were observing the activity without taking part.
Two of them held torches sparking with fire.

The man who spoke to him in Antioch pulled Shimon by
the neck, forcing him to look him in the eyes.

"You are going to swear by your god, by Yeshûa, that
you'll never bear witness about him. Never, do you
understand me?"

As if to give clout to his words, a stone whistled by
Shimon's ear hitting Perpetua in the stomach.

"Speak, or the next one will be higher, you hear me?"

Shimon was trembling like a leaf. "Perpetua," he
whispered.

Another stone whistled past him.

"Perpetua," he cried out, agony in his voice.

He couldn't let it happen. He couldn't let her die. Not
now. Not now...

Just then a cockerel greeted the first rays of the sun rising
over the mountains. Shimon closed his eyes. Not for the first
time he heard Yeshûa's words. It was the last supper they
were having together. The Master said...

*Truly I tell you, this very night, before the rooster crows,
you will disown me three times.*

Not again, Shimon whimpered. Please, Master, not
again... He set his teeth, shut the world out and called out in
a powerful voice.

"My wife, remember the Lord!"

And then he collapsed in his fetters like a doll made of
rugs.

***

21

ABA'YE

Aba'ye bent low over Shimon's body still slumped against the apple tree. He'd already cut his fetters asunder, and threw them away with disgust. Yet, the Rabbi remained immobile. He looked dead, as indeed, in some respects he was. His heart died with Perpetua—even as the mortal rock hit her temple. He didn't want to live. Not without her. Not after all this time—time of waiting, hoping.

Time of loneliness.

Even now, feeling moisture on his lips, for a moment he couldn't collect his thoughts. He was lost. Perhaps his mind refused to focus on what must have transpired.

"Drink… drink, Master," Aba'ye whispered.

Though he felt water touching his lips, then running down his cheeks and chin, Shimon's eyes remained closed. The cool water didn't bring him back to reality, not immediately. He blinked, repeatedly, and looked around.

It was quite light already. There was enough light to see, though the morning sun was still behind the ponderous clouds. It was the beginning of a somber day.

Shimon pushed himself up, stumbled, then stood up leaning against the tree trunk behind him. Again, he looked around. There was blood everywhere. Five corpses were lying, their arms and legs at odd angles, like grotesque manikins that someone threw around in a haphazard fashion.

Am I in Sheol?

In horror he looked at Aba'ye. He, too, was awash with blood. Other people' blood?

"It is I, Rabbi," Aba'ye said. "I was too late, Rabbi. Forgive me…"

And the giant fell to the ground putting his arms around Shimon's knees, begging for forgiveness.

Slowly Shimon was regaining his senses. His arms freed from ropes, he held Aba'ye gently, stroking his hair. He didn't dare to look at the apple tree straight ahead. He saw, instead, a short Roman sword, also red with blood, thrown some paces away. Shimon remembered that sword. It was Paul's. And now, in Aba'ye's hands, it had saved his life.

"Too late?" he asked, still stroking his head.

And then the horror of the night came back to him. Yes. Aba'ye was too late. And so was he. Much too late.

And yet… a momentary hope crossed his mind.

Then he saw her. Her body was lying quietly on his right, seemingly relaxed, with no more cares to trouble her. She didn't seem to have changed at all. Not in his eyes. Her face ashen, with just two blue-black bruises on her forehead and temple. She couldn't have suffered long. The bruises looked deadly. They were. Shimon closed his eyes again, in a vain attempt to shut out reality. In absurdly slow motion, his legs refused to support him.

"Rabbi," it was Aba'ye's voice again, strangely soft for a man his size. "She's at peace now. She's with the Lord."

His words reached Shimon through a fog of pain. Aba'ye was right, of course. She was with the Lord, now. She was at peace…" Shimon opened his eyes and saw Aba'ye's large face covered with tears. The giant felt his pain.

"Thank you, Aba'ye. I needed that reminder," Shimon whispered. And with half-closed eyes he wiped Aba'ye's tears with the hem of his coat. "Don't cry," he said, "you have saved my life," he added, straightening up.

Slowly, his joints stiff, Shimon raised himself, again, to his feet. Aba'ye was too distraught to help him.

"We shall have to burry her," Shimon said, as though to himself.

And then he smiled. In spite of the bruises on her face, Perpetua looked truly at peace. There seemed a wisp of a smile at the corners of her lips. Perhaps she saw the Lord even before she joined Him, he thought. Goodbye, my love. I shall always be with you.

Then things got dark again.

Shimon became aware of his surrounding when he saw himself sitting next to Aba'ye on the cart that presumably brought him here. Aba'ye was holding the reins and they were ambling along a road he found vaguely familiar. Soon enough they arrived in Bethsaida. Aba'ye went inside the house, took out some implements, and began digging a grave. Shimon looked on, still in a daze that refused to lift from his awareness.

The next thing Shimon remembered was nearing his house in Antioch. Aba'ye helped him to get down from the cart, then took the donkey and cart round the back of the house, into the yard. When he came back, Shimon was still standing where he'd left him. Aba'ye helped him inside and laid him gently on the bed. Shimon's face relaxed. Merciful sleep descended on him immediately. He slept till past midnight. When he came to, he saw Aba'ye sleeping on the floor, at his feet.

Shimon reached down and stroked the giant's head. "He save my life," he murmured to himself. "The Master would have forgiven them... they knew not what they were doing..." He stroked his head again. "Thank you, Aba'ye. Thank you..."

And then Shimon lay back once more and slept, again, till sunrise.

Soon after losing his wife, and with his children scattered Lord only knowing where, Shimon no longer had anything to

208 Stan I.S. Law

lose by staying in Antioch, other than protecting his own life. He packed his meager belongings and set out for Jerusalem. There, after a long separation, he joined his old friends James and John. By now they unreservedly supported Paul's apostolate to the Gentiles, although they, themselves, laboured principally among the Jews. For a while, at least, Shimon decided to join them. He was sorry to leave Aba'ye, but his inner voice had told him to go to the City of Peace. This is where the Master had ended his life. This is where Shimon wanted to be.

Poor Aba'ye, he murmured. Poor Aba'ye...

First he'd lost Paul to his travels, and now Shimon to the Jews in Jerusalem. For a while, at least, the giant would remain all alone. Perhaps that too was necessary.

Autumn came early that year. On Paul's return from Jerusalem, Shimon was gone. They must have passed each other on the way. Paul learned about Shimon's tragedy from Aba'ye. He offered the big man comfort as best he could; he knew that Aba'ye loved Shimon.

They all did.

Paul spent the winter writing epistles to the many brethren he'd visited on his first and second journey. It kept him busy as, in Shimon's absence, he had to look after the Antioch Christians as well. And there were more of them, day by day.

All has remained quiet until spring, when Shimon visited Antioch with a group of converted Jews. It was during the Spring Holiday season. It soon transpired, that while celebrating the Feast of Unleavened Bread, Shimon declined to eat and to share fellowship with the uncircumcised Christian Gentiles. He chose the company of the Jews he brought from Jerusalem, sitting apart. Paul knew that Shimon had no such needs in the past, when living in Antioch. In fact, until his departure for Jerusalem he treated Christian Gentiles as equals in all respects. Now he set himself and his party apart. Was he afraid to hurt their sensibilities?

Paul, always full of fire, saw red.

Publicly, without mincing words, he accused Shimon of hypocrisy. Harsh words were exchanged between them.

"I remember when you were Kepha," Paul muttered, his blood boiling.

"I would not hurt those who uphold the Law," Shimon answered.

"If you, being a Jew, live in the manner of the Gentiles and not as a Jew, why do you compel Gentiles to live as Jews?" Paul replied, staring him in the eye.

"Christianity is not a new religion, Paul, it is Judaism brought up to date," Shimon replied, but his argument did not carry any weight. Paul suspected that Shimon knew that, but he needed to be accepted by his new friends even more. At least, it certainly looked like it.

It seemed that in spite of the Jerusalem Conference of some years ago, there were many who only paid lip service to the agreement.

Paul was bitter.

It seemed that the rest of the Jews played the hypocrite with him. Even Barnabas, once his personal friend, turned against him, carried away by their hypocrisy.

Not for the first time in his life, Paul felt alone. Very alone. He found more courage among the Gentiles than among his own people.

A day later, Shimon's friends left for their return trip. Shimon remained behind. He had to. He could not leave with Paul holding anger in his heart. He waited until dusk, and walked up to Paul's house. He found him, as was usual for him, bent over the table, his face carrying a pensive expression, apparently writing one of his many letters.

"May I?" Shimon asked, putting his head through the half open door.

Contrary to his own habits, Paul usually kept his door ajar. Perhaps he thought he was more agile and faster than anyone who might wish him harm. Perhaps someone in need of help would not have walked in if the door were shut.

Or… Shimon thought sadly, perhaps his faith is stronger than mine?

Paul jumped to his feet, gesturing Shimon to enter.

"My home is your home, Rabbi," he blurted, sounding a little embarrassed.

He realized instantly that it ought to have been he, the younger man, who should have approached Shimon to still the stormy waters between them. After all, they both served the same Master.

Paul's house was little more than a room with a loft for sleeping. Downstairs there was a table, four chairs, and a bench on which Paul would stretch, on occasion, to give his back a rest from being constantly bent over while writing. A small oil lamp cast dark shadows all around. Only the table was illuminated. Attached to the room was a small annex, which Paul used as both, kitchen and a place for ablutions. When necessary, he squatted in the backyard, over a hole, which he topped up with soil after each successful evacuation. As he was seldom home, this arrangement suited him fine.

Shimon took a deep breath. He noted that in spite of their disagreement, Paul still addressed him as Rabbi. So, there is hope, he thought. Of course, he knew that there was always hope.

"I see you are writing, Paul, am I interrupting? Perhaps a bad time?"

"No, Rabbi, you are always welcome."

Paul sounded consolatory, almost servile. After the way he'd spoken out publically against Shimon's behaviour, he wished, belatedly, that he'd left it for a private meeting. It wasn't his job to correct Shimon's Christian mores in the company of others. Or ever, for that matter.

"I came to apologize…" Shimon started.

"No, Rabbi, it is I…"

Shimon raised his hand, quieting Paul. "We are not going to fight over who is more guilty, are we?"

This time Shimon's words were accompanied by a broad smile. "I came to talk to you as a friend, nothing more," Shimon added.

Paul moved a chair closer for Shimon to sit down, and then retuned to his side of the table. He, too, took a deep breath. Again he wished he'd had the courage to have gone and seen Shimon first.

"Your life has never been diminished by self-doubt, was it Paul?" When the younger man didn't answer, Shimon went on. "You were always sure of your ground, Paul. You put equal passion into whatever you are doing. Total commitment."

This sounded halfway between a question and a statement. Paul's face showed agreement, but also a suggestion of fear. He'd once put equal passion into destroying the Christians, as he now did into sharing with them the Good News. He wondered if Shimon was always right, but wouldn't dream of disagreeing with the Rabbi again.

Nevertheless, he nodded, partially against his better judgment.

"It is not so with me, Paul. Some people are strong and face boldly every adversity. Others have to overcome their innate doubts, even fear."

Paul slowly looked up. He was beginning to understand what Shimon was talking about. We are all endowed with different talents. We have different challenges to overcome. He looked at Shimon with new, or more precisely with renewed respect.

Shimon didn't find it necessary to tell Paul that he had decided to side with the young Jewish acolytes for two reasons. The first was to increase his influence over them in

Jerusalem, and thus have the power to try and keep them on the straight and narrow. Recently there were literally dozens of sects forming in the south. Some were even deviations from the teaching of the Master. It wasn't easy to maintain his own disciples on an even keel.

And the second reason was much more important. He wanted to be the subject of Paul's wrath. He wanted the young Jews to see how the Gentiles felt about their own hypocrisy, as against how the Master would have wanted them to feel. By now Paul's reputation was spreading far and wide. His reaction to their, let alone Shimon's, behaviour would not be taken lightly. It most certainly would not be ignored.

The Gentiles wanted not just to be equal, but also to feel equal. Not just mentally, but emotionally.

"Do you know why, my friend, Yeshûa told us not to judge one another?"

Paul looked up, again, questioningly.

"Because, Paul, we would have to enter a man's soul to know what are his motivations. And we can never enter that. Yeshûa could, and that is why he always forgave everyone."

Paul dropped his head. He had so much to learn.

"I am sorry, Rabbi. I am sorry…"

And for the second time in his life Shimon rose and gently stroked Paul's head. Then he walked to the door and gently closed it behind him.

There was one other reason why Shimon dallied behind after his Jewish acolytes had left for Jerusalem. He had to know what happened before Aba'ye had found him on that fateful night. He asked Aba'ye about it early next morning.

"Tell me, my friend. Tell me what happened before you saved my life."

It was history, now. Shimon could talk about it with only an echo of the pain that once tore his heart. Aba'ye seemed to still suffer from a lingering guilt.

"I couldn't help it, Rabbi. I was unconscious," was his cryptic reply.

Then Aba'ye blinked a few times and sat down. They were in Shimon's old room. The brethren still kept it for him, although it was Aba'ye who now stayed here, as though looking after it for Shimon, in case he needed it, and as a place where he kept Paul's money hidden.

"We did everything as you told us, Rabbi. Your wife was already packed. She didn't take much, and your sons came back to dispose of the house and the rest of the belongings. They knew you'd ask them to do so. We set out on foot—I carrying what little she took with her. Just some memories, she'd said..." and Aba'ye again dropped his head at his recollection of that day.

Shimon waited patiently for the big man to continue.

"She didn't want to wait. We set out in the afternoon and walked through sunset and into the night. We reached the turn of the road which led to that house..."

He couldn't continue. His face broke into an expression of such sadness as Shimon had never seen.

"She was such a kind Lady," he whimpered.

A while later Aba'ye collected himself. Shimon didn't rush him. For a moment he regretted asking Aba'ye to fill in the blanks in his memory. It was selfish of me, he thought. But, it was too late.

"We were just past that turn, when all things went blank. In the last seconds I realized that a rock hit me in the back of my head. I went out cold. When I came to, I was alone. They pushed me into a ditch, I suppose, on one side of the road and covered me with some debris. I guess I was too heavy for them to lift. I think they left me for dead."

Shimon nodded. Things were beginning to fit into what must have happened. Aba'ye was becoming calmer.

"When I woke up I looked for your wife. Then I realized that they, whoever they were, must have taken her. There was no sign of anyone up or down the road. I don't know how long I was unconscious, but I have a hard head. I assumed if they went north or south, I would still see them afar. There was no one."

Aba'ye's face was showing signs of anger.

"It had to be that side road, a while back. I got up and walked back a few hundred paces, and turned into that lane. When I got to the house, they were already..." and again he couldn't continue.

Shimon waited, knowing what was coming.

"I was too late, Rabbi," he whimpered. "I was too late..." he repeated, as though asking Shimon to tell him otherwise.

And for the third time Shimon stroked a grown man's head, as though he were a little boy. Then he sighed deeply.

"It's all right, Aba'ye. It's all right..." he muttered, and rose slowly.

He was ready to return to Jerusalem.

***

22

THIRD JOURNEY

Now that **Shimon and Paul** had reconciled their differences, Paul felt strangely relaxed. No matter what disagreements they had, Paul always held Shimon in highest regard, recognizing in him the Kepha, the rock upon which the Church of Christ would be built. Not that Shimon did more apostolic works than others; all apostles worked wherever the spirit moved them. It wasn't that. It was something intangible about Shimon, something that had escaped him at their first meeting, and, frankly, ever since.

Shimon had no regard for himself. None whatsoever. What people thought of him was of no consequence to him. All that mattered was being true to that which Yeshûa had implanted in his heart.

Although paradoxically, and still inexplicably to Paul, Shimon was hardly the Rock he was reputed to be. Paul was forced to reanalyze the meaning of the word Kepha. It did not represent that which never moved—that remained static through the ages.

It was something quite different.

Paul realized that when referring to Shimon, Kepha meant that no matter how many mistakes he's made, how many errors he may have committed, no matter how often he tripped on his path to enlightenment, he always returned to the center, the immovable center of his being.

To the immovable, endless, immortal power that welled within him. That center was rock-solid, static, unchanging and unchangeable—not the universe that swirled around him and all of us.

Shimon was not the Kepha that never moved. He was the Kepha that always returned to the base upon which he was building the church. Not to his power, but to the power within him. To Yeshûa.

Refreshed by his realization, Paul immersed himself in his writing with renewed enthusiasm. Not that it took much to enthuse Paul. He was not a man to spend hours on meditation. His mission was to act, to stay busy. And that he did in an exemplary fashion.

After spending most of autumn and all of that winter in Antioch, visiting the surrounding cities, and towns, and villages, Paul's feet began to itch for another journey. He felt it was his duty to visit the towns and cities where he and his friends had planted the seed; and perhaps to plant a few more on the way back. By the following summer he was ready to go.

As for Antioch, the church was now well established. There were many evangelists capable of taking the reins and keeping the church going and expanding, according to the Lord's will.

Paul left on the first days of spring.

First, he revisited the churches he'd already established in Galatia and Phrygia. He wanted to see how the letters he'd written to them a year ago were received. From what he's heard to date, the churches flourished.

In early autumn he moved to Ephesus.

Situated in a valley between two hills gently sloping towards the river Cayster and then toward the Aegean Sea, it was in the central location of Asia Minor. Long before Christianity took its roots there, the Temple of Artemis, hardly a league from the center of the city attracted many worshipers. Artemis, the daughter of Zeus and twin sister of Apollo, was also the goddess of hunt, wild animals and fertility, powers desired by many. Her temple was reputed to have brought many blessings upon the city. Paul was quick to take advantage of the throngs of visitors to share with them the Good News.

Paul also liked the easygoing, tolerant people who lived there. He liked them all so much that he'd spent more than three years there, preaching to pagans and sharing the Good News with nonbelievers. He also continued writing. It was in Ephesus that he wrote his letters to the Corinthians. He also delivered powerful messages in the synagogue that strengthened the faith of many Christians.

Yes, Paul really liked the city of Ephesus. As did a number of other evangelists, including John and Timothy.

And then, one day, a strange event took place. Seven sons of a Jewish priest named Sceva arrived in town unexpectedly. The group travelled from place to place, claiming to exorcise people from evil spirits: an ability claimed by many, possessed by very few. The seven brothers watched Paul casting out demons in the name of Yeshûa. As Paul was very successful in this endevour, they attempted to try out his method themselves. When they came across someone who evidently was in need of mental liberation, they decided to try Paul's method.

"We exorcise you by the Yeshûa whom Paul preaches," they proclaimed in unison.

And then, a funny thing happened; funny, though not for the seven brothers...

They heard a powerful voice saying:

Yeshûa I know, and Paul I know. But who are you?

What followed was totally unexpected. The man who's evil spirit the sons of Sceva were trying to cast out by the authority they did not possess, leaped at them, overpowered all seven of them, so much so that the all the sons of the

Jewish priest run out of the house, reportedly both, beaten up as well as naked—although why naked it was never explained.

It must have been quite a sight.

The news of the event spread quickly. The name of Yeshûa was magnified, Paul's influence increased, even as fear of false prophets fell upon them all. As for the sons of Sceva, they'd learned their lesson. They repented, gave up their practice of magic, and burned their books of spells and evil practices.

Peace returned to Ephesus—but not for long. All too soon, the easygoing tolerance was suddenly exhausted. Business does not like competition, and the nonbelievers regarded Paul's preaching as business. A lot of people lived off the benefits of Artemis: donations, souvenirs, mementos, meals, overnight stays, and other profitable endeavours. Paul had to pay the price. Again.

There were riots.

In the meantime, Shimon left the conquering of new grounds to others. He realized, instinctively, that other apostles, even evangelists, let alone Paul, were much better at presenting pertinent facts about the Good News to the masses. He decided that his job was to visit various churches, far and wide, quietly, and make sure that they did not waver from the new Path. By that time, there was a great many of them. Left on their own, the acolytes were in danger of deviating from the straight and narrow.

Paul wrote letters to them. That helped. But what was needed was a dose of human touch, and few men were more human than Shimon.

People, it seemed, tended to adapt the gospel to their old ways, their own needs, to make it more acceptable to their mindset, their old beliefs. Paul would sweep them with his rhetoric, and soon move on to conquer new territories. Paul was laying the foundations. Or, to put it differently, he was planting the seed, but the fresh seedlings had to be watered with spirit. It was true that Paul would revisit periodically the cities he'd awakened to the true reality, but the reality was still mixed with the environment in which people had grown up, with the customs that had been entrenched in their minds and hearts since childhood. And there were a great many gods and goddesses in that environment.

They, those acolytes, had to be born again.

Their minds and hearts had not been cleansed of all the erroneous knowledge imbedded in their heads for many past generations. They had to start with a completely clean slate. Paul couldn't do that. What he did was wonderful, but it did not go deep enough.

Neither do men put new wine into old wineskins...

Shimon remembered the words. He remembered most words of the Master. Paul had never met Him. How would he know?

This life suited Shimon. Like the Master he'd served, he had nowhere to lay his head. No place to call his own. As Paul got older, he'd sometimes stop on his journeys of raising awareness of the Christ for months, even years in one place, as Shimon did but once, in Rome. Paul did it quite openly. He no longer felt the need to hide his identity.

Shimon preferred to travel incognito, listen to people before he'd gently point them in the right direction. Sometimes the new Christians didn't even recognize him. They thought that he might be a new prophet, sent to them by heaven to help them understand the Word. By the time they realized who he was, or may have been, Shimon was gone. Only the news spread that a strange man appeared to them, wise in the ways of the Lord.

And they rejoiced.

Shimon was finding the physical reality more and more in direct opposition to that which has been taught by

Yeshûa—taught to the few, to the chosen ones. The more he thought about it, the more he realized that Yeshûa, while living in this world, considered it but a transient phase in his, what Shimon could only infer from His words, eternal life.

Be in this world but not of this world.

Shimon remembered those words. Recently, the echoes of that secret knowledge never left him. The Kingdom to which the Master referred grew in intensity. Shimon's visions, or perhaps waking dreams, became more vivid. Sometimes they included conscious participation in that inner, seemingly chimerical yet very tangible, reality. Somehow, that inner reality—that which he previously always regarded as dreams—was being influenced by his will. He called it lucid dreaming, although that only partially described his awareness.

Was that the Kingdom the Master had referred to?

Shimon was finding that other world more and more fascinating. He felt drawn to it with an inexorable force. Even as he travelled, some years ago, by ship to Rome, he recalled the ever-receding horizons, so it was now, with Yeshûa's Kingdom. The more he approached it, the more its boundaries receded. Not that it became any less real. It was more real by the day, only the horizons receded. At sea, there was always a line where the sky touched the water, or the land. In the Kingdom there were no horizons. It was infinite. Limited only by his ability to perceive it.

And then Shimon sat up with a shock. What, he mused, what if even as I can gain control of my dreams here and now—what if He whom I've seen in my dreams gained control of this, our wakened reality. What if my dream reality to Him is that which this reality is to me. What if even as I visit His reality in my dreams, He visited ours in His…

My Kingdom is not of this world…

Was He the eternal dreamer…

Is that why He'd said that His Kingdom was not of this world—meaning not of this reality?

It was after He'd risen...

We were alone, no... there was James the Just, and John, and myself. We were sitting together... and then He appeared. He'd said something about, yes, he'd told James to leave Jerusalem...

No, that's not it... well, there was more. He appeared to us, to some of us, so many times...

Then He'd said something about there being many heavens, seventy-two measures of heavens, wasn't it?

Ah, yes. And then He'd told us not to worry, not to be sad, not to be concerned...

I am he who was within me. Never have I suffered in any way, nor have I been distressed...

There was more... ah, yes...

And this people have done me no harm...

I remember it all, now. James was crying and on hearing these words, he'd wiped away his tears. The rest of what the Master had said was unclear.

"Perhaps James will remember better," Shimon murmured. "I'll have to ask him. I must."

And then his eyes drifted again beyond the horizon to another reality. Perhaps closer to His reality?

If the Kingdom of Yeshûa is not of this world, was He an alien here? Could He manifest in this world even as I manifest in my lucid dreams?

Sometimes Shimon wondered if Paul ever ventured into that inner Kingdom. Not whether he had dreams—all people have dreams—but if he ever assumed conscious control of them.

Some years ago Shimon struggled with problems of other people, with his own, even with the future, as though the present didn't have problems enough. He struggled until he remembered Yeshûa's words.

My peace I give unto you...

Poor Paul, Shimon mused, why must he struggle so?

The silversmith was jealous. Pure and simple. Paul's preaching caused many people to stop purchasing replicas of the goddess Artemis. The original sculpture carved out of white marble adorned the entrance to her magnificent temple. The replicas were guaranteed to bring good fortune. Or so the silversmith named Demetrius claimed.

Now, Paul ruined it all. He had to be punished. He was responsible for the loss of a considerable profit.

"Idols," Paul kept repeating. "They are all idols!"

Artemis was worshipped in Ephesus and across the entire Roman Empire. She was their goddess from time immemorial. Even the Romans worshiped her, though they changed her name to Diana.

Paul would have probably lost his life if it hadn't been for the city clerk who told the rioters to take him to court.

"Artemis is protected by Zeus," he declared, "no harm will come to her. If anyone has a case against Paul, the courts are open, and there are proconsuls. Let them bring charges…"

The city did not tolerate uproars. There were laws to protect its citizen. Ephesians were civilized. Had been, for a long time.

Paul breathed easier but he thought it wise to make a quick getaway. Quietly, he skipped town. He walked through many cities, visiting new acolytes, as his feet took him back to Troas, where he celebrated the Feast of the Unleavened Bread. It was good to encounter tradition in which he'd been raised. Some of his old friends came to visit him, to compare the joys and tribulations they experienced in their churches. It transpired that they were all successful, but people, they say, seemed to be drifting back to their old ways.

Paul felt tired. He met with the elders and warned them about the oncoming apostasy. They nodded gravely. They all seemed worried. They could read the signs. They had their own suspicions.

Soon after the meeting Paul boarded a ship for Miletus, and stopping only for a short while in Patara, he sailed for Phoenicia.

There, it was almost like home; almost like Judea. With only short stops on the way, he arrived safely on the shores of Palestine. His spiritual home. The place where the Master lived and preached. They say that all roads lead to Rome. Well, not yet, at least not for Paul. For now all Paul's journeys took him to Jerusalem, though not always with pleasant results. There were memories there, and some bruises, which took a long time to disappear. No matter, he returned to all the places where those he'd spoken to had accepted the Word. They were the only family he had.

But people, it seems, are fickle.

No sooner had Paul arrived than Jews assailed him. Word travelled fast—they could not stand his ongoing successes. As in Ephesus, jealousy raised her ugly head. Here, too, he was beaten up by his own people. Again. It was almost their regular sign of welcome.

For the first time since his vision on the way to Damascus, Paul wondered if he was on the right track. He wondered if quality was not of greater value than quantity. He'd spent the last few years conquering thousands of people for the Empire of Christ. He worked day and night, ceaselessly, without rest. When he stopped in his travels it was only to recover his strength and to write letters to all the churches he'd initiated. There were so many of them. They all needed his help. His concern. Like children who are in need of their father. It never crossed his mind to stop and just pray.

Didn't Shimon say that by your deeds they shall know you?

Something like that.

Well, he gave them deeds. And what did they do? They'd beaten him up. Again and again and again…

Lord, why can't I pray?

Why do I cause a riot wherever I go?

Why don't my own people understand my words?

He taught so many others to put their trust in the Master. In the power of the Lord. Yet he, himself, continued to work like a slave. Am I not a Jew, he asked himself?

Am I not a citizen of Rome?

This realization had saved him. It saved him from further beatings, and from a scourge by the Romans.

Paul should have known better. On the way back to Jerusalem, he'd stopped briefly in Caesarea where he'd met the prophet Agabus, the man who'd once warned them about the coming famine in Jerusalem. On that occasion, guided by Shimon, they'd all listened. The prophet spoke of spiritual famine, although some people were also short of food.

This time Paul looked for spiritual interpretation of Agabus' words, instead of taking them literally. The prophet saw Paul bound, hand and foot. He demonstrated the event using Paul's own belt. He showed Paul what the Jews would do to him, should he continue to Jerusalem.

Paul was not inclined to listen to other people's spiritual insights. He was a very practical man. He would not be persuaded.

Now, belatedly, facing the angry mob, he wished he had listened.

***

23

THE PRISONER

Paul was lucky. When the Jews beset him with very nasty intentions, the scars of which he carried for some time, Romans had come to his rescue. In spite of his humble demeanor, Paul was a proud man. He tried to resolve his problems himself. But when his arms were tied and blows started landing, he needed help.

The mob activity was watched closely by a passing detachment of Roman soldiers. The Romans didn't like mobs; they were hard to control. When the detachment came closer, Paul shouted to them that he was a Roman citizen himself.

Although many Jews vowed to kill Paul, right there and then, the soldiers had to act. Roman citizenship offered extensive protection anywhere within the Empire. It was a highly coveted prize, desired by many, possessed by few. Paul, thanks to having been born in Tarsus, was among the lucky ones. The soldiers dispersed the Jews, and led Paul to the nearby barracks. There, the Commander himself confirmed his Roman citizenship.

For now, Paul was safe, though… not for long.

Released the next day by the Romans, he was, nevertheless, led before the Sanhedrin, to determine the cause of the riots. Paul's pleas of innocence meant little to the Sanhedrin. He'd been a flea in the midst of their garments for a long time, and he was never among their favourites. Except when he had been beating up those blasphemers, of course, but that was a long time ago. And now, Paul was in trouble, again.

Nevertheless, he was released.

The Romans were watching the Sanhedrin. The Pharisees, and the Sadducees, and most of all the priests, had to play it safe. Particularly the priests. Romans didn't like priests of other religions.

That very night Paul had a vision. He saw Yeshûa standing before him, saying:

Be of good cheer, Paul; for as you have testified for me in Jerusalem, so you must also bear witness in Rome.

Paul was never much for listening to visions or prophets. He could never tell the difference between a vision and a dream. He was planning to preach to the Jews, again. His own conversion was initiated by a vision, yet he appeared to be a slow learner; or else his intuitive faith in divine protection went a long way. What he did learn came mostly at the feet of Ananias. He'd never forget him.

At the time, his problems were far from over.

By next morning, a band of irate Jews swore that they would starve themselves until Paul was killed. The chief priest, presumably after a healthy breakfast, urged them on. Paul had been a thorn in their side for a long time.

"If only he hadn't been a Pharisee," they said, "not to mention a son of one." That last was adding insult to injury.

But Paul was smart and, in spite of the troublemakers outside, he'd already developed many friends. At the last moment he learned from his own people about the plot and made sure the Romans heard about it.

It worked.

As mentioned, the Romans looked after their own—their own citizens. Before the Jews could carry out their threat, the Romans, two hundred of them, escorted Paul out of Jerusalem under the cover of night. They took him all the way to Caesarea, where the commander submitted his case to be heard by Felix, the governor of Judea.

In the absence of any evidence of Paul having broken any *Roman* laws, the Most Excellent Governor Felix decided to put Paul in protective custody.

Paul spent the next two years in the Praetorium of Herod of Judea, i.e.: in the military headquarters. In other words, in prison. Perhaps the good governor was hoping for a bribe from someone, anyone, to release him. No matter, Paul was given a lot of freedom to move around, even to receive visitors. It was almost like a long awaited holiday.

And then, the Most Excellent Felix had been replaced by the Most Excellent Festus.

Tempus fugit.

Also about that same time, Paul recalled the dream he had had about Yeshûa commanding him to testify for Him in Rome.

"I stand at Caesar's judgment seat, where I ought to be judged," he declared when standing before Festus. "To the Jews I have done no wrong, as you very well know."

When Festus nodded, Paul continued.

"For if I am an offender, or have committed anything deserving of death, I do not object to dying; but if there is nothing in these things of which these men accuse me, no one can deliver me to them."

And then, raising his voice, Paul announced:

"I appeal to Caesar."

When the Most Excellent Governor Festus weighed Paul's words, he had an inspiration. In an attempt to gain favour with the Jews, he decided to grant Paul his wish. He offered Paul a chance to have his case tried in Rome by Caesar himself. Paul agreed readily.

But not all was done yet in Judea.

While Festus had already agreed to send Paul to Rome, King Agrippa, accompanied by Bernice, his wife, who some say was his... sister, arrived in Caesarea to allow Paul to defend himself against the charges the Jews brought against him. After all, he was the King, and he ought to decide, right?

Paul must have had moments of concern when Agrippa arrived. After all, King Agrippa II was the great-grandson of Herod the Great, the homicidal maniac who killed as many baby boys in Judea as he could in the hope of murdering infant Yeshûa. Not a nice man at all.

Then, Agrippa's father had the apostle James beheaded, and had arrested Shimon. He had had great hopes of murdering Shimon also, before the apostle was miraculously freed from jail.

And now Paul was facing a worthy successor of this charming, if bloodthirsty, purportedly perverted family. There was a very subtle but fundamental difference between Paul's one time persecution of the Believers, and that practiced by Agrippa. Paul persecuted them out of a misplaced religious conviction. For Agrippa the motivations were exclusively those of political expediency.

Nevertheless, in Festus's Palace Agrippa had to play it with care. As was to be expected, like Festus, Agrippa found nothing in Paul's behaviour worthy of imprisonment—let alone death. He must have been dreadfully disappointed.

"Should Paul choose to forego his plea to Caesar, you might as well free him now," he declared. I could always get him later, he must have thought.

But, by then, Paul had different plans, and he most certainly didn't trust Agrippa to keep his word. He decided to stick to his plans and hold the Proconsul to his word. Surely, a Roman's word was his bond?

It was.

Under the circumstances, Paul would get a free ride— sail rather—to Rome, though in theory at least, he was still a prisoner. Nevertheless, Paul counted his trip to Rome as his fourth missionary journey, as indeed it was, even if unwittingly financed by Rome.

It could have been clear sailing, henceforth, if it hadn't been for bad weather. His ship ran aground in the storm, and Paul was forced to spend the winter in Malta. He could have done worse.

Nevertheless, Rome had many resources. Once the weather improved, Paul was put on the next available ship and sent to the heart of the Empire. There, a little to his surprise, and in conspicuous contrast to Jerusalem, he was warmly greeted by Believers. It seemed that, long before Paul's arrival, Shimon has done great work there.

The trial before Nero was little more than a subterfuge. Once the Jews got rid of Paul from Jerusalem, they never pursued him. Other evangelists, who continued to disturb their peace of mind, let alone their conscience, kept them busy. Paul rented a house, and continued with his work. He preached, wrote letters, and received visitors.

At long last, life was beautiful.

Paul had written more letters to the various churches he'd initiated, one could say established, than he could remember. Some of them were even delivered. Others... perhaps we shall never know. Starting with Thessalonians, later he wrote again to Corinthians, then to Galatians, Romans, Ephesians, Philippians... they all benefited from his inspiration, from his need to share. He'd even written to the Hebrews who had so often rejected him. Towards the end, he even wrote to his friend Timothy, in memory of having travelled together. Paul couldn't sit still and do nothing. He was also a good friend endowed with a good memory. He wrote in every spare moment. Whenever he wasn't busy preaching. Which, in spite of his literary output, was rarely. After all, he was an apostle.

And, as for his memory, well, it wasn't getting any better of late—he hoped Timothy wouldn't notice.

Other than the time Paul had spent in the desert, time was now principally needed not to learn new but to cleanse himself of the old wine, for the first time in his life, Paul felt truly relaxed. In all his previous journeys his head was always filled with things he'd have to do, with letters he'd have to write, with sermons he would have to deliver. Not now. For a time, although a prisoner, he felt free. Dangers were inherent in such a condition. When he was not kept busy, he was apt to stop thinking. He would be in danger of calming the turmoil invariably going on in his head. And he might succumb to the counterpart of thinking.

He might succumb to listening.

He was beginning to wonder if his constant labours were not a form of escape from having to stop and listen. Shimon once told him to stop. Just that—to stop. He'd never explained what he'd meant.

Although officially Paul was still a prisoner, there was only one soldier guarding him. He could still preach, teach, meet with friends and confer with Jewish religious leaders.

There was only one thing missing. Shimon. Shimon was the one man, the only man he'd ever met, who did not follow the established ways, who thought beyond the expected, established ways.

Just stop, he'd said. Just stop.

The more Paul thought about it the more he realized that only when one stepped beyond the transience of time the true reality would begin to lift its veil. True reality of what? Of the Kingdom? Didn't the Master say that it was here and now? That's what Ananias had told him.

Here and now?

If so, then why am I running up and down the Empire, crossing seas, persuading people to listen to the Word of Yeshûa when I hardly know what it was? I am creating a church for Him, but the church has hollow walls. It is not filled with the substance of His Kingdom; just with its promise. Promise of the Kingdom hereafter. Not now.

Not as He'd promised.

Paul thought that he was beginning to understand the difference between his own understanding and that of Shimon. He, Paul, preached always about the future. The future life, the future churches, the Christ's Empire about to come to earth and sweep the nations. Surely, it had to happen. Was he not chosen to spread the Word? To build that very Empire where Christ ruled supreme, above all others?

Not so was Shimon. Paul realized that he was always down to earth. Whereas Shimon? Only Shimon's feet may have been touching the earth we all walk on, but his head and his heart were already in heaven. Right here on earth, yet in heaven.

"What does Shimon know that I don't?" he murmured.

Paul had too much time. He was not used to it. He was becoming like the Greeks who created their gods out of philosophy. Out of the process of thinking. Out of their needs. Their gods were the personification of logical thinking. At least, Paul thought wistfully, they lived in the here and now.

I, too, am only partially on earth, he mused further. Only I have no idea where the rest of me is.

And then there was the question of Power. Not his, but the Power that, on occasion, manifested Itself through him. How did that work? What made him the vessel that the Power chose to manifest through? He could never invoke It, yet It was always there when needed.

In the name of Yeshûa I heal thee…

He'd spoken those words in the past and the Power responded. It was as though the Power was life itself. What was the Power hidden in His name?

Yeshûa. The late form of Yehôshûa. Meaning? He tried to recall Gamaliel's lectures. In Hebrew it meant 'Yah is salvation', or 'salvation through Yah'. So what was meant by Yah? The Greeks call it Jah, as in Jehovah. It was a poetic form of Yahweh, the Existing One. Or YHWH. Or according to Moses, what it really meant was I AM THAT I AM.

His head began to hurt. When Gamaliel had given his lectures all this was just theoretical, now... now he was no longer a boy. Now he had to understand it.

"Would I?" he asked himself. "Will I ever understand it? Would I ever understand the power of the real I AM?"

The power of the real ME?

Paul had been brought up in Greek culture, and only later he continued his education in Jerusalem. Gamaliel had spoken of some such things but he wasn't clear. Paul vaguely remembered Gamaliel trying to explain the meaning of the Hebrew word *shem*, or *shum*, which the Greeks translated into *onoma*, meaning 'name' or 'renown.' Neither, Gamaliel had said, meant renown or an appellation to tell people apart.

Paul closed his eyes, and the silhouette of the old Rabbi wavered, then solidified behind his closed eyelids.

"All words are symbols," Gamaliel was saying, "symbols of things they stand for. *Shem*," he affirmed, "symbolizes the nature of that which is being named; all that comprises the sum-total of the character of an object and or a person thus designated."

Gamaliel was a great teacher.

But, wondered Paul, what is the real nature of I AM?

A moment later the contours of the old Rabbi dissolved into the air around him.

Funny, Paul thought. Yesterday when I was busy preaching, I wouldn't have remembered a single line of Gamaliel's lecture. It was too long ago. And today I am relaxed. In a way I stopped thinking and, perhaps, just perhaps, I have just began to listen?

Is that what I have to do more? Just listen?

I thought I did. I thought that was what enabled me to preach, to win souls...

I thought... I've done a great deal of thinking. Like the Greeks.

And then Paul closed his eyes again and asked: What was Yeshûa's nature? What were the elements that comprised the sum-total of His character?

And then he stopped thinking and just listened.

Two years later, Paul was acquitted of all charges—not that there was much to acquit him of. He was free to leave Rome and return to his favourite pastime. To conquering new lands, new people for the church of the Christ. But, though he'd never admit it even to himself, he was reticent to return to his journeys. He had just tasted the antechamber of inner peace.

Nevertheless, next spring he boarded a ship for Crete to confer with Titus. Paul had written some letters to him, and it was time to meet him face to face.

It was a perfunctory meeting. Paul had to make sure that Titus was following the instructions he'd sent him. That done, Paul left Titus to do his work and boarded another ship. This time, stopping but briefly in Nicopolis, he set sail for Iberia. He had written to the brethren in Iberia almost ten years ago, and it was high time to follow up on his letters in person.

The Empire was growing larger. He was beginning to realize that he must delegate as much as he could to others. The vast majority of Christians were very good men. Men he trusted. Some of them, more so than himself.

But his passion remained. There were still parts of the Roman empire where the Word hasn't reached. It was up to him. It was his job to plant the seed, no matter what the ground. He had no control how it would grow, although he tried hard to follow up. He couldn't be everywhere at once, so he wrote letters. Many letters. What else could he do?

After a season in Iberia, he was ready to leave the spreading of the Good News to younger men and return to Rome. Had he not done enough? Was not the Empire of

Christ growing faster than any other? Even Alexander would have been jealous.

And it was my making, Paul mused.

Sure, others helped, but it was he, Paul, who actually made it happen. He inspired not only the pagans, the believers in idols and false gods and goddesses... he'd inspired the evangelists. He created...

And then an opportunity presented itself that Paul couldn't resist. He was ready to leave Iberia for Rome, when news came of the revolts in Britannia. The ship with reinforcements was leaving the next day. Paul bribed the captain to be taken along. The captain was a curious man. Paul offered him private tuition in the Word of Christ.

"And why should I listen to the words of a Jew?" the captain asked, his Roman pride showing.

"A Roman Jew," Paul corrected. "You are a soldier, your life is in constant peril. I cannot offer you more then Nero does, here, on earth, but I can offer you eternal life."

The captain listened. Romans believed in many gods and goddesses. One more wouldn't hurt. It sounded like too good an offer to miss.

Once again, Paul set sail into the unknown.

The days on the sea are long, the nights longer. When Paul talked to the captain, the time passed easier. But the captain had duties. Paul, yet again, was alone.

"Why am I always alone, Lord?" he asked, looking at the shimmering waves made alive by the moon. The whole sea seemed alive. Breathing.

I am always with you...

Paul spun on his heel, nearly falling overboard. He distinctly heard the voice. Then he stopped and sat down on the deck, his back against the gunwale.

For the first time Paul realized that he was looking for Yeshûa everywhere except in the depth of his heart.

By the time they reached Britannia, Nero's general Suetonius Paulinus crushed the revolt with his usual brutality. The ship turned back, with only some soldiers replacing those that had fallen in their struggle to sustain the glory of Rome.

There was little chance that another ship would take Paul back in the foreseeable future. Suddenly, though not for the first time, he felt tired. Very tired. He preached to the people in the harbour. A few dozen of them. He planted the seed. Let the Lord water the ground that it might grow.

"What shall I do?" he asked the captain.

The Roman was halfway to becoming a Christian. He was almost convinced.

"Come home, Rabbi. People in Rome need you even more."

Paul went. The captain was a good man. He would make a good Christian, Paul thought. Perhaps he would spread the word in the Roman navy. And what about me, Lord. When shall I find the peace that You offered?

My peace I give unto you…

This time Paul didn't spin around. He knew from where the voice had originated. Outside, in this world, only silence surrounded him. Silence enhanced by the humming of wind against the tightly stretched shrouds keeping the mast straight; that, and the occasional creek of timbers. The sails themselves made no sound.

***

24

SHIMON AND PAUL

For the first time at the end of his journey there was no crowd waiting to greet him on his arrival. Perhaps I am spoiled, thought Paul. They've spoiled me. Or perhaps, in the past, it had been their way of saying thank you.

No matter.

Paul was one of the last to leave the ship. Soldiers had priority. By the time they left, the crew had the sails tied down and was in a hurry to get back to their families. Can't blame them. They were away a long time. At least it was still light, in Ostia, the ancient port of Rome he'd visited before. And the weather was fine. Not too hot, just right for a good walk.

But it was dark by the time Paul got to Rome. It was a long walk, or maybe he was just getting old. When he got back to his house, no one was around. The door was ajar as though someone had just left. Not even a soldier for company, he mused.

Surely, am I not still a prisoner?

The first thing he discerned on entering into the gloom of his house was a pile of clothing someone had thrown, in a haphazard fashion, into the corner of the room. Probably to be taken out for washing the next day? It was too dark to see. Paul was tired and ignored the mess one of his young acolytes must have left behind. Young people were like that. Everywhere. They did not clean up, even if they slept for free in someone's house.

"Of course, they couldn't have known I would be coming back today," he murmured, trying to justify the action of conspicuous absentees. Then he cleared his throat. He sounded harsh even to himself.

"May the Lord be with you, Paul."

The voice emerged from a heap of clothing in the corner of his room. The heap moved, slowly rising, to unveil a human shape. Paul took a step back. He believed in spirits, and in miracles, he'd witness some himself, but he did not believe in ghosts.

"Sorry to startle you, Paul. Your man let me in. I told him I wouldn't need him any more tonight." Then, seeing that Paul was still looking lost, he added, "I was praying."

That would account for the heap of clothing. Paul recognized Shimon's voice immediately. Shimon must have been on his knees. Why do people kneel down to pray, Paul wondered? Isn't Yahweh omnipresent?

"And with you, Rabbi," Paul responded belatedly.

Paul walked up to the only window to draw the curtains and let in at least some of the moonlight.

The next words Paul heard were tinged with humour.

"Don't, my friend. Yahweh made the night to be dark. Your eyes will get used to the gloom." Then he chuckled, "People will say that I was never here," he added, as if sharing a joke.

Paul had to smile. It was as though he weren't here either. As he'd already noticed in Ostia, whenever he returned from a journey, there were always people awaiting him. Always. They were friendly or otherwise, but they were always there. Except for this time, he had to admit. But people knew where he was going to after leaving Iberia. Britannia is a long way off. The news of his departure must have reached Rome, but no one could possibly expect him to come back so quickly. He never had in the past.

"You surprised us all," Shimon said, after Paul remained silent.

"I am sorry, Rabbi, I should have greeted you. I am a bit disenchanted with my last voyage. Have you eaten?"

Paul spoke before thinking. He had no idea if there was any food in the house, of any sort.

Man shall not live by bread alone, but by every word that proceeds out of the mouth of God.

The words reached Paul as though spoken through a veil. He turned, straining his eyes.

"What did you say, Rabbi?" For some reason Paul was getting nervous.

"I have eaten, thank you," Shimon assured him. "There is some *matzah* in the kitchen.

"*Matzah*? But it's not Passover...?" Paul was surprised.

Matzah is a Jewish symbol embodying duality. It is both, the meager sustenance of slaves, and yet it also commemorates the bread the Jews ate when escaping from Egypt. Thus, it is a symbol of liberation.

"It is good bread, Paul. There is also water to quench your thirst."

Paul wondered how could Shimon possibly know that he was thirsty. He hasn't drunk anything since early morning. No wonder he sounded harsh. Paul also wondered if Shimon was suggesting a different kind of liberation altogether.

Paul went to the kitchen, drank deeply from a Roman ewer given to him by one of his disciples, and came back holding a large piece of *matzah*. Once his thirst was sated, he realized that he was also hungry.

Shimon was right. Usually by the time it got so dark, he would be already asleep. No need to light any candles. And by now, his eyes were getting used to the darkness. He could even make out Shimon's features. There seemed to be a slight glow on his face, as if he'd smeared some oil on it. It wasn't hot enough to be perspiration.

Paul wondered why Shimon came to see him, particularly since he was unlikely to be in Rome at this time. For a while they sat in silence, enveloped in the dark stillness of the night. After spending months on the ship rubbing shoulders with soldiers and the crew, Paul found the relative privacy of space, even in the small room, relaxing. Also, not for the first time, he found himself strangely alone. For a moment, even Shimon's presence eluded him.

"Did you think about our last discussion, Paul?"

Paul shook his head; the reality of where he was returned to him abruptly. The walk, the journey, the constant movement of the ship, even the virtual uncertainty he always felt at sea, sapped strength out of his body.

"You have done a great deal for the Lord, Paul. And the Lord has sent me to share with you that which He told me after He has risen."

This brought Paul into sharp awareness of his surroundings. If there was one thing he was jealous of it was the knowledge Yeshûa had imparted to the apostles after His resurrection. They never talked about it, as if it had been given to them in confidence. Suddenly the darkness surrounding him seemed filled with light, though not an earthly light. Not light visible to the eyes, but the light that only knowledge can offer.

Just as suddenly, Paul became agitated.

"Stop!" It came like a thunderclap.

Paul had never heard such power in Shimon's command. He took a deep breath and let it out slowly.

"You must stop. Your mind is racing, hoping to uncover that which is beyond the reach of the mind."

This time Shimon's tone of voice, rather than his words, had a calming effect.

"Stop? I am not travelling any more…"

"Your body is no longer travelling, Paul, your mind is still searching. Whatever you're looking for is already within you. You will not find the Master by standing apart, only by coming in."

"What am I to do, Rabbi?" The plea in his voice was close to resignation.

"Stop," Shimon repeated, this time gently. "Just stop. Don't search for Him far and wide, when He's already right here."

Paul was glad there was darkness around. He didn't want Shimon to see near despair on his face. I tried, he thought, I tried and tried…

"Stop trying, Paul. Just stop…"

Is he reading my thoughts?

For a moment Paul thought that the room was flooded with light. He saw himself sitting within this light. Then he became the light and merged with it to the exclusion of himself. He and the light became one.

He gasped, and the vision was gone.

"He is always within you, Paul. Always."

And then there was silence. For a moment Paul tried to grasp the image of himself within the light, and almost immediately he gave up. That for which he yearned was not of this world. Yet, it was he, it was himself that he saw. But it was also not he. It was that that resided within him. Like… like…

There were no words that Paul could find. Neither in Greek, nor in Latin, nor in Hebrew, nor in Aramaic. And then, as though from a great distance he heard the words he's heard so many times before. Words of assurance, of consolation. Words of Good Cheer.

I am always with you.

For some time Paul sat, silent, no longer searching. He found what he was looking for. After all the journeys which he thought would bring him closer to his quest, the search ended right here. It ended in silence. In peace beyond human understanding.

I am always with you.

Paul turned to share the good news with Shimon. His eyes, already adjusted to the darkness, searched the room. Shimon was nowhere to be seen. Paul was completely alone, yet... yet he also knew beyond the shadow of a doubt, that he'd never be alone again. Never.

And his heart was filled with joy.

The next day Paul wrote more letters. He was resigned in knowledge he could not convey that which was now in his heart, that which cannot really be shared. We already are all one, he mused, how can I tell that to people when I couldn't understand it for so many years myself?

He wrote letters all day. He had to. He had to try, at least; try to help those who were still searching. He knew how painful the search was. How often disheartening. Later, towards dusk, he closed his eyes and just listened. It took only a short time for him to see Shimon.

"Welcome back, my friend," Shimon spoke as though only a moment separated them from having been together.

Paul smiled. He never imagined it would be so easy. So effortless.

"You must slay that which binds you. Then you are free," Shimon said. He, too, was smiling.

"It is like going to heaven, Rabbi..."

"We don't go to heaven, Paul, we return to the place whence we came. To our home."

Paul was on the verge of becoming disappointed, again.

"Only remember the Master's words, Paul. Heaven is within you. It is a state of consciousness. Each man's heaven

is different. We create our heavens. We store our treasures
there, for us to enjoy. Heaven is also a condition of infinite
possibilities, where everything already exists in its potential
form. It is up to us to make it real, for ourselves, in our own
consciousness."

Paul remembered the words he'd heard from one of the
apostles: *whatsoever a man soweth, that shall he also reap.*
Didn't I write something like that in one of my letters? Only I
thought we would reap the results soon, right here, on earth.
But it is not...

"Then why are we here," he interrupted his own
thoughts. "Why did we ever leave the heaven you
described?"

"Life here, in the condition of duality is a great gift. In
heaven we are one. That is what love is—being one. Also in
heaven we cannot be injured. We cannot be harmed. Thus,
we learn slowly. The knowledge gained there, although
seemingly enormous compared to here, on earth, is... you
might say, theoretical. It carries no consequences. We are like
children playing with fire without fear of getting our fingers
burned."

"So we shall always come back to learn, ah... faster?"

"We are the living embodiments of spirit. We can do
whatever we want."

"...but, we choose to return..."

"In order to rise higher."

"So there are many heavens?"

"Yahweh is infinite. There is neither beginning nor end.
In Yahweh we have our being. On earth—our becoming. But
we are all one."

"Yahweh is One."

"And we are the embodiments of Yahweh."

For a timeless instant of infinity, Paul and Shimon shared
that which made them one. They both shed that which kept
them apart. Their bodies. Paul experienced a sense of

incredible lightness. As though he were in a dream, yet he was fully aware of his surroundings. His chimerical eyes were filled with wonder.

He thought of the sky, and in that same instant he found himself suspended high above the ground, smiling at the ocean of stars. His heightened senses allowed him to see countless swirling universes that he'd never imagined existed.

"Yahweh..." he whispered, his lips wide with awe.

"Endless, Infinite..." Shimon nodded at his side.

"Worlds without end..."

And they inhaled the infinity of the universe, recognizing their endless playground. They were like children who were allowed to see a room full of toys for the first time. An infinite playpen of infinite potential.

"Let us stay here," Paul whispered.

And in that moment the universe with all its toys vanished into the penumbra of Paul's room. It was getting gray outside.

Paul sat up to share his wonder with Shimon. Only, once again, he was alone, though in a very different way. Shimon was not there, any more, but for some strange, inexplicable reason, Paul didn't feel alone at all. He would never feel alone again.

"Thank you, Shimon," he whispered, his heart replete with gratitude. "Thank you, Yeshûa."

The Master taught all the apostles the mystery of life, but only after His resurrection. Life eternal? And then Paul understood. While walking this earth, Yeshûa was teaching us how to conduct our condition of becoming. Later, when he shed his physical body, he showed the few chosen ones the mysteries beyond the horizon of physical reality.

Now, Shimon had passed it on to me, Paul mused, enchanted. The wonderful Shimon...

It was getting light enough to write. He had started this letter sometime ago. He sharpened his quill against a stone and dipped it in ink.

Charity suffers long, and is kind; charity envies not; charity vaunts not itself, is not puffed up...
It does not behave itself unseemly, seeks not her own, is not easily provoked, thinks no evil...

After a moment he leaned back. There was so much more. So much...

And what of the empire? What of the empire for Yeshûa?

It was a cool, comfortable night. A fresh breeze coming from the West ruffled his papers. Yet, suddenly, he began perspiring. He wiped his forehead with his sleeve. Then he shrugged. Looking back had given him ample evidence that he'd been given enormous powers of persuasion. He'd used them to the full. He organized the incipient churches as a general would organize his army. He developed a hierarchy, demanded obedience, appointed his successors.

My successors?

He shrugged again.

He believed in what he was preaching. Was it too late? Had he planted the desire for an earthly empire in too many minds? Will the seed of an empire here and now grow in peoples' minds, hearts, eradicating Peter's image?

Yeshûa's image?

Let the dead bury the dead, he remembered Ananias telling him. That's what He'd said. At least, Ananias insisted He'd said so.

Paul looked down at the letter he was writing.

That's all there is, he thought. Love. It's all about love. Love that makes us all one. The unifying force. Charity. How can that be?

He picked up the quill. Was he too late...

Rejoices not in iniquity, but rejoices in the truth:

Bears all things, believes all things, hopes all things, endures all...

He couldn't write. His hand was trembling too much.

Sometime later, Paul tried, for the last time, to imagine a Kingdom, a Kingdom of Yeshûa right here, on earth. Only now he realized that it didn't make sense. He knew that the Kingdom really was not of this world. Nor did his dreams of an empire make any sense, either. The whole Kingdom, the whole of the Empire already was here. It was whirling countless universes within the hearts of all who could only stop. Stop and listen. Even for a moment.

Infinite, endless, universes, with neither beginning nor end.

Like Yahweh.

Paul was so lost in his thoughts that he hasn't heard the unmistakable sound of a troop of soldiers marching, in step, along the paved road. He'd heard them many times before, but his mind was elsewhere. Moments later, there was a knock. Opening the door, he saw a contingent of soldiers on his doorstep. Two of them came in and took Paul by both arms.

"In the name of Nero, you are under arrest."

And they took him away.

The soldiers couldn't understand why, for some inexplicable reason, Paul kept smiling. Being arrested by Nero's orders, especially of late, did not bode good fortune. Particularly, if you were a Christian.

"The fool thinks he'll get away with it because he's a Roman citizen," one centurion sneered. He didn't like Christians. They were a humble lot. No pride in them. No pride at all.

They walked in step, with only Paul missing the beat.

Later, the same centurion looked at Paul and shrugged. Paul didn't stop smiling even when the soldier pushed him harshly onto the ground of the small, dark cell.

"I am coming home," Paul whispered. "I am coming home..." And he continued to smile.

***

25

NERO

I t wasn't easy being an Emperor. Not even with the greatest army the world has ever known. What made it hard were not the wars, the constant rebellions that had to be squashed like vermin under his foot. He had excellent generals for that. No. What needed care was Rome itself. As the center of the world it had to be more than it was.

"Am I the only one who understands that?"

The Emperor would ask this question *urbi et orbi*. No one ever knew how to answer this question. Damned if you said yes, damned if you said no. It was best to look attentive and say nothing.

Poor, poor, Nero.

Nero, as so often in the past, was feeling sorry for himself. He almost reached for his lyre to compose a sonnet, or at least an ode, in praise of the only Emperor who cared.

Nero never expected to become an Emperor. His uncle, Caligula, had enough time to produce an heir of his own. He even exiled Nero's mother, Agrippina, after her husband's death. Not that Nero blamed him for that—she pushed her nose into men's business all too often. Still, Caligula also ceased his inheritance and sent him out to be raised by his aunt, Lepida, Claudius's third wife. That wasn't nice.

"It is true that my father, Gnaeus Domitius Ahenobarbus they called him..." he threw in, in case someone was ignorant of his heritage. "It was true that daddy eliminated a few inconvenient people and was a cheat who was charged by

Emperor Tiberius with treason, adultery and incest. We all make mistakes, don't we?"

'Eliminated' was a euphemism for murdered. For a murder that was deemed necessary—for the good of Rome.

"Well, don't we?" Nero repeated, a supercilious smile playing about his fat lips.

If you were a member of Nero's entourage, like Otho, or Nerve, or even Vespasian, you would be wise not to answer this question either.

Nero always thought of himself as being very forgiving. Even so, just then, he felt a slight shiver running down his back. He shrugged, again. He did a lot of shrugging lately. Daddy was not always easy, he thought. And then he sighed. He did a lot of that, too.

"May Jupiter protect me from my family," he murmured.

No, it hasn't been easy.

But Fortuna Primigenia, fixed his destiny at birth. The goddess of fate was, above all, fair. And as the daughter of Jupiter she had more power than any mortal. Including his uncle. She wielded more power than anybody.

Except for Nero, of course, the Emperor.

Except for Nero Claudius Caesar Augustus Germanicus. There. The Emperor of the Roman Empire. The Emperor of the World.

Some said that he only cared about Rome itself. He denied that.

"It is not that I don't love my Empire," he declared, "it is just that I love Rome more!" For Nero, Rome was the Empire. The only Empire that really mattered.

They all got the message. They've been warned. They understood. Nero Claudius... and so on and so forth, had a job to do. And a job he would do. For the glory of Rome.

He had to start building Rome again. Not rebuilding, but building it from scratch. In a different location? No. That wouldn't do. So to do that, he'd have to get rid of the riff-raff; get rid of the squatters; the dilapidating wooden shacks—all stacked one next to another, all full of vermin. Full of rabble that did not deserve to be in Rome.

Wooden shacks. Ha!

Rome will shine the world over as the city of noble marble. Breccia, Botticino, Golden Sapphire, Travertine… And granite, of course. All noble materials. All Roman stone…

Rome is for the Romans!

This time he did reach for his gold-leafed lyre and seemed determined to ejaculate rhyming couplets to his eternal glory. And the glory of Rome, of course. This he usually accompanied with most unholy noises by strumming its strings.

Roma, Roma… Rooomaaa…

He smashed the lyre against the wall. For the life of him he couldn't find a word to rhyme with 'Roma'.

Nero didn't like the Rome that his predecessors had built. Or allowed to happen. Without planning, without organization. He, Nero, was a poet. An artist. Not just on his lyre, or as demonstrated by his brilliant acting, or even at driving a chariot with ten horses at the Olympic Games. No. Art was in his blood. The Rome he would build would be a monument to humanity. To the whole world.

To his name.

A good way to start would be to clear the streets of what shouldn't have been there to start with. As this idea percolated into his mind through the diffusion of self-centered minutia, his face began to display a beatific smile. Nero was definitely inspired. He knew exactly how to start. Too many of those shacks were occupied by Christians, by Jews that weren't even Roman citizens.

"Arrest all Christians," he proclaimed. "They have never produced anything of value. Anything lasting or to the glory of Rome. Arrest them all."

Two of his secretaries hiding behind the columns, yet at the ready for his every call, made notes. Arrest all Christians, they wrote; then rushed to pass on the orders.

The remaining aid, Epaphroditus, a Stoic by nature and conviction and a secretary to Nero by profession, the one who knew Nero best, stayed behind. He sighed deeply, then walked slowly to the Emperor and handed him a brand new lyre. He knew his master would be in need of one. And then he walked as far away as he dared to hide from the hideous noise that was about to reverberate throughout the palace.

Paul was in the first sweep of arrests. He had no idea why he was arrested—after all he'd been officially released on his own cognizance, but, with Nero, one never knew. At least now, with all the other Christians lumped together, he could continue to preach. To deepen their faith.

For a moment Paul wondered if he ought to tell his brethren about what Shimon had told him. Would they understand? Or would they think that he was attempting to create a new sect to compete with… with what? There were too many offspring Jewish sects already.

"With what I've created myself?" he mused, a sad smile, the smile he carried so often on his face since Shimon had visited him in Rome. No, the smile wasn't sad. It was a smile of acceptance. Of an inner peace?

"Sorry… With what Yeshûa has created through me?" he corrected, feeling slightly ashamed.

He did visit me, didn't he? Sometimes Paul still wondered if any of that recollection was real. What was reality, anyway? Isn't it whatever we create in our mind? He shook his head.

During all these years, Paul didn't understand the inner teaching himself. What chance would they have? They might lose what little faith he was able to instill in them. People

were weak. Even as he was. Until that night with Shimon...
He had been there, hadn't he?

"Would people understand that heaven is here and now,
and all they needed was a change of heart?"

Paul shrugged.

For them heaven was a place in the hereafter. A place
they'd go to, eventually, one day, after... well, after they
died. It made the prospect of death much easier. Or living in
poverty—that made it easier, too. Or helping one another,
which was so necessary these days.

Nero was helpless against them. Being a Christian meant
just waiting to go to heaven. Sure, you ought to accumulate
good deeds, but you didn't expect any reward right now. It
was like working on credit, with interest accumulating in the
hereafter. For later. For ever?

That's what they thought.

They weren't that far out...

It wouldn't do to tell them what Shimon had told him:
that after this life, they'd come back, again and again, to
continue in their becoming. The fact that the prophets of old
came back, now and then, was another story. They were the
prophets. Even His own closest disciples thought that
Yeshûa, the Master Himself, might be Elijah, or some other
reincarnation. Paul tried to remember. Ah yes. It was in
Caesarea Philippi...

"Who do people say I am?" He'd asked them.

"John the Baptist, or Elijah or Jeremiah or one of the
prophets..." they replied. They had no idea either.

Only Shimon knew. It always came back to Shimon.
"You are the Messiah, the son of the Living God," he'd
replied. Shimon knew.

And now I also know... there was that smile again. Not
just I hope, or feel—I know. I know what is the saving grace.
It is knowledge. It is real knowledge of who you are. Did He
not say that we are all children of the Most High? Yeshûa

knew it. King David knew it. Didn't he say, Ye are gods? And then... you are all sons of the Most High.

All of us... if we do His will.

Only they all forgot. So many years... No one else knew it until Yeshûa reminded a few of them after He'd risen. He'd also mentioned it before but it had fallen on deaf ears. If it hadn't been for that, we wouldn't know it to this day. We would know the words but not understand them. The knowledge would die, with Yeshûa and King David. Forever?

And even now there is no way I know how to explain it to them. To the brethren. To my friends. To the people with whom I worked so hard to give the Good News.

And now?

And now I can't take their beliefs away from them. Should Nero murder any one of us, at least they'd believe that they were on the way to heaven. On the way to everlasting happiness. Everlasting joy for having given their life for the Christ.

After all, it was I who taught them that. And it was why they became Christians.

What would Shimon do?

Where was Shimon anyway? Paul hasn't seen him since that night when he'd visited him in his house.

What would he do?

Paul wished he'd listened more to what others had said about Shimon's preaching. It was just that their work kept them many leagues apart. Often thousands of leagues.

It was at this moment that Paul heard them singing. The Christians sat together, against one stone wall, huddled and yet seemingly relaxed—and they started singing. They must have been Jews. Paul remembered *Tehillîm*, the songs of praise. As an ex-Pharisee, he remembered most of the Book of Psalms by heart. They were songs expressing happiness. How come, he wondered? They are not privy to the secret knowledge that Shimon shared with him, yet they sound happy. They sound as though they were looking forward to going home. Not coming back, but going, nevertheless. Was there really such a difference?

And now they were singing *Shir Lashalom*. The Song of Peace. Was there really so much peace in their hearts? And then Paul remembered Shimon. And he smiled.

Nero defined exactly where the new Rome should stand. He delineated the new, wide streets, the plazas for the Imperial Legions to march, the places and palaces for arts and entertainment. And sculptures, of course. Lots of sculptures. Preferably of himself. Of Emperor Nero.

He did a thorough job.

"Why, some of our Provinces have better amphitheaters than Rome has!" he spoke out, waving his arms in frustration. "All we've got is a Circus," he added sadly. He was close to tears.

All he needed now was a way to clear the way for his vision to come true. He needed space and a way to induce people to leave the designated area. Only, there were just too many of them. They were clustered together like a herd of wild animals.

His vision was as vast as were his needs. All land around the Forum, around the Temple of Jupiter and, of course, down to the Circus Maximus where he'd raced chariots himself, had to be cleared of all obstructions for his dream to come true. The three buildings would be spared, of course; after all, they were structures worthy of Rome, but the rest?

And then he had it.

With only the major buildings and temples having been built of stone, the rest of the wooden shacks would serve as kindling for the great fire. A cleansing fire. A fire of purification?

The fire would be an offering to the gods. After all, Nero was a deeply religious man. Almost a god himself. Almost.

He would help those who would lose their homes unwittingly, but Rome had to come first.

The rest was in the hands of Vulcan.

"We, Romans, can start the fire, but only Vulcan can control it," he murmured, divine sparks dancing in his eyes. And again he reached out for his lyre. This time the words and the notes flowed directly from Erato. He wiped a tear of joy at the thought of his Master Plan. The gods were with him. They inspired him.

Nevertheless, Nero made a mental note to make a substantial offering during the next Vulcanalia of live fish and small animals. Vulcan seemed to favour them.

Six of his most trusted men moved into positions on the southeast corner of the city. They had instructions to start the fire halfway between the densely populated Esquiline and Aventine Hills. That would minimize the damage, and yet clear enough land for the Grand Plan to come forth.

Nero was becoming impatient.

They already waited a whole week for the propitious wind to blow from southeast, to cut a clear path towards the Forum. Then it would stop on the Tiber River and the work could begin.

At long last, the wind blew from the southeast. Nero was sorry to miss what would surely be a grandiose spectacle. He saw it in his mind's eye. Was he not a great artist? Yes, he saw it… a most splendid sight, worthy of Vulcan himself.

Yet Emperors have their responsibilities. If he were to rebuild Rome, he had to remain innocent of any wrongdoing.

It was getting dark.

It wouldn't take long, now. It had to be done at night—the artist in him demanded that. And then gods inspired him once again. On the spur of the moment, he took his wife and made for his villa in Antium, overlooking the blue Mediterranean. He drove the chariot himself. Four horses and his wife. The horses were in front, of course. In less then two hours he gave the reins to his henchmen. The palace was always ready to receive him at a moment's notice. After all, he was the Emperor, and no one, no one ever dared to forget that.

Nero knew that his plan was brilliant. His only regret was that he couldn't share it with anyone. Even the six most trusted men he'd sent to set the spark in six different places, all southeast of the center of Rome, would meet with unfortunate accidents within the next four hours. He used only officers, men he could trust to keep quiet. Nevertheless, just to play it safe, other centurions had already been dispatched to cut the arsonists' throats in punishment for their dastardly deed.

Time dragged.

How he wished he could be there, looking at Rome burning, from up close. He couldn't wait for the evening. He bit his fingers. Then his nails. Then his knuckles.

He felt like biting.

The moment it turned dark he went out onto the wide southern raised terrace, which opened views to both east and west. The night dragged on, and on, until midnight. He sniffed the air. Not yet, he thought. Soon. Would he smell it from here? The wind blew from the right direction; it should carry it. It wasn't far. The sweet smell of success...

He had to wait long.

"*Vino!*" he rasped. His throat felt dry.

He watched the moon casting shadows on the hill to his left. He drank three chalices and still felt thirst squeezing his throat.

And then he caught his breath.

Far, far away, a little to his left, he saw a strange light growing in intensity even as he looked. It seemed as though the sun was rising early that night. Some little time after midnight? Nero felt elated. His right arm stretched out and immediately a beautiful slave placed a lyre in his hand. The slaves knew his habits, his gestures. They had to—so as to stay alive.

In order to improve his popularity, Nero had begun singing in public, in Neapolis, in 64 A.D.. A few years later he still hadn't become any more popular, but, at least, on his private terrace, he had become a seasoned performer.

His fingers caressed the gilt instrument, then struck the strings. First gently, then with renewed force. He thought of himself as a true virtuoso. After all, nobody, but nobody, has ever denied it. His lips curled in a peculiar smile and then a sound came from his throat reminiscent of a dog howling.

Nero was singing.

Another slave, lithe, beautiful, raised the hem of her dress and began dancing. He didn't even glance at her. His eyes were riveted towards the east, his nose sucking air to feel his Great Plan coming into manifestation.

And then he threw his head back and laughed.

"They will never know," he snorted. "They might suspect, but they will never know!"

He thought himself lucky. He felt kinship with Romulus. He, Nero, also had to kill the old city even as Romulus had to kill Remus. Romulus would be proud of him.

Roma, Caput Mundi, the City on the Seven Hills...

He sang, his voice filled with euphoria, with images of the future. He was witnessing the rebirthing pains of the Eternal City.

His lips curled even more as he began to compose an air to the gracious god Vulcan.

***

26

THE BANE

It started with the arrests. No one knew why or wherefore the Christians were being arrested. It had begun with just the Jews, though two days later the Romans of Christian persuasion were also arrested. Still later it seemed that only some parts of the city had been cleared of Christians, while in other parts they were left alone. For how long they wondered?

Soon, most of the streets between the Esquiline and the Aventine Hills were quite empty of people. None of this made any sense. At least, not to the Christians. Of course, there were no houses left there to live in. All they had was a piece of land on which to pitch a tent. And now, not even that.

Even non-Christians weren't sure of their ground. No one was. And there was danger in the air.

"The gods must be angry," they said. No one thought of Nero. Not yet.

And then came the fire. It spread quickly, much quicker than anyone could have expected. Although local fires happened in Rome quite often, no one had expected a fire of such magnitude. This fire seemed to have started in the east end, and spread with amazing speed towards the center. The wind blew the sparks that ignited the dry wood of the small wooden dwellings—most of them previously occupied by

Christians. Small insignificant dwellings occupied by small, insignificant people, who never did anyone any harm.

The fire burned, smouldered, and filled the air with sparks and a pungent stench for six days. It completely destroyed the center of Rome.

Why was it that the poorest of the poor always gravitate towards the center of every city? No one knew. Such is the nature of man. Perhaps they want to be in the center of things that seems so unattainable to them? Or perhaps they want to observe, or to take part, vicariously, in the life of others. Once Rome was a Republic where all people were equal. Perhaps the poor wanted to watch those who were more equal than others? More equal than they were? Perhaps it gave them a sense of belonging.

No one knew.

No one knew how the fire had started, either. Surely, someone had to be blamed?

By noon of the seventh day, Nero drove back from his villa on the coast. He was always proud of his acting ability. On arrival in Rome, his face assumed a studious image of great concern.

We are not like dictators, the heathen to the east or the north, or anywhere outside the borders of the Empire, he mused. We, Romans, were born of a Republic. Well, we were, until we became an empire. We must convince our citizens that what we are doing is for their own good; that we are doing things on their behalf.

"We must help people who lost everything," he declared, making sure that a good number of citizens had heard him. He really suffered from a deep need of being popular. He needed to be loved.

"We must help them!" he almost shouted, his bleary eyes travelling, with great concern, over the still smouldering embers. He looked magnificent in his full battle regalia. He had to use both hands to control the horses, which objected to the smoke still drifting from the ruins. But from his chariot he stood head and shoulders above all others.

Later that day, surrounded by only a few choice centurions—hardly his usual Imperial Guard of hundreds—he went meandering, on foot, among the cooler remains of Rome.

"What care, what concern. Viva Emperor Nero!" people exclaimed.

A handful of farthings had been thrown in their general direction. Still, there were not many people. Most had been arrested, many were dead, and some had escaped with their lives. But those few that remained took up the chant:

Viva Emperor!
Viva Emperor Nero!

They love me, he thought. They really love me.

The shouts soon ceased. Apparently, during the last six days, the wind hadn't quite cooperated. Fed by the abundance of fuel it spread at an alarming rate, reaching far into both the Esquiline and the Aventine Hills. What came to Nero as even a bigger shock was that the fire travelled uphill to raze *Collis Capitolinus* and even *Collis Palatinus*, both hills, as well as the other two, that had previously been densely populated. At least from those farther away from the source of fire, more people had a chance to escape with their lives.

Nero's thoughts travelled along slightly different lines.

So far so good, he thought, the more land the better. But his eyes also showed a shadow of concern. There was a lot more damage than he'd ever imagined there would be.

I must find someone to blame, he mused. Quickly!

What would Agrippina say? Nero was afraid of his mother but didn't have the courage to eliminate her himself. She often had some good ideas, however.

He raised his eyes to Jupiter. The next moment a beatific smile lightened his frazzled features. He had it. By the grace of goddess Minerva, or Athena, or whatever her name... he had the answer from the goddess of wisdom. For a moment he was annoyed at the Greeks for confusing him.

"Who better than the Christians?" he asked himself, almost out loud. He forgot he had them arrested already. He wanted to scream his answer, to share it. He couldn't. It wouldn't be politically wise. At least, not yet. But the Christians were the obvious answer. Most Romans hated them. Weren't they the troublemakers who denied Roman gods their dues?

"I shall fasten all guilt to them and devise the most exquisite tortures on those who are already hated for their abominations. On Christians!" This time he had spoken out loud.

Alas, this time he was alone, stamping out the smoke from some debris. His entourage stayed back to protect their immaculate sandals. Nero had actually found a piece of wood that was still making halfhearted attempts to smoulder. He was rather proud of himself.

"By Jupiter," he growled, even louder. "By Jupiter, they will pay!"

He felt better already. What made him tired were the constant decisions he had to make. It wasn't easy.

The Christians continued singing. There was little else for them to do. They were all clustered against one end of the elongated rectangle with oval ends, inside the Circus Maximus. The fire passed them by, to the north of the arena. They were all safe.

"Praised be the Lord!" they sung. Loud. Perhaps, to cheer themselves up?

Their voices resounded, bounced off the bleachers, soon to be filled with tribunes and ordinary people. Not that any Romans were ordinary. Romans were noble. The choicest in the world. For now, voices of the Christians reverberated in the air loaded with expectation. None had any idea why they were there. None wanted to know. They refused to think.

Paul, sitting on the sand, his back against the solid stone wall that surrounded the whole arena, watched them with a mixture of admiration and concern. Those people, he thought, have no idea what they are doing. He had a vision last night of what was in store for them. A vision, or a dream, he could no longer tell them apart. He saw blood on the sand. Blood everywhere. Including his own. By now he was resigned— the others were still living in hope.

For them, the truth would be too terrible to accept. He told them to love one another. To love their enemies.

To love their enemies? It will not be easy, he mused.

Then Paul's eyes travelled over the length and width of the arena. More than two thousand feet long and four hundred feet wide it was the largest chariot racing stadium, and by far the largest mass entertainment venue in the Empire. It had been built for *populus Romanus* and the gods. All the gods— Romans were careful not to offend anyone. Large religious festivals were held there annually. Smaller festivities counted up to fifty-seven in a single year. It was a popular place with the Roman people.

Paul sighed heavily.

And now this, he mused, his heart in a knot of pain. His people, his brethren, were all innocent—every single one of them. They were the innocent lambs here to be offered as sacrifice. To Roman gods? To Roman people?

Here and there, in groups of three or four, some brethren would kneel down and pray. He taught them to do so. A vain prayer, he thought. A vain prayer.

Whatsoever you ask in my name...

Paul remembered the words. Ananias had told him of the Master's promise, so many years ago; and later, many years later, Shimon had explained their meaning. In my name, the Master had said. In my name. In my nature. And my nature, He'd said, is that of spirit, of that which cannot be hurt, or injured in any way. It was too late to tell them, even if they could understand. It took more than thirty years before I understood, and only because Shimon took pity on me. He must have seen what was coming; what was in store for us all in Rome. For them? For them it was too late. Unless...

Unless Yeshûa takes pity on them.

From the top of the bleachers, Nero regarded the same group of people. Were there enough of them, he wondered? He wanted a real show. A classic. A festival that would go down in history. Even as he watched from above, some groups were being led away to the inner holding areas for questioning. They wouldn't be let out into the open area again; not until the games began. It was better that way. They would enjoy the surprise.

For now, Nero kept those below in ignorance. Once they were questioned, they might begin to suspect something. They might rebel or try to escape.

He preferred peaceful, obedient actors. For now, he had to gather evidence to present it to his people. Romans deserved to know the reason for the fire. A little torture, he knew, would go a long way to procure a requisite number of confessions. He suspected that many of them, those confessing to setting the fire, weren't even Christians. Still, it was all for the greater good.

For the good of Rome.

Once a convincing number of confessions of guilt was announced, always *urbi et orbi*, to the whole city and to the whole world, the rest of the Christians would be judged guilty by association. Perfectly reasonable assumption, Nero thought. He liked to be fair to his people.

He allowed himself a puerile chuckle. He hadn't had such fun in a long time. He'd already issued instructions to bring to the Circus wild dogs, and keep them starving. Also some big cats—like lions or panthers. The bigger the better.

As many as they could get. That too was his mother's idea. He was beginning to like her. Maybe he'll spare her life, after all. If only she wouldn't butt in so often.

Luckily, the Circus had a good supply of leopards and bears and even elephants, although those last would hardly be needed; not until it was time to cart away the corpses.

Nero was looking forward to tomorrow, or the day after. Or as soon as they could gather enough people, the games would start. Then he spun on his heel and walked quickly away. That stupid singing was getting on his nerves.

A lot of people had run away from Rome. They had to be brought back. Nero knew he'd need a lot of labour force. Labour of thousands—to build the new Rome. There had to be a way to show them that it was safe to return.

Once again, it was his mother, dear Agrippina the Younger, who'd given him the idea. His friends, particularly Seneca, warned him against her, but she was proving to be all right. It seemed that brains run in the family. And, after all, he could always have her killed later.

So there. All was well.

Nero issued an order to drive piles into the ground on all roads leading to Rome, and attach Christians to them.

"Then," he told the men chosen to carry out the task, "you will wrap them in thick cloth and douse them with oil. When darkness comes, you will set them afire to show those who ran away that it was safe to come back."

There. He'd taken step one. Now for step two.

He had to take peoples' mind away from their tragedies. He announced festivities. They would take place in Circus Maximus. The Christians would perform. He knew that the Romans liked theater. They would come to watch in droves.

They did come, but only a week later. They seemed more attracted by the aftermath of the fire, than by the promise of games. The delay was expensive and inconvenient. The Circus had to cancel the practice of the charioteers for a whole week. Also the Christians had to be fed, and be given some water. They had to be kept alive, a little longer, and then show some spunk. Some vitality. It would be no fun watching them otherwise.

The bleachers began to fill a little after midday. Circus Maximum was large. It could hold easily some 150,000 spectators. Probably more than Rome could boast, right now. No matter, the show would be worthy of Rome. Worthy of Nero. The Emperor.

He picked up his lyre.

"Let the games begin," he intoned.

There was an air of expectation. Then, the trumpets sounded. The trumpeters were stationed on both sides of the lengthy arena, equidistance from each other. On command, they rose to their feet and blew their instruments in perfect unison. Then, lowering their arms, they repeated the Emperor's words in loud, penetrating voice.

LET THE GAMES BEGIN!

The audience hushed. When silence returned to the arena, the trumpeters once again rose to their feet. Also, once again, they spoke in perfect unison, sounding as though a single person was speaking.

In the name of Nero Claudius Caesar Augustus Germanicus, the Illustrious and Benevolent Emperor of All Rome, let it be known that, after extensive questioning and research by the Imperial Guard of our beloved Emperor, the Christians living amongst us as our guests, have mocked our grace and munificence by setting fire to our beloved city. Furthermore, while admitting to having started this reprehensible deed, they have offered neither reason nor excuse for their shameful and inexcusable act. Under the circumstances, I ask the citizens of Rome to pass judgment over them at this time.

There was more, but this was the essence of the speech, which the ten speakers conveyed to the remaining citizens of Rome, in Nero's name. In the meantime, the beloved Emperor was leaning against a smooth marble column, a lyre in his hand, shedding tears over his beloved city.

It wasn't easy.

This announcement was followed by more fanfare from the ten trumpeters, which was soon drowned out by the shouts of "death to the Christians", while some one hundred and fifty thousand thumbs were raised into the air, performed a circular motion as though to gather speed, and descended downwards towards the earth. The judgment had been passed, as expected.

Almost immediately after this momentous decision, five groups of about ten Christians in each bunch were let into the arena along its whole length. The people, the announced performers of the games—looking emaciated but still cheerful—wandered about on the pristine sand, not knowing what has been expected of them. No one told them anything.

"Just go and enjoy yourselves," some centurions told them, their grim faces twisted in peculiar smiles.

Some of the soldiers had nothing to do with the Imperial Guard. They were regular army. They didn't like what they suspected their Emperor had devised to entertain his people.

"Just go," others added, a vicious smile showing their true feelings. Then they pushed the Christians into the arena at the point of their short Roman swords.

A roar of approval swept the bleachers. Everyone had first class seats. And then came the moment they'd all been waiting for. Even as the iron gates on both sides of the arena had been lifted and a mass of angry dogs ran into the main area, Romans rose to their feet. Soon the sand showed red splotches of blood. Human blood.

The crowd roared.

Viva Emperor Nero!

The gracious Nero struck another chord on his lyre. He was truly inspired today.

"My people," he crooned, "they love me…"

And then another roar from one hundred and fifty thousand throats filled the air. When the gates opened again, a dozen leopards entered the arena. They, too, had been starved for a few days. They were also thirsty. When the roar stopped, fewer than a dozen people were still singing. Their faces were filled with joy at the thought of going home.

***

27

THE END OF THE BEGINNING

The carnage went on for many months. Every time Circus Maximus was filled to the last seat. The crowds came from far and wide, and were ecstatic. Each time Nero himself greeted the *populus*, enhancing the occasions with his noble presence. Each time Nero's throat needed to be repeatedly refreshed with red wine, as red as the blood now mixed abundantly with the sand below him. He needed wine to be able to continue singing immortal odes to Rome, to the gods, and finally, humbly, to himself. More than once he wiped off tears of elation at the wonderful shows he's been inspired to produce for his people. In his mind he saw new Rome, new splendid buildings, shimmering in white marble, to his eternal glory.

"... *la vita pulchra est... la vita bella...*" his voice, now throaty and fairly drunk, intoned for the tenth time.

"...*la vita bella...*"

People had also been given ample barrels of wine. When local vineyards dried up they reached out to Umbria, then Tuscany and Mache, Abruzzi and Molise, finally to Campania and Basilicata and Calabria. And when those cellars ran dry, Nero sent ships to Sicily.

He looked after his people well.

And outside the walls of Circus Maximus, slowly, but slowly, Rome grew.

And people learned fast. They dipped their own chalices, or even hands cupped together, and splattered their mouths and faces with red wine in wild abandon.

"*...la vita pulchra est...*" they picked up the chant. "*La vita pulchra est!*"

Life is beautiful!

What else could they have hoped for? What more could they have asked? Blood, song and plenty of wine. Was not life beautiful?

Each time the show ended when the well-fed animals were slowly enticed to return to their pens behind the iron grills. Then the elephants dragged the corpses scattered haphazardly all over the once yellow and now red sand. Ropes were tied to human legs and thrown to handlers seated on the elephants in elaborate *haudahs* imported from the Far East, designed for that purpose. Soon the arena was cleared of bodies. Body parts were collected into baskets and cleared by guards alone, to be fed to animals between the games. Nothing was wasted.

Two or three drinks later the arena was cleared. Until the next time. Each time fewer Christians were brought out and thrown to the wild beasts. Each time, fewer of them...

They were beginning to run out of Christians.

But it remained great fun, and Nero still needed more workers.

Tempus fugit.

Time flies. It went on, inexorably, and the rebuilding process had hardly begun.

Circus Maximus was used regularly to amuse the people of Rome. It had to be. In order to gain sufficient labour force to rebuild Rome, people had to be entertained. They had to be drawn, attracted from the outer limits of the Empire.

On specific order from the Emperor, all ships were directed to bring workers to Rome. Slaves or free men. No matter. From far and wide.

Shimon took advantage of one such opportunity. He looked, and was, too old to be a construction worker, but he had considerable experience as a fisherman, and offered his services to feed those coming from afar by providing them with fresh fish. It worked. Within three months he landed in Rome.

He didn't come to Rome to preach. Paul has done a great job of that. He came to Rome to strengthen people's resolve. It was growing thin. After all, for many just a few months have passed since they first heard the Good News. Their faith had not yet taken deep roots. Shimon wondered how he might help them. How he might deepen their faith. Not by dying in the Circus Maximus, but by making their life more abundant.

He didn't preach openly. He laboured in secret.

He went from house to house, pleading, persuading, and blessing the Believers' strength. He reached farther and farther out, farther than Nero's men, to find Christians who were still awaiting miracles. And then, slowly, very slowly, the periphery of Rome also began to run out of Christians. They seem to have disappeared.

My work here is done, thought Shimon.

"Lord," he asked, "what would you have me do?"

Yet the festivities went on. They supplemented the butchery with gladiators. Blood is blood by any other name.

Shimon prayed all night, and then decided that he'd do more good alive than dead. So many people still haven't heard the Word. And of late, Paul was nowhere to be seen. Some said that he'd been arrested with the others. No one knew if he was still alive. And so many have died. Shimon needed to go farther out, away from Rome, and spread the Word.

So many people…

Tired, dejected, he bid farewell to the few friends who remained in hiding in the few wooden shacks that escaped the fire on the outskirts of Rome. What little he owned, he carried with him in one hand—mostly a little food and some water. He had no idea where he was going. He knew the Lord would lead him wherever the need was greatest. Wherever he could do the most good. He took Via Ardeatina, which led him directly towards Via Appia. He was alone on the road. People were afraid to wander about. Too many soldiers were looking for cheap labour—forced, if need be, or to gather the rest of the Christians for Nero's games.

Shimon prayed as he walked, until his legs wouldn't carry him any farther. He found a shaded spot under a tree that would support his back. He closed his eyes, exhausted. He had no idea what tomorrow might bring, but today he was reaching the end of his strength. He was not a young man any more. He has served the Lord for a long time. Surely, he deserved a little rest? Yes, surely he deserved a rest...

And then he saw Him.

"Lord, where are you going?" Shimon asked, surprised.

"I am going to Rome, to be crucified again," Shimon heard, and then the vision was gone.

Shimon opened his eyes but could see no one. And yet, there and then he knew exactly what he must do to get the rest he yearned for.

Yet, another surprise was still awaiting him.

For at least five hundred years, it has been forbidden to bury people inside the walls of Rome. For miles and miles along Via Appia, tunnels had been cut into the tufa, the soft, highly porous rock, which only hardened when exposed to the air. Side branches and niches were cut from the main tunnels for individual burial sites, for both Christians and pagans, although the latter soon joined the brotherhood of Believers.

Many burial places had been prepared in advance for members of the families that settled in and around Rome. And in the meantime, since Emperor Nero began his holocaust, Christians found the tunnels, the catacombs, ideal hiding places. There were literally thousands of them in the tunnels that stretched for miles.

And, they soon realized that soldiers were afraid to enter the domain of the dead. There were whispers about vengeful ghosts and demons.

It is here, at the entry of one such tunnel that Christians found Shimon, lying down on his back, seemingly in a daze. When he came to, they did their best to persuade him to join them in their hiding places. They offered him food and water and shelter. Some, among the older Christians, even remembered Shimon from years ago.

But Shimon's mind was made up.

The next day he was back in Rome. He walked up to the group of Christians being taken to Circus Maximus. They looked scared. They were new Christians, like babes in need of a mother.

"I, too, am one of them," he told the centurion. "Don't I deserve to be freed?"

"Fool!" the centurion sneered, but grabbed Shimon by the collar and tied his neck to the rope binding others. Then he looked at him again.

"Aren't you a Jew?" The soldier was hoping for a reward. Jews were scarce in Rome these days. Not many were left any more.

That same day Shimon met many friends among the prisoners. He spread cheer among them. Slowly, very slowly they understood. As slowly fear was leaving their faces. Like those first brought in—those who already knew the Lord. Shimon's certainty grew now that his own journey was coming to an end.

That very evening he and the soldier who commandeered him were both rewarded. The soldier got a whole silver denarius for bringing in Shimon. They saw how the other Christians regard him. The Commander, too, heard about him and decided to kill him as an example to others. To show them that their Master had no power in Rome. These Christians were altogether too placid. Not enough drama in the arena. People were getting bored.

"Aren't you Pétrus, the Rock?" one centurion asked with a sneer, as they led him out into the arena.

They crucified Shimon in the middle of the arena and left him there, for others to see him the next day. It was a Roman custom to grant a dying man his last wish. For some reason, Shimon asked to be crucified upside down.

"I am not worthy to die as He did," he murmured.

Needless to say, the vast majority of Christians, or Jews for that matter, had never been asked about their particular preference. For some reason, which no one seemed to explain, in Shimon's case they obliged, with hardly a chuckle between them. It wouldn't have been polite.

De gustibus non est disputandum, they said.

Then they stood back and laughed.

The trumpeters rose to their feet. After a brief fanfare, the ten men stationed along the bleachers made another announcement. The games were nearly over. About twenty Christians had been torn to shreds. Nero thought that a pity. Some of them looked strong enough to be workers. He needed more men. At the same time he'd lose the men he had, if he didn't entertain them.

It wasn't easy.

By then, the games have been going on for four months. Originally once a week, then every second, and soon he might have to space them even farther apart. They were really running out of Christians. Or Jews. Or anybody willing to provide entertainment. Jupiter only knows where they all disappeared.

The last week or two, the gamekeepers used only thirty Christians, six in each group along the length of the stadium. It wasn't much but, it was the best they could do. If they lost more, too early, there would be none left for later. And building new, eternal Rome would take a long time.

Nero issued orders to look for Christians from Calabria to Rubicon. Farther if they had to. It took time.

"Bring me Christians," he screamed. "Is my Empire not large enough?"

He took to screaming lately. It didn't do his singing voice much good. On the other hand, in his case, it didn't do it much harm, either.

Nero was beginning to find the games boring himself. And then his personal entourage promised him a surprise. Not before, but after the usual show. After the arena was cleared of corpses.

Without warning, the fanfares blared again. People looked up in surprise, as did Nero. Then the five speakers made the announcement.

And now, for your lasting pleasure, Emperor Nero offers you the leader of those that committed the crimes against Rome. His crime is so much greater… he is a treacherous citizen or Rome!

Hush followed, all waiting to hear who was the scoundrel who burned their beloved city. The announcement was preceded by another blast from the trumpets. Then came the name:

Saul of Tarsus

Not many knew who Saul was, let alone Paul, but the announcement that he was the leader, the most vicious of all the Christians, was enough. Another roar filled the air even as Paul was marched into the arena, escorted by a group of six centurions, three on each side, decked out in ceremonial uniforms of Imperial Guards. They really gave Paul an imperial treatment, one worthy of a Roman citizen.

Even as Paul walked to the center of the arena, thumbs rose in the air, performed a few gyrations as though gathering speed, and descended decisively towards the blood-splattered sand. People didn't even have to be asked to pass judgment. They knew their duty. They were Romans.

There were advantages to being Roman, or at least a citizen of Rome. You were not crucified, nor nailed to a tree, nor torn apart by wild animals. You had the privilege of being beheaded.

Paul knew that. He walked unassisted, free to run at any time. At the centre of the arena he was told to bow to the Emperor. He didn't. He remained standing. At such lack of respect the centurion behind him kicked him in the back. Paul staggered and fell to his knees. In the same instant a short Roman sword descended on his neck. His head rolled in the sand.

People roared.

Nero smiled.

Paul was home.

There was talk later among the centurions. Just before Paul was beheaded, those standing closest heard his last words. "Take me, Lord. Take me."

They didn't understand those words. "Who was this lord he spoke of?" they wondered.

And later, two or three, were even more surprised. In Paul's voice there was hope, and commitment. But there was also something they didn't recognize until long after the beheading. In his last words they thought they also heard a hint of daring.

Three heads had rolled in the sixth decade of the New Era. One that was already mostly engulfed in spirit, one that provided a link between heaven and earth for the benefit of many; and one that was anchored firmly on earth, or even in lower strata of human existence.

In 68 AD, the year in which Paul was beheaded, a year after Shimon offered his life, Nero's head still remained on his shoulders—though not for long.

Cruelty, lying, dishonesty, hate, wrath, sloth, greed, pride, envy, depravity and gluttony were not the only vices that Nero suffered from. He was also terribly bad at economics. Normally this wouldn't matter a whit, but he was the Emperor of the Roman Empire, and thus his errors in judgment had colossal consequences. They affected the whole civilized world. There were rebellions to quench, wars to be fought, lands to be conquered, enemies to be destroyed... normally those would have been normal, everyday activities.

But the cost of rebuilding Rome forced Nero, for the first time in the Empire's history, to devalue Roman currency. He reduced the weight and the purity of both the golden *aureus* and the silver *denarius*.

While this did not advance, let alone solve, any of the activities listed above, it did give Nero enough money to build a hundred-foot statue of himself. *Colossus Neronis*—a bronze colossus adorning the vestibule of his imperial villa complex.

Then, things went from bad to worse.

By March 68, there were rebellions against Nero's newly imposed taxes. After all, before Nero took over, Rome was based on vaguely republican principles, and no republican ever wanted to pay taxes, let alone have them raised.

In May 68 various armies in various provinces began to fight each other. The victor's legions attempted to declare their own commander an Emperor. Though the victor refused to act against Nero, further discontent of the legions of Germania and Iberia did not bode well for Nero. In Iberia, Galba, the governor of Hispania Tarraconensis was gaining support from Nero's enemies.

The Prefect of the Praetorian Guard, the commander of Nero's personal bodyguards, came in support of Galba. Nero had to run.

He had a few choices left.

The port of Ostia was not far away. He could take a fleet to one of the still loyal eastern Provinces. That idea misfired. The naval officers refused to carry out his orders.

"Is it so dreadful a thing then to die?" they asked, quoting Virgil's Aeneid; their faces showing contempt.

There were other options, but all offering little hope of survival. Some, none at all. Ever more gloomy, and by then ashen with fear, Nero returned to Rome. To his palace.

He was exhausted. On waking at midnight in his own bed, he found that the palace guard had left. He wandered the chambers, at night, looking for anyone. The palace was deserted. He, for the first time in his life, was alone. No one to blame, but worse... no one to kill to vent his anger. No one to even take his own life, to end this charade.

"Have I neither friend nor foe?" he called out.

He heard footsteps. The man bowed deeply. Of course. It was Epaphroditus. He once was a slave, and now, for a while already, he was his private secretary. Nero had once granted him his freedom. The man was still grateful. And now Nero needed a place to hide. The freeman offered his villa, some distance outside Rome.

On arrival, Nero ordered the freeman's servants to dig a grave for him. His host was risking his life. By then, he knew, Nero has been declared an enemy of Rome. He was to be beaten to death. An unpleasant demise.

Nero was not a complete imbecile. He knew that time had come to take his own life.

Only he had no previous experience. He only knew how to kill others. He asked for a demonstration from one of the servants. The servant refused.

Alas, Nero had no guts. No courage had ever invaded his heart.

And then he heard the sound of approaching horsemen. He ordered his secretary to perform the task. The freeman obeyed. The blood flowed freely.

"Qualis artifes pereo!" he exclaimed, even as blood gurgled in his throat.

People repeated those words long after his death, with nothing but derision. "What an artist dies in me," he'd said. And those were his last words.

So ended the Julio-Claudian dynasty.

And then chaos enveloped the whole of Rome.

However, in many ways this was just the beginning. The three deaths, particularly those of Paul and Shimon, announced the beginning of an Empire that Paul foresaw almost forty years ago, on his way to Damascus. No martyr ever died on earth without inspiring hundreds if not thousands of others to take up the banner and march towards the ever-receding horizon.

Christianity was no different.

The names of Shimon and Paul inspired thousands of followers, filled their hearts with courage, with desire to espouse the faith that gave them all incredible courage in the face of all diversity. No Roman Emperor ever wielded such power as Shimon and Paul had. And, contrary to the earthly rulers, Shimon and Paul's influence grew even after their death.

Perhaps they never died. Not really. Perhaps they only changed the venue from which to inspire people. Perhaps they only followed their Master and offered His promise to people they'd left behind.

"We shall never leave you," they seemed to say.

One other thing had changed. For every five or ten Christians martyred in Circus Maximus, ten or twenty other people who had never heard of Christianity began to wonder. Soon they'd begin to ask questions and then, they'd start knocking on doors, searching for the Word. And these were no longer just Jews. It began with the slaves, and they were soon followed by their masters, the almighty Romans. And a new fire began spreading across the Roman Empire which, day after day, lit new hearts with desire to spread the Word.

And there again, there are some who say that, one day, perhaps when we least expect it, Yeshûa will come back. That He'll walk the earth once more. When He does, one can but wonder if Shimon and Paul will come back with Him. Whenever that might be, we can be sure that, until then, all three of them will watch over us.

And in some ways, all three of them are still with us.

To this very day.

Even now.

***

The Future

The persecution of Christians by the Romans began with Nero. As best I could determine, the Roman Emperors who persecuted Christians after Nero included Domitian, Trajan, Marcus Aurelius, Septimius Severus, Maximinus the Thracian, Decius, Balerian, Diocletian and Galerius, and finally Julian the Apostate.

It is more than evident that each new persecution strengthened the Christian movement, which, though undergoing almost unrecognizable changes, gradually transformed itself into a religion, the distant echoes of which appear to last to this day. It can be assumed that it was only thanks to Paul's exceptional organizing ability that the 'church' survived at all. We must also assume (from very insufficient data) that he invariably appointed bishops, devised methods by which local Christians could elect their own by public acclaim (both men and women were so chosen), and to delegate responsibility for spreading the "Good News", far and wide, by his own carefully chosen disciples. As indicated in the novel, while Peter was committed to the theological or metaphysical aspect of the teaching, Paul decided that quantity was what counted if the 'church' were to survive.

Briefly, we can conclude that while Peter inspired the spiritual aspect of the new faith, Paul took it upon himself to make sure that sufficient number of believers existed from which the "chosen few" might emerge. What enabled him to do so was his fluent knowledge of Greek, the *lingua franca* of his day, and his determination to take the teaching outside the confines of Jewish society. We must remember that for a long time Christianity was recognized as "just another" Jewish sect. Nevertheless Paul laid the foundation stone upon which the Empire of the Catholic Church was built—an empire whose influence surpassed that of Alexander the Great. Later history seems to suggest this thesis, as the Church has grown its own castles, army and incredible, extremely material riches. To this day, Peter's teaching remained only for the few.

This last statement is, of course, only an opinion which the writer of this novel holds, and should not be regarded as a historical fact.

It wasn't until the year 313AD that Emperor Constantine the First legalized Christian Worship, thus stopping the persecution, which allowed Paul's vision to flourish. The consequences were predictable.

While Julius II may not have matched the thirst for secular power demonstrated by his papal predecessors, such as Gregory VII (1073-1085), or Innocent III (1160-1216), or even Boniface VIII (1235-1303), the final nail in the coffin of Peter's vision of Yeshûa's teaching, of the original Christianity, came from within the Church itself. The

following is an excerpt from my book VISUALIZATION—
Creating Your Own Universe:

"In the early 16th century, pope Julius II (1503-1513)
decided to destroy, literally raze to the ground, one of the
largest and most ancient churches in the Western world,
in order to build a bigger and better and more splendid
testimony of the church's temporal power. The old
basilica of Saint Peter was certainly the most venerable
church marking the place where St. Peter was supposed
to have been martyred. No matter. The new St. Peter's
was certainly more pompous, acclaiming greater secular
power, more impressive to the sheep"

"Although the new basilica had been completed only a
century later, it befell the sovereign pontiff to start a new
tradition of what is commonly described as the
decadence of the papacy."

My own opinion is that the decadence had begun very
much earlier, and continues to flourish to this day. More on
the subject of decadence can be found *et alibi* in the book *"I
segreti del Vaticano"* by Corrado Augias.

Whenever men want to build an empire on earth, an
empire here and now, they will always have to face those
who are willing to give their lives for the enigmatic Kingdom
that is not of this world. And, surely, we can't really blame
them. After all, their Kingdom is eternal. Even as other
empires wither and die, the Kingdom that is not of this world
goes on. And on.
Forever.

***

Lexicon

ANCIENT MEASUREMENTS

Length
Handbreadth—width of four fingers closely pressed together.

Span—width from end of thumb to that of little finger.

Cubit—length of the arm from point of elbow to end of middle finger (about 18").

Distance
Furlong—about 600 feet

Mile—eight *furlongs* (1618 yards, less than American mile of 1760 yards). A day's journey was deemed between 20 and 30 miles.

League—a distance a person or horse could walk in an hour or 1.5 *Roman miles*.

Weight
Shekel—varied, (silver) usually form 1/3 to 1/2 of an ounce.

Talent—about 3000 shekels, (90 pounds, all that one man could carry).

Value

Farthing—smallest Roman coin, equal to 1/64 of a *denarius*. A *denarius* was average wage for day's work.
Mite—Smallest Jewish coin, about 1/2 of farthing.
Penny—equivalent to Roman silver *denarius*
Denarion or *denarius* - see above
Lepta - a small value Greek coin
Kodrante - about 1/16 of a soldier's daily pay

FOREIGN WORDS

Hebrew days of the week:
Yom Ree-Shon - first day, Sunday (starting at preceding sunset)
Yom She-Nee - second day, Monday
Yom Shelee-She - third day, Tuesday
Yom Re-Ve-ee - fourth day, Wednesday
Yom Hah-Mee-Shee - fifth day, Thursday
Yom Shee-shee - sixth day, Friday
Yom Sha-Bat - Rest day, Saturday

Essenes - flourished from 2nd century BCE to 1st century CE. Some claim they were instrumental in early upbringing of Yeshûa.
Shamayim - Hebrew word for heaven. Dwelling place of God and the abode of the righteous dead.
Quid pro quo - (literally) this for that
Nec plus ultra - (literally) nothing further beyond
Sic transit gloria mundi - thus passes the glory of the world
Urbi et orbi - for (of) the city (Rome) and for (of) the world
Erato - Greek muse of lyric poetry

De gustibus non est disputandum - (literally) There must not be debate concerning tastes.

Lingua franca - the working language used as the most common means of communication outside one's own mother tongue.

et alibi - among other places.

ℐⅽᴋⁿoⱳⱡeⅆℊⅿeⁿⱦ₷

I would be remiss were I not to thank my many friends who read the galley proofs, none more so than Ronald Piecuch, whose proofreading efforts helped to make this book a success. But most of all, I welcome the return of Madeleine Witthoeft who, after a brief rest, returned to offer me her editing and proofreading skills. As usual, my gratitude to my wife, Bozena Happach, who put up with being a grass widow for weeks on end and then allowed me to benefit from her insights.

Some of the subjects mentioned in this novel are derived from following sources:

King James Version of the Bible, as published by Thomas Nelson Inc., in Jew Jersey, USA.

ACTS 13:9-11
ACTS 14:11-13
ACTS 17:16
ACTS 17:17
ACTS 19:13

ACTS 19:18-19
ACTS 19:35-36, 38, 40
ACTS 21:10-12
ACTS 22:1-8
ACTS 23:11-12
ACTS 23:23-24
ACTS 25:10-11
ACTS 25:13-26:32
JOHN 20:19-31
GALATIANS 2:11-14
HEBREWS 11:1

Additional information was gleamed from:
THE NAG HAMMADI LIBRARY, James M. Robinson,
The First Apocalypse of James, and The Gospel of Thomas.
Quotation: *De Natura Deorum*, was taken from:
http://www.epicurus.net/en/deorum.html

A point of interest

Although the Polish writer and Nobel Prize laureate
Henryk Sienkiewicz had written a novel entitled: *Quo Vadis*,
on which a famous Hollywood epic of the same name had
been based, both, the book and the movie perpetrate great
historical error. Although they present a lot of the action
taking place in the Rome's Coliseum, in fact, the arena had
been built only two years *after* Nero's death, in 70 AD.
My novel corrects this mistake.

***

Preliminary Research

(Blog)

When starting this novel, I began to share with some of my friends my preliminary research, leading to the first few chapters, which inspired this book. The reader might find it of interest to see how the story evolved, and what may have motivated my need to share with you this ancient story. Most of the blog is still available on the URL below, although, hopefully, the actual novel has been improved since. Below, I stopped with the draft of Chapter One.

> http://stankapuscinski.blogspot.com

Jan, 23, 2012
Peter & Paul (#1)

A good way to celebrate a new blog (you can find my previous attempts on Author's Den and at Goodreads) is by sharing with you the research I just began for my new historical novel. My preliminary title is Peter and Paul. *Yes, the biblical duo who were often accused by some accredited by others, for creating a religion, which conquered the minds of the western world.*

Few of us know that Peter and Paul did not see eye to eye. In fact they differed greatly on the interpretation of

Yeshûa's teaching. Yeshûa, or more correctly Yehoshûa is the real name of Jesus, supposedly the Greek equivalent. And even then Jesus has been pronounced Yesus; thus when one attempts to "speak in the name of Jesus", one ought to know what the name stands for. And that is, more or less, how the book has begun. With the real meaning of Yeshûa, who never intended to create any religion. This privilege, apparently, was taken up, firmly by his followers.

Jan. 25, 2012
YHWH and Peter & Paul (#2)

Theoretically, the book should be called "Shimon and Saul". The problem – most people wouldn't know who those gentlemen were.

I need lots of research. To write about Peter and Paul, I have to get the feel of the man who influenced their lives. I touched on the subject of Yeshûa, the late form of Yehoshûa. Well, the name Yehoshûa is a rare Hebrew surname, but the etymological meaning gets to be more complex, though when uncovered, it throws a different light on the very principles of Christianity.

In Hebrew, Yeshûa (in Greek Jeshua) means "Jah is salvation". Yah (or Jah), in turn, is a poetic form of Yehovah (or Jehovah), which as Yahweh represents the Hebrew YHWH (Yodh, He, Waw, He). This tetragrammaton is the expression of the male and female universal principles, and appears to be the equivalent of the Mosaic I AM THAT I AM.

Now the problems really begin.

So far, we have regressed from Yeshûa backwards to Moses. And, you will note that there is absolutely no mention of any god, with or without a capital G.

Surprise?

I am reminded of a Bergman movie "The Seventh Veil" wherein Max von Sydow makes this statement: "We carve an idol out of our fear and call it God". We all know the story of the Golden Calf and the Ten Commandments.

Jan. 27, 2012

Peter and Paul and Omnipresence (#3)
(Continuous research for historical novel)

I am beginning to see Peter and Paul's problem.
The dogmas with which I have been brought up state that God is omnipresent. Thus, perforce, I am within God. However, since God is omnipresent, likewise perforce, She (It? The Universal Principles?) is (are) also within me. Interesting. I'm not sure how this fits in with the tenets with which Peter and Paul have been brought up. Hopefully, we shall find out.
Perhaps the fullness of this understanding explains the indescribable expressions of euphoria depicted by the old masters on the faces of mystics. The many martyrs of Peter and Paul's days are said to have met their death with a blissful smile. It is as if they knew something we don't. In a way, this book is an attempt to unravel this mystery.

Shavuoth or later, Pentecost (#4)

(Continuous research for historical novel)

Apart from Yeshûa, my outright bestseller, writing a historical novel is nothing like any other novel I've ever written. It is still "fantasy", an expression of writer's imagination, but, to be honest, if one describes real people of the past, one is obliged to do them justice as best one can. Is it not easy if they've been dead for some 2000 years.

I had to learn about Peter's village, his life as a fisherman, perhaps even his state of mind. And then to retrace how his life may have unfolded. My book will probably start the day before the Pentecost. That Greek word meaning 50th. It refers to 50th day after Passover, the day the Jews commemorate as the day on which the Hebrews had been promised enlightenment. The Ten Commandments. Of course they didn't call it Pentecost. That is the name the followers of Yeshûa adopted from the Hebrew feast of Shavuoth.

And, surprise, on that day a bunch of (with the possible exception of Matthew), uneducated, illiterate guys, hiding, scared stiff, cowering in their own shadow, suddenly got up and began preaching the Good News.

Coincidence? Myth?

Fascinating. Should be quite a book!

The Secret of Shavuoth (#5)
(Continued research for historical novel)

It is obvious that Peter and Paul could not benefit from later terminology to express emotions, metal states, deviations, and suchlike as we have now. Yet mental aberrations, deviations from the accepted norm must have existed. One can but wonder how P & P dealt with them, how they described them. It seems that symbolism to explain the unexplainable must have been in high demand. The apostles could not benefit from the achievements of Sigmund Freud, Carl Jung and a number of other psychiatrists/psychologists/students of human nature.

Yet they, P&P, managed to completely change the state of consciousness of tens of thousands of people, without driving them mad. Amazing! What fantastic powers of persuasion! And... what they offered must have been completely revolutionary. The question is what???

It is evident that something unexplainable must have taken place on the feast of Pentecost. What was it? What was, what must have been, the secret of Shavuoth?

The Mystery of Yah and El (#6)

(Continued research for a historical novel)

I've learned about Yah, or Yahweh, but there is a new problem. There is also El. It is to be found in compound names only. It stands for (symbolizes) the divine principle in human consciousness. You could say, your Higher Self. It is that through which we can contact the Existing One, the Jehovah or Yahweh. As such, (to quote from my <u>Dictionary of Biblical Symbolism</u>, see above), it symbolizes the union of the Father (masculine) and Mother (feminine) principles, making the Third, thus El represent the trinity or completeness. You can find it in Is-Ra-El: the feminine, the masculine and the unifying principle.

Interestingly enough, we all know where Is and Ra originate. Is - (I suspect from Isis) the feminine principle, Ra - (the Egyptian sun god), the masculine principle or our conscious mind.

*And this is where the problem really drift away from any Christian teaching I ever heard. Names like Eliah, or Elijah, or Eliel, all biblical names, state that **the two are one**. They state that El and Yah (Jehovah) are inseparable, that they are one. Echoes of "I and my father are one" (John 10:30). Interesting? Not even close to Christian teaching. The problem is that long **before** Yeshûa was born, this statement applied to everybody. Not just to Yeshûa, later, as the Christian teaching proclaims. Hence, so many Hebrew names listed above. That is how we are made. Constructed. Created. It must have been equally as shocking, as blasphemous, to them, to the Gentiles as it sounds to us.*

And yet? The Bible is supposed to be right. Right?
Peter and Paul had quite different problems than I ever
imagined. They had to convey this knowledge, or philosophy
to the gentiles.
Wow! Do you think they made it?

**Is this Blog for You? A little Break... from Peter and
Paul (#7)**

(Continuous research for historical novel)

Half in jest, and I suspect half-earnestly, my friend asked
me, "...can you explain to me why on earth I would want to
blog through minutia of the making of a novel that I'm not
sure I'm that interested in reading when it's finished."
Why indeed!
Well, there is an answer, but it will probably appeal only
to people who may not have written any books, but always
thought that perhaps, one day, they might pick up the quill...
Don't we all want to say something, sometime, without being
interrupted? (This applies to married men only).
Such people might find it fascinating what research
method would a writer use to write, e.g., a historical novel. I
remember when writing Yeshûa, I went through a dozen thick
books on philosophy, ancient customs, history and suchlike,
before I wrote a single line on my trusty Mac. Writing the
book took me about 7 weeks. The research about 2 years. Not
to the exclusion of doing other things, but it took about that
long before I was ready to just sit down and write. You
accumulate knowledge in your subconscious and then let it
flow. Preparing to write a book is, sometimes, like studying
the piano for 5 years to be able to play Chopin's Minute
Waltz in... 60 seconds. (Actually it takes just under 2
minutes; 'minute' stands for 'small', or 'tiny', but the
sentiment is there).

Of course, most people won't care how many years the pianist studied as long as he plays well. But some do. And when they find out they might, just might be in awe. Or they may decide to never, never attempt to write a book.

Miracles (#8)

(Continuous research for historical novel)

The Bible abounds in "miracles". They are as much a daily occurrence as eating and sleeping. How come? Until the Shavuoth following the ascension of Christ into a reality where the apostles couldn't follow, none of them could perform any miracles.

Again, how come?

When writing a historical novel one has to attempt to make it real by the standard of the prospective reader. How can a modern man, a writer, accept events, which seemingly deny the laws of nature?

I have two options. I can either write a book that would sound like a religious dissertation, or assume that magic of yesterday is the reality of tomorrow. Perhaps it is we who cannot understand, as yet, the laws of nature, as they really operate. Perhaps we did once, and lost it...?

Perhaps we have become too materialistic?

Below an excerpt from my book "DELUSIONS".

"At the onset the last century, Sir Arthur Eddington, an British astrophysicist and philosopher of science, declared that, taking into account the distance between the nucleus and the orbiting electrons, atoms were mostly empty space. More precisely, he calculated that they were approximately 99.9999999999999% empty space."

The Hindus claimed for thousands of years that our material world is an illusion. They called it Maya. Now science seems to confirm it. Miracles have a very different feel in the light of the above. Perhaps the apostles learned something the way many scientists claim when they say that he woke up with a new idea?

The Secret of Shavuoth (#9)

(Continuous research for historical novel: Peter and Paul)

I think I'm beginning to get it. It seems that without the study of symbolism one is unlikely to uncover the secret discovered by the few, some 2000 years ago.

Going back to Is-Ra-El, I forgot to mention that Is, the feminine aspect, also stands for our subconscious, which is the sum-total of all the knowledge we have acquired over our individualized existence. That would account for billions of years.

We must remember that Is-ra-el is an androgynous concept. It applies in all its components to both men and women.

Now, perhaps the intense desire of the apostles, probably anchored in genetic memory of expecting the enlightenment associated with Shavouth, caused them to finally understand what Yeshûa had been trying to tell them for 3 full years. Was he telling his disciples that when you enter a state of mind wherein the conscious and the subconscious become unified (as in OBE or lucid dreaming), then you acquire powers that seem miraculous? We think nothing of performing miracles, in our dreams, outside the confines of time or space. Yet, when we wake up, we lose this capacity.

Well, at least for a while, the apostles didn't. Apparently the Christ could invoke this mental state at will. Perhaps, one day, we all shall.

Perhaps...

To achieve this end, however, we need a complete change of attitude, perhaps best explained in my <u>Key to Immortality</u>.

Can anyone perform Miracles? (#10)

(Continuous research for historical novel)

There are more things on heaven and earth, Horatio Than are dreamt in your philosophy.
Hamlet, Shakespeare, Act 1, scene 5.

Or could it be that we have the capacity to unify the two hemispheres of our brain? In my novel The Avatar Syndrome I discussed the possible consequences of such a union. The book is a novel, but, as usually, I've spent endless hours on trying to learn how our brain works.

This was getting intriguing. Did people in the past have abilities that were since lost?

Peter and Paul did not have my options on hand. It seems that they conquered the mystery by an effort of will, or of meditation – as eastern yogis are said to do. I've read of many cases of humans performing acts that defied physical limitations – yet, they have been confirmed by many unbiased witnesses. The problem is how to perform what we regard as miracles at will. How to create conditions which awaken within us our dormant, latent power.

And make no mistake about them. The latent powers are there, waiting to be rediscovered. As a species we are becoming more and more materialistic. Perhaps we ought to look back and see if there isn't something we might learn from the past.

My job as a writer is to make this human potential real and believable to the readers of Peter and Paul, without using any modern terminologies that, obviously, didn't exist in their time. And... to make the novel exciting.

I suppose you'll just have to wait and see... (please, do!). But one thing I can promise you. You will get the answer to the quandary of miracles.

Let the Dead Bury the Dead (#11)

(Continued research for my next historical novel: "Peter and Paul")

In the teaching imparted to Peter, the concept of death must have been quite different to that assumed by us. It seems that the dead were all who have not been, as yet, spiritually awakened. Yet there is no clear explanation what constitutes spiritual awakening.

Yet, it seems very apparent that something very fundamental must take place in our psyche.

We have two clues.

1. Let the dead bury their dead. (Luke 9:60)
2. Among them that are born of women there hath not risen a greater than John the Baptist: notwithstanding he that is least in the kingdom of heaven is greater than he. (Matthew 11:11)

It sounds as though John did not quite make it through the Pearly Gates. On the other hand, it seems that no matter what we do, or how good we are, this has nothing to do with entering the kingdom of heaven.

*A mystery? Peter **must have solved it** in order to teach as he did. In my **BEYOND RELIGION** series, I discuss*

Salvation and a number of subjects that weigh on the mysteries I must resolve for this book.
I must solve them by the time I write the novel! Mystery, suspense and magic? The science of yesteryear?

What happened to the Gnostics? (#12)

Continued research for my historical novel: Peter and Paul.

There are two ways to practice religion: through faiths or through knowledge. The inner knowledge is referred to as Gnosis. Faith is often regarded as a 'gift', as in 'gift of faith'; knowledge requires effort. Lots of effort—as in this research for P and P.
It is my contention that Yeshûa was a Gnostic. His power and philosophy sprang from knowledge, not from an act of faith. Thus the Gnostic Gospels of Nag Hammadi (see my **KEY TO IMMORTALITY***) must be closer to his teaching that the 4 gospels, written 100 years+ after his death, translated hundreds of times, rewritten by hand, and adapted to various predilections by various Christian churches. The matter is further discussed in the chapter Reviewing the Elements in my book* **VISUALIZATION – Creating your own Universe.**
No matter.
While Bishop Irenaeus (2nd century AD) of Lugdunom (now Lion in France) had been canonized most probably for his infamous "Adversus Haereses", (Against Heresies), might be forgiven in his day for attempting to destroy Gnosticism, we have no such excuse. The Gnostic Gospels survived in spite of his unholy onslaught on Yeshûa's teaching, extended to this day by dubious 'scholars' of 'established' churches.

To put it differently, when you know something, it is easy to have faith in it; faith "greater than a grain of mustard seed." (Luke 17:6). Indeed, you could move mountains...

Where did Yeshûa's Gnosis come from? (#13)

Continued research for a historical novel: Peter and Paul

Unfortunately for the so-called 'believers', unlike all the gods of the past (Krishna, Osiris, Zeus, Jupiter, et al.), Yeshûa was not born omniscient.

In Luke 2:52, the evangelist states that: "Jesus increased in wisdom and stature, and in favour with God and man." Surely such a process of amelioration is hardly necessary for a god.

In my book Yeshûa – Personal Memoir of the Missing Years of Jesus*, I attempted to show how Yeshûa, the apostles' mentor, acquired his knowledge. It took him 18 years of hard work to prepare himself for his mission. Not many people, of whatever profession, are willing to spend such length of time to acquire their knowledge. In addition to external sources (books, teachers, universities), there are two principle sources from which we can draw information.*

First, our subconscious, which supplies us with the knowledge acquired over, perhaps, millions of years of our physical or material existence.

And then there is the other source, which many tend to ignore. I'm talking about our **unconscious***. This latter source seems to give us access to ideas not previously experienced. Carl Jung's archetypes of collective unconscious? We can but speculate.*

But how can we access this Source? They say that few years of meditation (or contemplation) will show us. It took Yeshûa just eighteen short years. I suspect this is the Gnosis

Yeshûa was trying to impart to his disciples. It couldn't have been easy.

A Secret Place? (#14)

Continued research for a historical novel: Peter and Paul

Peter asked Yeshûa, "Lord, where go you? Jesus answered him, Where I go, you can not follow me now; but you shall follow me afterwards." (John 13:36)

The response Peter got implies that Yeshûa knew his destination, thus he must have visited it before. Likewise, it states that Peter will follow him, i.e. Yeshûa later. It suggests that Yeshûa was familiar with his impending destination. Where?

To quote Shakespeare, "that is the question".

It seems to me that there is only one 'place' one can 'go' without physically leaving the earthly environs, and that is to go within. The travel takes place within your consciousness. There are ways.

Ye are gods? (#15)

Continued research for a historical novel: Peter and Paul

In Blog #10, I quoted the scriptures that, under certain circumstances, we have the power to "move mountains". While the statement is probably symbolic, 'mountains' symbolizing raised states of consciousness (see Dictionary of Biblical Symbolism), the statement assumes new meaning in the light of today's knowledge of physics. Firstly, we already move mountains by 'hands', i.e. by our advanced machinery.

The question is can we move them by the power of our minds – directly, without resorting to our heavy equipment? Modern physics state that matter surrounding us, indeed of which we are all composed, is... 99.999999999999% empty space (see discussion in <u>Delusions – Pragmatic Realism</u>). In the light of this fact, moving mountains is paramount to moving the lightest of feathers, indeed, a tiny spec of dust.

It seems that Yeshûa must have known of the illusory nature of the world we live in. But our faith, rather than the truth (which has been predicted to "set us free") is much stranger. We know that the chair we sit on is virtually empty space, yet we believe it to be solid and thus it supports our (equally illusory) weight. Please note: all this is science, not religion. Pure 21st century science.

Atheists or believers (#16)

Continued research for a historical novel: Peter and Paul

By Gnostic standards, only those people are true atheists who have not succeeded, as yet, in performing acts with, or by, their states of consciousness. Whatever that might mean. It is a sort of, "Look, Ma, no hands."

Yet this is, it seems to me, exactly what Yeshûa managed to convey to his followers. In those days, I assume, "to be born again", (as the saying goes amongst some people today, like George W. Bush), did not consist of walking around singing Jeeeeezus, or Loooooord, but in discovering within us the infinity and the affinity of I AM. Apparently Yeshûa managed to plant the seed of immortality in his immediate followers (see <u>Key to Immortality</u>). It's amazing what you can do if you consider yourself to be closely related to Mary Poppins.

BTW, I hate preachy books. Can anyone tell me how to write this novel without being preachy?

A Historical Novel or Murder/Suspense Story? (#17)

Continued research for a historical novel: Peter and Paul

Could there have been a high-level plot to destroy all early followers of Yeshûa's teaching? Particularly the apostles? If the answer is yes, then my historical novel might turn out to be a historical murder/thriller novel.

It was a question of business—of economics.

One gold talent was worth approximately 27 silver talents. At 3000 shekels per talent, that's a lot of tithes (see Tithing, essay #39, in Beyond Religion vol. II).

Who would get the new tithes? How much would the Sanhedrin lose? We know how today's politicians react to any diminution of their income. IRS is on your doorstep in no time at all. The Great Sanhedrin of Israel consisted of 71 members—that's a lot of people to support. And then there were the priesthood. A whole tribe of them. Add to it all the other assemblies (each town had one) and you need a tax base. With the new Christian sect siphoning off people, the Christians couldn't have been popular with the ruling classes. Somebody, somehow, had to protect the status quo. What best way is there than to get rid of them altogether. Dead men don't pay taxes, but they provide a good example. Isn't this what all the established oligarchies did do in those days? Or later days. Now?

A Christian What? (#18)

Continued research for my next historical novel: Peter and Paul

In the beginning of the new era, the Christians were just another Jewish sect. The others were the Pharisees, Sadducees, Essenes, Zealots, and many we probably never heard of. By the end of the first century, "thirty sects of Christians might be reckoned in Asia Minor, in Syria, in Alexandria, and even in Rome" (Beyond Religion vol. I, *The Carrot and the Stick, essay # 28).*

Peter had to find a way to establish his, or Yeshûa's, followers as a recognized entity, which followed a similar set of rules, or at least the same teaching. With others competing for the hearts and minds of people around, it couldn't have been easy.

And the teaching of Yeshûa was characterized by the Master's often-repeated phrase: "Why do you not understand my speech?" (John 8:43). There is a touch of mystery there; perhaps even irony?

Do we understand the teaching today? Yet Peter had to. He was the 'Rock'. What could have it been that was so incomprehensible even to his chosen few?

And what Paul? (#19)

Continued research for my next historical novel: Peter and Paul

Paul never met Yeshûa. He taught what he thought Yeshûa may have taught. Rather like the priests, padres and preachers of today, not to mention TV evangelists.

Researching the Nag Hammadi Library, it seems to me that Yeshûa imparted secret knowledge to his immediate entourage only. Perhaps only the apostles. Thus Paul's knowledge was secondhand. Paul may have had his visions and inspired revelations, but not direct knowledge or gnosis.

There is, it seems, no substitute for the real thing. I wonder how I can convey this fact to my readers without diminishing his, i.e. Paul's, contribution of the spreading of the 'faith'. No matter how wrong he may have been. (see: KEY TO IMMORTALITY).

Paul's Visions (#20)

Continued research for my next historical novel: Peter and Paul

Below a quote from my book Visualization—Creating your Own Universe.

"All visions are subjective. Subjective religious visions are called Revelations. Subjective non-religious visions (unless held by famous people) are often referred to as hallucinations. Hallucinations can be subdivided into artistic, political, social, idealistic, and a whole array of inspired non-religious fantasies, delusions or insights."

The problem is: Who is to decide which is which?

If I am right in my analyses, what should we think about Paul's contribution to Christianity? Would he and Peter invariably agree?

Or could there have been a profound schism in their thinking? Historical novels are not as simple as I thought they would be. Not if one is to deliver the truth... as best one can.

And yet... did not Yeshûa's gnosis come from within?

Historical novels are not only difficult to write, they are fascinating to research!

Apostles and Demons? (#21)

Continued research for my next historical novel: Peter and Paul

Not everyone realizes that the story of Peter and Paul is also, if not essentially, a powerful murder story. We know that eight of the twelve apostles have been murdered in vile, horrifying ways; echoes of the popular 'thriller' Angels and Demons.

At the beginning of the modern era, just following Anno Domini 1, things were tough.

A small group of people dared to stand up to the powers that be, against the mighty Rome, the Jewish oligarchy, against various factions, both secular and religious, which wanted to maintain status quo. There was no freedom of religion in those days. Remember Socrates some 400 years earlier? (I touch on the subject in <u>Alexander - Alexander Trilogy Book II</u>). He dared to think for himself and was forced to drink hemlock. Not much has changed in the Middle East since his day. Now that you mention it, in some mid-eastern countries, not much has change to this day. Could that be karmic justice?

It is time to start... (#22)

Continued research for my next historical novel: Peter and Paul.

The time comes to start writing. Not that I have all the answers, but I think I exposed most of the questions; at least enough of them to start the story.

I may or may not continue with the research, although I usually do while I write. Below a short sample how the story could (but not necessarily will) start.

Chapter ONE (draft)

"I miss fishing," he said out loud to no one in particular, his mind drifting back, far, far back to a different life, a different reality. His eyes wandered aimlessly, reaching beyond today, beyond the immediate, a wistful smile barely widening his mouth.

"I miss fishing," he repeated, seemingly to himself.

They were all gathered, still together, in Bethany, were the Master had left them. Only one week ago. He didn't say goodbye. No, not goodbye, just so long. In fact He'd said that He'd never leave them. Never.

It didn't feel like it.

"I miss fishing," Shimon said, once again, his tone filled with longing. It was beginning to sound like a far-eastern mantra the Master once told him about.

Then he sighed deeply. He always sighed when he thought of the Mount of Olives. That is where he escaped into memories of way-back-when. When he'd first met the Yeshûa. Then he relaxed and allowed his mind to retreat even further back. Back to when he'd cast nets in the Lake Gennesareth. The Lake of his childhood.

"I'll make you fisher of men," He'd said.

Only He didn't. And now, He'd left. And I am still here. Alone. Quite alone. Why do they look up to me? I am nobody. I'm ignorant. I know nothing. I am a fisherman. A fisherman of fish, in my lake.

His eyes reached far from shore, fishing for memories.

(to be continued)

The Dark Days, cont. (#23 and #24)

Continued research for my next historical novel: Peter and Paul.

I am trying to visualize how a simple fisherman from a village in the middle of nowhere, who'd since proven a man of relatively weak character, perhaps even with a yellow streak, would handle himself when tremendous responsibility has been thrust upon his shoulders. Surely, he'd take time to adjust... For a while, I suspect, he'd escape into his memories of innocence and youths.

Chapter ONE (draft, continued)
The Dark Days (excerpt)

Shimon used to enjoy over-night fishing the most. Heaving off with the last rays of the sun dying over Mount Tabor, just missing the peek on the south side. Even from the shore the view was breathtaking. From the shore of Bethsaida—the Place of Nets; little more than a village. Soon after they cast of, they'd watch the night fires beginning to twinkle, afar, long, long ago, before Tiberias grew into a city.

He missed the western breeze carrying them to the middle of the Lake on a broad reach. Just a small sail, knit by his mother and sisters, was enough. They were in no hurry. They had all night. They didn't have far to go.

His friends, in their prouder moments, liked to call it the Sea of Galilee. It sounded more important. Some sea—from every place on its near-lustrous surface you could see the shore, and not very distant, at that. But it was their lake. Theirs for generations. Sweet water where his father, and his father before him, fished for fresh-water fish.

He was a fisherman then. Carefree.

And then He came. Quiet, unimposing. Just his eyes. There was heaven in those eyes. Infinity? Andrew had seen him first. You couldn't escape those eyes…

"Shimon?"

Shimon, He called him, long before He'd changed his name to *Kepha*. All too soon the Romans began to refer to him as *Petrus* taking their translation from *pietra*. The Greeks would give him their own version, naming his *Petros*, from their own rock or *petra*. Later, much later, some Gentiles coming from afar would call him *Peter*. Wherever he'd go, people would give him names of their own. Yes, he sensed the future and he was afraid.

Yet it all happened in just three short years. Just three…

When did He first call me Kepha?

"What? Shimon, you must eat!"

Andrew proffered a wooden bowl of steaming soup.

Later? It all happened in just a few years. Just a few…

He didn't feel like a rock. He felt weak, fragile, inadequate, scared… like that night on the boat when…

"Shimon?" the sound of his name reached him from afar—perhaps the other shore? He ignored whoever tried to invade his memories. It was good to remember, even knowing what followed. After all, He did come back. He was real…

"Shimon?" this time the voice was louder.

It must have been Andrew with something of no importance. It could wait. Back then he was happy. So happy. No decisions, few responsibilities… His mind drifted back, again, far, far back…

"Shimon, you haven't eaten for three days…"

(to be continued)

The Dark Days, cont. (#24)

Continued research for my next historical novel: Peter and Paul.

It is hard to imagine how a group of men who never faced any challenges other than keeping "body and soul" together, were suddenly thrust into an existence well beyond their means to comprehend. I repeat, those early followers of Yeshûa were simple, (with one exception) uneducated men, who must have felt completely out of their depth.

Chapter ONE (draft, continued)
The Dark Days (excerpt)

Andrew was worried about his elder brother. He'd aged, fast, during just these last few years. Already his short trimmed beard was showing signs of gray hair. Andrew suspected that since the Master's departure Shimon felt great weight pressing him down to earth. Literally, down to earth. Perhaps he was trying to reconcile heaven and earth into a single entity, like two sides of a single coin. Perhaps it was all the decisions he had to make. Everyone wanted his opinion, his advise.

I'm a simple fisherman, Andrew heard him say. Many a time. *A simple fisherman...*

But no one believed him. He really had to be *Kepha*, a rock; strong; unbending; not to cave in under all the expectations.

Shimon looked up for an instant. The next moment his eyes lost focus and drifted back, to the world of his own. Then, a gentle smile broadened his mouth. Andrew wondered if his brother would ever share his daydreams with him.

The wind was rising...

Just sitting there, amidships, on the rough-hewn board spanning from side to side, his two friends stretching abaft. A gentle sway of the dying wind... then silence, darkness, the sky punctured only by the stars of Yahweh. We cast our nets and waited, he recalled, catching a few hours of sleep.

"Not I. I'd sit silent, listening to the stars," he murmured, hardly aware of Andrew's presence. And then he repeated softly, "I miss fishing."

I miss fishing... It really did sound like a mantra.

The waters rose with restrained anger and instantly he began drowning. Have faith, He said. Have faith. Trust me. The power lies within you.

Yeshûa was standing, seemingly on the water. He watched the Master walk towards him hardly touching the waves. Almost floating.

Come to me," Yeshûa tempted, his voice relaxed, encouraging him with a smile. "Don't be afraid..."

(to be continued)

The Dark Days, cont. (#25)

Continued research for my next historical novel: Peter and Paul.

It seems evident that Andrew, Peter's younger brother would have to take over the role of Peter's protector. Peter, or Shimon as he was then known, was trying to find his footing in the role of a leader of... of a bunch of men with an absurd, revolutionary idea, left them by Yeshûa.

Chapter ONE (draft, continued)
The Dark Days (excerpt)

"Shimon!" This time Andrew's voice was more insistent. It no longer sounded like the Master. Andrew didn't like Shimon drifting off, so often lately, when there were decisions to be made. As the younger brother he felt the need to look after Shimon. Funny how roles change. Until the Master left them, Shimon was the one who looked after all of them.

"He hasn't left us," Shimon murmured. "He's still within us."

"What's that?"

Andrew looked concerned. He was really worried about his brother since He'd left. Since He'd left them alone. It seems, Shimon missed Him the most. Still, they had to cope. And Shimon had a lot on his mind. The Master had left his brother in charge.

Shimon was really not himself, lately. Not since the Master's departure or even before. He seems to have lost all confidence ever since that night he'd spent on the courtyard. Even now he seemed to grow weak and agitated each time some cockerel sang; even during his sleep.

Actually it's been a while. Apart from Andrew, the others didn't really know what had happened. Shimon had no inclination to tell them. Three times... three times the cockerel sang. Three times...

"Never mind."

Shimon was tired of explaining it to his friends. He blinked a few times to shake off the images of Gennesareth. For a while they wouldn't let go. Then he thought of the others, and the boat dissolved in the water. The others wouldn't understand. They'd spend just as many years with the Master as he had, yet they didn't seem to understand his teaching at all. "Why can't they understand my words?" He'd asked them, many a time. Ah, yes, many a time. *Why can't they understand my words?*

To understand that none of this is real?

My kingdom is not of this world...

Andrew drew back from his brother recognizing the signs when Shimon was in a morose mood.

"I suppose Stephen arrived?" Shimon asked without looking up.

"Not yet, Shimon. We expect him shortly."

Andrew just didn't have the heart to tell Shimon that Stephen had been murdered. Stoned to death. In the days that followed the Believers have scattered throughout Samaria, yet preaching the Word as they went.

(to be continued)

The Dark Days, cont. (#26)

Continued research for my next historical novel: Peter and Paul.

Undoubtedly the conditions in which the early followers of Yeshûa lived must have been considerably more barbaric than we are used to today. While Rome was spreading its victorious legions across the Middle East, at local level riff-raff must have held their own. Also, the Pharisees and the henchmen of the priests were a constant threat. Under such conditions implementation of Yeshûa's teaching had to present a virtually impossible challenge.

Chapter ONE (draft, continued)
The Dark Days (excerpt)

"You could never be sure, these days. The roads, such as they were, seemed the favorite haunt of the bandits in search of easy money," Shimon murmured. He ought to know. He'd been beaten up, twice, by total strangers.

Love thy enemies...

Again Shimon's lips widened in a wistful smile. His thought seemed almost like a joke; a joke that was painful and not at all funny. Yet, Yeshûa'd insisted.

"I'm sorry, I though he'd already arrived," Shimon replied, another sigh escaping his parched lips. He still had time. Andrew would look after things. Shimon didn't want to treat his brother badly, nor to ignore him. He loved his younger brother. And, after all, it had been Andrew who recognized the Master first. Back then, at the shores of Gennesareth. Before anyone even began to suspect who Yeshûa was.

Ah, yes. Back then, by the Lake. But now it was time for Shimon's daily walk. The time he hated but promised himself to do no matter what.

(to be continued)

The Dark Days, continued (#27)

Continued research for my next historical novel: Peter and Paul.

While the challenges facing all the apostles, particularly whose of Peter, were extraordinary, life had to go on. Nevertheless, to reconcile the Teaching with everyday life was more than, at the time, than Peter could handle. His effort must have been directed at staying reasonably sane...

Chapter ONE (draft, continued)
The Dark Days (excerpt)

He made a point of going out, every day, alone, even if just for an hour or so. He hated this commitment to himself, but knew that if he didn't he'd crawl into a hole and pull the lid over him. He was afraid. He couldn't even define of what

he was afraid of. Not precisely. Perhaps just of not being able
to conquer his fear. He almost smiled at the thought. Could it
have be that simple?

Yeshûa was never afraid. He walked into crowds, hordes
of total strangers, often showing signs of anything but
friendly disposition. Yet, He was never afraid. How did He
do it, Peter asked himself many a time. How on earth did his
do it?

"It's not real, Shimon," He'd said. "None of it is real,"
He'd often repeated, a mysterious smile lighting up His face,
his sky-blue eyes piecing Shimon's to his soul.

It's not real...

He was always like that. Nothing seemed to matter
much. Not really. Except loving one another. How on earth
can one love a total stranger?

It was real to Peter. It was real and, most of the time,
scary. That was why Peter went out every day. Since He'd
gone, Peter had to conquer his reticence of meeting other
people. Especially meeting strangers. His band of men went
out to preach, daily, but not he. They understood. He was in
charge. He had to hold the fort. Fort? What fort. A mud hut
just big enough to hold a dozen people. Yet he did go out.
Once a day. He'd never met anyone who'd given him a glad
eye. Not since he'd left Bethsaida. His home. His lake. His
family. Now?

Even surrounded by ten of his best friends he felt alone.

He looked left and right, and breathed easier. The street
was empty. Yesterday he turned left; today he'd go right,
wherever it led him. He promised himself that he'd stop
stealing glances over his shoulder. At least for twenty paces
at a time. It wasn't easy.

He imagined that He was walking with him—that made
him feel better. Much better. If he really concentrated he
almost heard His steps—right there, besides him.

"I'm always with you," He'd once said. Seems like so long ago. Just a few days had past since He left them.

I am always with you...

This time Peter was sure he'd heard His voice. He nearly spun on his heal to see His face. Then he remembered the twenty steps. Six remained. He smiled to his own thoughts. If only, he thought. If only my faith were stronger.

(to be continued)

The Dark Days, conclusion (#28)

Continued research for my next historical novel: Peter and Paul.

And then, of course, there was the tradition of completely distorted Hebraic or Mosaic teaching, which not only the sacerdotal classes but the man of the street practiced. While Yeshûa's teaching was intended to change all that, in those early days only the "believers" made an effort to love one's neighbour, let alone one's enemy. As for defenseless women, they didn't seem to matter at all.

Chapter ONE (draft, continued)
The Dark Days (excerpt)

It was a quiet late afternoon, hardly a breeze in the air. He was crossing the square, keeping close to the wall to take advantage of the shade. Half-dozen children were playing hide and seek, in the side street, using the merchants' carts as hiding places. Nothing much happened. It was too hot for adults to take even a leisurely stroll along the dusty streets. And then they came.

Instinctively, Peter backed up into the penumbra of a doorway. Two men were dragging a woman, perhaps no more than twenty years old, by both arms. Five other men followed, grim smiles on their faces. Her bare feet were rubbing against the hard-beaten sand. Must have been sore, skinless, by now. It wouldn't be long now.

Two of the men tied her arms, then legs, then pushed her against the stone wall, which was already splattered with blood from previous occasions. The other men watched, their smiles getting wider. Then one of the men picked up a stone and threw it at her. He didn't have a good aim—it missed her by a handbreadth. She didn't utter a sound. Resignation? The other men were better. Perhaps they had more practice? By the tenth stone she lay crumpled, unconscious—by twentieth, probably dead. Nobody cared. The men wiped their hands on their coats and walked away. No one even stayed behind to bury her body. She was left there as an example.

The children played on.

He would have forgiven her, whatever the transgression. The body doesn't sin, He'd said, only the mind. Or, He would have stopped the men from doing anything. He had that power.

And I just stand here, cowering, Peter thought. A deep, tearing, silent sob heaved his chest. Oh Master, please give me strength. Give me courage. You called me a Rock, yet my heart is like putty.

Yeshûa was never afraid. Never. It was as though He was immortal. It was as if he could never die. And yet...

It all seems so very short time ago.

(Read on in the book...)

[I think the rest you'll find in the novel. I hope my introduction which, by way of originality, I've placed at the end, was of interest to you. If not... you should not have read it. After all, the novel itself should have been enough.]

Regards,
Stan Law

A Word
about the Author

Stan I.S. Law (aka **Stanislaw Kapuscinski**), architect, sculptor, and prolific writer, was educated in Poland and England. Since 1965 he has resided in Canada. His special interests cover a broad spectrum of arts, sciences and philosophy. His fiction and non-fiction attest to his particular passion for the scope and the development of Human Potential. He authored more than thirty books, nineteen of them novels.

Under his real name he published seven non-fiction books sharing his vision of reality. He also composed two collections of poems in his original native tongue in which he satirizes his view of the world while paying homage to Bozena Happach's sculptures.

***

If you enjoyed this book
PLEASE, WRITE A (brief) REVIEW BEFORE YOU FORGET.

INHOUSEPRESS presents a natural Prequel to PETER&PAUL:
YESHUA – Personal Memoir to Missing Years of Jesus

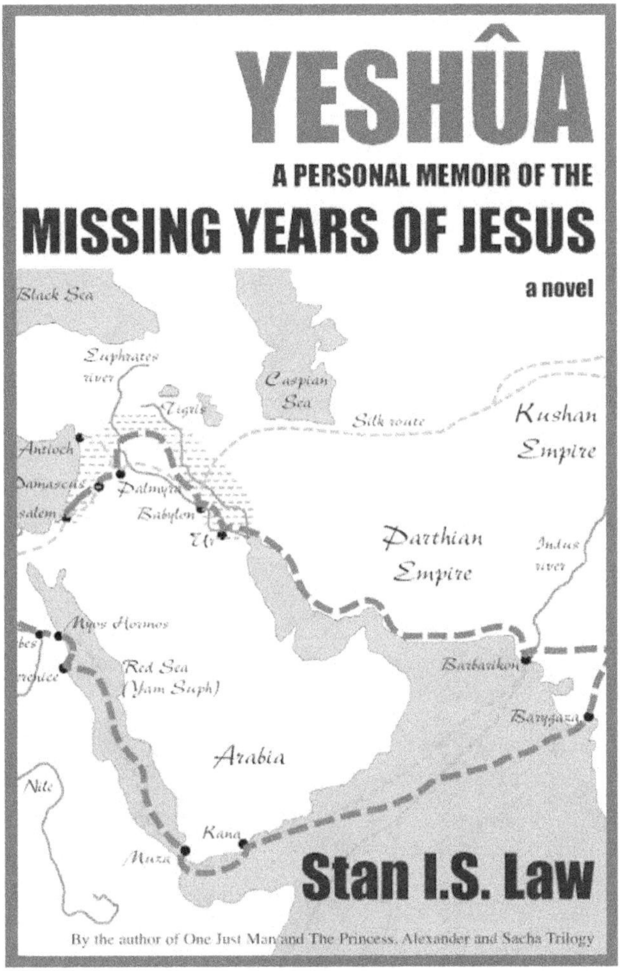

YESHÛA

A PERSONAL MEMOIR OF THE

MISSING YEARS OF JESUS

a novel

Stan I.S. Law

By the author of One Just Man and The Princess, Alexander and Sacha Trilogy

INHOUSEPRESS Montreal, Canada
info@inhousepress.ca